FORD ROAD

FORD

ROAD

Amy Kenyon

The University of Michigan Press
Ann Arbor

Published in the United States of America by
The University of Michigan Press
Manufactured in the United States of America
⊗ Printed on acid-free paper

2015   2014   2013   2012   4   3   2   1

A CIP catalog record for this book is available from the British Library.

Library of Congress Cataloging-in-Publication Data

Kenyon, Amy Maria.
    Ford Road / Amy Kenyon.
       p. cm.
    ISBN 978-0-472-11820-5 (cloth : acid-free paper) —
    ISBN 978-0-472-02829-0 (e-book)
    1. Self-realization in women—Fiction. 2. Family secrets—Fiction.
    3. Nostalgia—Fiction. 4. Grief—Fiction. 5. Michigan—Fiction. I. Title.
    PS3611.E676F67   2012
    813'.6—dc23   2012005004

Grateful acknowledgment is made to the following publisher for permission to reprint material:

HAVE YOURSELF A MERRY LITTLE CHRISTMAS
Words and Music by HUGH MARTIN and RALPH BLANE Copyright
Copyright © 1943 (Renewed) METRO-GOLDWYN-MAYER INC.
Copyright © 1944 (Renewed) EMI FEIST CATALOG INC.
All Rights Controlled by EMI FEIST CATALOG Inc. (Publishing)
and ALFRED MUSIC PUBLISHING CO., INC. (Print)
All Rights Reserved   Used by Permission

for Isaac

Crowds of emigrants were taking shipping for Michigan. . . .
I had often wondered at advertisements hung up in barrooms,
stating that, as such a person had taken the Michigan fever, he
would sell off all his stock by vendue—as he was to clear out for
Michigan by a certain day. I went on board one of these vessels
bound for Detroit; we had steers, cows, horses, wagons—in short
we were like the followers of an invading army, and every one
building castles in the air.

—RICHARD WESTON, *A Visit to the United States and Canada*
  in 1833: With the View of Settling in America, Including a
  Voyage to and from New York (1836)

BACK

ON MAY 2, 2003, MARION SEGER DIED IN HER HOMETOWN OF MID-
dleville, Michigan, just a short drive down a gravel road from Parmalee
Cemetery, where she was to be buried. She was eighty-six years old and
the daughter of Fred and Ada Gaillard, whose graves were also in Parmalee.

It was what you might call a lucky passing. Marion died, and would
be buried, back in the places of her choosing, although she had lived
away from them for her adult life as a wife and mother. It was lucky too
that everybody arrived in time, Pam from the northern suburbs of Detroit, Sid from Chicago, and Kay from Los Angeles. Marion's three
grown children, the *family*—is how they were collapsed into one and
named by the hospital workers.

Marion had been moved from an elderly care ward to a quiet,
lavender-colored room in the hospice wing. Each room looked onto a
courtyard where there were rosebushes and park benches donated by
grieving families, and where each bench bore a small plaque with the
name of a former patient, now deceased. The hospice people gave out
pamphlets and spoke in low, practiced tones. But the pamphlets did
not help as much as everyone expected. It is true they prepared Marion's children for the physical process of imminent death, its stages
and signs. But they also reduced Marion's passing to something
prescheduled, a course to be followed step by step. At times, the pamphlets encouraged them to watch like overanxious parents checking a
child's milestones. If anything, they became so absorbed in following
the guides and pleasing the hospice workers that they lost sight of their
mother. They did not know what she felt anymore, what they felt about
her or about themselves.

Pam, who had been attending to Marion regularly, saw that they were failing. She taught Sid and Kay to remain practical. They learned how to wash and gently handle and turn Marion's wasted body, administer liquid morphine, and give water. She was so dry. Pam found the thought of Marion's thirst unbearable. So they took little sponge cubes stuck to the end of cocktail sticks, dipped them into a glass of water, and then lightly ran them across Marion's cracked lips and inside her mouth, moistening her gums and tongue. Reading became irrelevant, and it was Pam who said, finally, that the leaflets should be put away. After that, with less than a week remaining, they took it in turns to hold their mother's hand; they talked to her, said nothing, softly sang her favorite songs from the thirties and forties, and stroked her cheek.

For a few days, she was in and out of sleep. When awake, she wordlessly tracked faces and movements, emitting shallow puffs and sighs. Soon, there were brief cessations in her breathing—she might stop for twenty or thirty seconds, abruptly breaking what few outward bodily rhythms remained, causing the room to fill with dark silence, then come sputtering back, startling them with loud and husky congestion. Her fingers and toes grew cool and bluish. She dozed for minutes at a time, only to open her eyes suddenly, wakened by pain or perhaps a physical urge not to miss her own death. Finally, and this in the last hour of Marion's life, her eyes remained open, but now dark and fixed. At last, she released a low, gasped breath, and her mouth dropped wide and did not close again, giving her a parting expression of faint bewilderment. It was over.

THE THREE CHILDREN CAME INTO A LARGE INHERITANCE BECAUSE Marion, besides being Fred and Ada's daughter, was the wealthy widow of Jake Seger, an accountant who had risen through the corporate ranks to become a top automobile executive during the final glory years of the American car. Kay Seger, born in 1954 at Henry Ford Hospital, was the youngest of Jake and Marion's children, and so, too, the youngest of Fred and Ada's grandchildren.

There is no adequate explanation of what happened to Kay after Marion was gone. The simple version is that grief sent the youngest child off the rails. The people who had grown up with Kay, in the same neighborhood, could still recall how they once teased her about being a "mommy's girl." They could remember watching from the sidewalk while Kay's dad dragged her from home to go to kindergarten. She kicked and screamed and tried to grab the front door handle, the corner of the brick house, the mailbox, anything to prevent being detached from the house and the woman inside it. She even escaped school a few times and ran home. But it didn't last. There were sessions with the school psychologist, a transfer to an extremely patient and devoted teacher, and Kay settled down. True, she did think she was a little special after all the professional scrutiny, maybe a bit prettier and smarter and more talented than the rest of the kids. Which she *wasn't*. But such distorted thinking was not entirely Kay's fault; her parents, in that fifties suburban way, had lavished too much attention on her. And as the youngest child and a girl, Kay had been tightly bound to her mother. Marion's affection was immense and genuine, but also controlling, snagged by expectation and a narrowness of feminine vision. Even the other kids, fighting their own domestic battles, could see that this had somewhat impaired Kay's image of herself, and they mostly forgave her for it. There were things about her to like. She was lively. She was a fast runner. Sure, Kay could be bossy and a little mean at times, but she was also enthusiastic and loyal; she happily shared Barbie clothes and didn't cheat at games.

Anyway, no, this wasn't Kay the mommy's girl, staging a return at Marion's death. Of course, something of the heat of that early devotion to her mother must have returned to bother the youngest child, but some other force was also at work. During those last days, when Sid, Pam, and Kay gathered as adults around the deathbed and watched their mother's eyes turn to black glass, Kay "caught" something that propelled her back home. She later joked that it was a bad case of Michigan fever. But if anything, it was Hofer's condition, catchable in all fifty states, she would say with a sad smile, before more reflectively explaining that Hofer's condition was an ailment discovered, or it might be better to say *reinvented,* as late as 2002 by Dr. Elmer Thisroy, a Baltimore psychiatrist.

"And I can't claim I caught it *from* Marion," Kay said. "Yet in retrospect, I believe Hofer's condition is an ailment which, to borrow an old phrase, runs in families. Lots of families. I want to say *every* family. I strongly suspect that my grandfather Fred Gaillard suffered from it and, very likely, Jacques Gaillard, Fred's father."

Hofer's condition is how Kay came to believe that her grandfather was not alone back in 1914 when he made his way across the state to the western counties to meet Ada Parker for the first time. Even as he headed west from Detroit, placing one foot in front of the other in a deliberate march to new life, Fred dragged a ball and chain of history. Really, he saw no possible approach to Ada except through the iron gate of his own loss, and hers. *Hello, Ada,* he might have said. *Ada, I've traveled more than a hundred miles to find you. A long way and a long time. I hope you'll want me. But first, let me give you your bitter past. Let me be the one to tell you what everyone else withheld.*

As for Ada, she did not wish to be told. Not really. But she was also tough-minded and practical. She understood in an instant that if she allowed Fred in through the front door of the clapboard house, he would put an end to her terrible waiting. Thereafter, he must have occupied a strange place indeed for Ada. He had gently delivered the news she needed but did not want. He had no part in her past, yet he knew of it; he was the last person to reach out and touch it. In that, Fred may have been the only man Ada would ever accept.

Yet they were nothing alike, Fred and Ada. How did they sustain one another? Through arcane laws of opposites and attraction? Scales teetering precariously and finally coming to rest? Kay said those were unanswerables; that was the word she used. "But I'll say this much," she added. "Fred was a carrier of Hofer's condition, while Ada was not susceptible."

The larger point is that many sufferers of this ailment can trace the first symptoms back to the death of a particular person. In Kay's case, that person was Marion, her mother, Fred and Ada's daughter. Moreover, there is no agreed treatment for Hofer's condition, much less an agreed definition or set of diagnostic criteria, because it has not been formally recognized by the medical establishment. It is not an imaginary disease, but it is one that has to be imagined. According to Kay, the only person actively researching Hofer's condition is Dr. Thisroy, down there in Baltimore. And in Kay's opinion, however unprofessional and uninformed, Elmer Thisroy will never be taken seriously by other medical or psychiatric practitioners. "When it hit me, I felt alone with my problem," Kay said. "I could do little more than stumble through it."

Marion's long illness and hospitalization had given Kay plenty of short visits to Michigan and ample time to plan any change she might make after her mother died. But she never planned a thing, never even saw it coming until a few days after the funeral. Like some of the acute cases recorded by Thisroy, it was a sudden onset. She returned to Los Angeles and terminated everything: job, house, furniture, accounts, subscriptions, and friendships. Then, on the first day of June 2003, just one month after Marion's death, Kay flew to Detroit and booked a room at one of the airport motels. There were too many motels to choose from, with their package deals, their late deals, with little icons on the websites indicating pool, gym, free shuttle service to airport terminals, minibar, cable TV. So she picked the Comfort Inn, if only for its name.

She checked in behind some loud and insular pilots and stewardesses who were flirting among themselves with tired abandon. As swiftly as possible, she found her room, let herself in with the swipe card, lifted her bag onto one of the two double beds, closed the curtains, switched on the television, and stretched out on the other bed. She watched the news, the weather, Oprah, back episodes of *Homicide*. Planes buzzed overhead. Occasional chatter and the high-pitched squealing of suitcase trolley wheels could be heard from the corridor. She emerged once or twice a day to buy cold drinks and sandwiches from a vending machine.

Kay might have rotted there in the Comfort Inn. Later, she swore she had not set out to contact Joe Chase. Not consciously, anyway. "I was almost as surprised as he was when the phone rang in his house and it was me on the other end of the line." But that is what took place. She had not seen Joe since 1970, the year the two of them were pried apart, when the Seger family moved out to one of the wealthier suburbs built for automotive executives, and Joe was shipped to Vietnam. Now she called Joe and told him her mother had died and she didn't know what to do next or where she belonged anymore. Marion was the last of the parents, the end of all that the previous generation had done right and wrong. Kay could no longer feed off her parents' actions and decisions and weaknesses as though she bore no personal responsibility for

5

her own mistakes. And at the end of the phone call, Kay told Joe she was sorry. For not keeping in touch. For everything. For things she didn't even know. She was sorry. She wasn't sure if they could put it right between them, but at least they might see one another, see what happened when they finally stood face to face. Joe listened.

It was only a matter of days, then, before Kay moved back to the old street in Garden City, to be with the first boy she ever loved. This is the story of what happened during the summer and fall after Marion died, when Kay found Joe again. It's a chronicle of the long past. And it's a cautionary tale about the perils of chasing dead times, people, and places, in Kay's case Fred Gaillard and Ada Parker, Detroit, Middleville, and Garden City. Joe Chase.

FORWARD

IN THE COUNTRY, A PERSON COULD BE SET UPON BY DIRT. BAD AS town. This was Fred Gaillard's discovery. But at the end of a dry spell, here on Shaw Road, a remote track in western Michigan, Fred found country dirt to be *dusty*. It chased him in gusts of warm wind, like swarming brown powder, infesting his eyes and hair. He brushed it off and saw its particles scatter, until the next gust came off the fields and sprayed him again. After a rain, surely the air would lose this gritty quality and the road sink into its historic ruts and tracks. Thick mud might spatter country clothes, lock hold of country boots, and pull them from the feet, but when that mud dried, all would be caked in powder once more. In town, especially at the automobile works, dirt was an *oily* problem, a layer of grime and soot that stained the skin, shirt-sleeves, and everything Fred touched. No matter how vigorously he scrubbed, the grease stayed under his fingernails and traced the lines of each palm. Once in a while, beneath someone's eyes, he hid his hands inside his pockets or under the table. But most of the time, he didn't think about the sticky black residues that marked him.

It was only now, walking this sunlit surface on the first day of September 1914, aged twenty-five, that Fred dwelled on such matters, silently comparing dusty dirt and oily dirt, and other discernable differences between the town and the country. He had rarely been outside Detroit, maybe once or twice to attend a race on the outskirts of the city. Since 1904, the year he started at Ford Motor Company, he had not even spent much time outside the factory. Fred was certain of this because he had passed a portion of his long journey calculating where and how the previous ten years *had* been spent. He counted the days worked and days out. The Sundays and the shrinking chances for piano and baseball. How the piano diminished imperceptibly, little by little, until it became a reverie, fluttering fingers without a keyboard. He added up the hours, and then he counted the number of Model T automobiles passing him on the road.

This situation—this carrying of bad news from Detroit to someone he had never met—the unexpected departure from the big town, ending in a hike down a long track surrounded by cornfields, coughing on dust raised by a late summer wind—all of this caused Fred to lose pace, move with doubt, as though each footstep to the west were too blindingly lit. There were no tall buildings to block the sun out here. He had set off in a hurry, full of desire and urgency, going *forward,* or so he had believed, but the nearer he came to his destination, the more he did not wish to arrive. Better to continue walking, get used to the wide space, calm down, and plan what to say when he reached the farmhouse. No sense arriving in a state of heart-thumping agitation, bowed by the big sky, racing and needy, without having measured and thought his own years, his place. Detroit and the accretion of things: the signs, the events small and large that had prodded him to this point.

Although he had never owned one himself, it was the automobile, its invention, and his small part in its production—from that first job at the Piquette Avenue plant—which once promised to carry Fred as far from the past as it was possible to go. One of the youngest workers, he had eagerly learned every inch and operation of the automobile, how to put it together and take it apart, how to repair engines. He had made the Ford factory his future, a Palace of Forgetting. But forgetting did not come naturally, and one person after another appeared to drag him back—his mother, whose eyes shone dark; his sister, Bell, with her unwavering loyalty to the dead father; even his best friend, Ralph, who had taken against Ford Motor Company long before it was a success.

He could hear Ralph now, badgering, arguing outside the Piquette plant on the last day of 1906. There, if he closed his eyes, glowed the high massive letters, grayish white in the freezing fog that New Year's Eve, painted across the top of the factory building. Fred could see himself too, standing beside Ralph on the opposite side of the avenue, the two of them barely out of boyhood, shoulders hunched in the December cold, hands in pockets, watching their breath in the Detroit winter.

8

At the age of seventeen, Fred was already in his second year of working for Ford.

"Home of the Celebrated Ford Automobiles," Ralph said, reading the sign aloud. "Yessir, I bet they been *celebratin'* this Christmas. How many cars you think they made this year? How many dollars? How many dollars did *you* see, Fred?

"Cover your ears next time you hear that factory siren," Ralph commanded, without waiting for an answer to his questions. "Pull down the flaps on your cap."

Whenever there was a layoff, Ralph had a go, tried to talk Fred into leaving Ford for good. Ralph worked for a builder, and swore no automobile boss would get him inside the factory gate. Ralph always gave about ten words for each one Fred spoke.

"The trouble with you is you're loyal to people who don't care a whit, that mechanic Spider Huff mostly." Ralph continued, unopposed. "When was the last time Huff spoke to you? Does he even know you're there?"

"I ain't seen him for some time now," Fred replied reluctantly.

It pained him to admit that Spider Huff no longer seemed to recognize him among the other workers. And he did not wish to fan Ralph's flame. His friend was still sore at Huff for interfering in their lives, beginning with a bet on a race way back in 1901, when Ralph and Fred were kids. It had been a playful, boyish bet between the two of them, until Henry Ford's mechanic stepped into the middle of it. Ralph lost his bet that day, lost his prized Civil War bullet to Huff, and to his thinking, lost Fred to the Ford Company.

"I ain't seen much of Huff since Mr. Ford had a secret room built on the third floor at Piquette," Fred finally admitted. "They're doing something up there, but it's not *my* business."

"*Mr.* Ford. He ain't the president, Fred. And it *will* be your business when they come down on the shop floor, tellin' you they got some new scheme, or they're shuttin' the plant for good or some such thing. *Mr.* Ford, my arse."

"No, you got it all wrong, Ralph. They ain't *working* up there. Mr. Couzens takes care of the company. *He's* the one to watch out for, keeps an office right by the machine shop. Nobody knows for sure what Mr. Ford gets up to on the third floor, but I hear he's so rich, it's

9

all jokes and fun now. He hands out fake cigars and wires up the door-knobs to play tricks on Huff. One day, I heard Mr. Ford and some other fella' stripped off and had a wrestling match. No, they ain't *workin'* up there."

But Fred was wrong. In October 1908, a new model, the Model T, was launched, having been planned and designed in great secrecy, in the locked room on the third floor of the Piquette Avenue plant. Henry Ford had put together a small research and design team drawn from his company favorites, including Joseph Galamb, a young Hungarian engineer, Paul Sorenson, a Danish-born pattern maker, and Spider Huff. Sometimes they worked until late at night; Ford brought in a rocking chair that once belonged to his mother. Huff designed the in-genious magneto, a flywheel studded with magnets and copper coil and capable of producing sparks for the cylinder, making heavy storage batteries unnecessary. No, Fred was wrong, very wrong when he told Ralph there was nothing doing on the third floor at Piquette Avenue.

Sometimes during his journey from Detroit to the western part of the state, even on the distant roads cut through fields without people, a Model T rattled by, bouncing up and down and tilting to one side, its owner perched proudly upon the seat. More than once, Fred was of-fered a ride by the driver, but he always declined. He had probably tightened a bolt on damn near every magneto on damn near every Ford on the road. For the time being, he preferred to travel by train, foot, even by canoe if it came to it. Plenty of time later to think about auto-mobiles; there would always be more Fords.

Finally, on this bright track outside Middleville, a town he had not known before, in Barry County, also unknown to him, Fred reached Shaw Farm. It was a simple but pretty, two-story, white frame house set back from the road, with grass and flower beds to the front and a large elm tree shading its porch. A woodshed could be seen to one side of the house, beyond which was a barn. The barn needed repainting and seemed generally less well tended than the house. Behind the house and barn, there was an orchard and then vast, planted fields that appeared to end at a row of trees in the distance. Fred guessed that to be where the Thornapple River ran through the farmland.

He was not ready. After lingering by the side of Shaw Road for an hour or so, Fred turned around and walked back into Middleville. It was dark when he presented himself at the James Hotel and rented a room for the night. An extravagant delay, leaving him barely enough funds to purchase train fare back to Detroit. He went without supper, finishing an end of bread bought that morning, keeping to his room because he had paid for it and the town outside felt small and strange.

All evening, Fred stood back a little from the window and watched the street, studying the passersby in twos and threes and their greetings back and forth. From time to time, he reached into his breast pocket to feel for the calling-card photograph, rubbing his finger around its stiff edges, finding the shape of it again. He had carefully trimmed the top right corner so that Ada, the girl in the picture, would never see it had been stained. Was she sleeping now, without knowledge, never imagining what was to come, never expecting him? Was it simpler and kinder to leave her be? He had looked at her too many times for his own sleep, taken the photo card out every day during his travels, in order to recall her face and steel himself to speak to her. She was always the same, sturdy but slender in a fitted white gown with lace and beads on the sleeves. Her gloved hands held a paper rolled and tied with ribbon. A diploma. She had finished her schooling.

The name of the photographer and the location of his Middleville studio were printed on the back of the photo card. Fred had visited the studio that morning, immediately upon his arrival in the town. That was how he finally knew the surname and precise whereabouts of the girl in the picture: Ada Parker of Shaw Farm.

For almost two weeks, without possessing these details, Fred had fixed on Ada's picture, held conversations with her in his head and sometimes aloud, imagined sitting beside her and taking her gloved hand in his, without embarrassment, and then touching the engraved band that hung on her left wrist. He had rested there with Ada until the whiteness of her dress emptied and blanked him, snowed over his grief and exhaustion. Night after night, he dreamed of heavy sleep, drifting snow, then dreamed of waking to find her unchanged and unmoved. Finally, he sat up and whispered the thing that must be told, whispered it in her ear, burying his mouth in the only color that remained, the thick brown of Ada's hair.

COMFORT INN

STRETCHED ACROSS THE DOUBLE BED IN THE MOTEL ROOM DURING those first few days back in Michigan, flipping channels with the remote, Kay thought about her inheritance. It was uncomfortably large and probably to blame for her recent impulsive actions. And it was old Hollywood. If there had to be so much money behind this dramatic movement backward, from west to east, she wished it had nothing to do with a death in the family. If only she had stumbled upon it accidentally. Like finding a dollar on the street and buying an ice cream she might not have had in the first place. Kay preferred to cast her disappearance as a very large ice cream.

The objects and trinkets left by her mother were simpler than the inheritance, cleaner than dollars, outside the frame. The best items carried no monetary value. A Thanksgiving platter with a winter scene in chestnut browns. Recipe cards in Marion's spidery script, stained with kitchen grease from as far away as the 1940s. Trails of dried ink beneath the fingertips. A pin shaped like a leaf, brushed silver with a light sparkle, as though it once lay on frosty ground, but flew up in a winter squall to settle on Marion's coat lapel. A half-finished bottle of cologne. The whiff of her, clinging to scarves and sweaters left behind. These items carried a deep pleasure to her children, as though her body were still present. Pam and Kay had sorted through their mother's things, dividing the jewelry, each selecting a few pieces along with some clothing from her once elegant wardrobe, before Sid drove the rest to a charity shop, his car piled high with black plastic bags. Pam and Kay watched him go, but they disliked the fact of their mother's clothes outliving her, being fingered and priced down, taken to hang on someone else, brush a different skin, acquire another's odors.

Marion was eighty-six when she died. She had been widowed for seventeen years and sick for nearly ten, first with cancer, then Alzheimer's disease. It was the cancer that killed her in the end; it came back and riddled her spine and, it has to be said, probably rescued her from the worst of the Alzheimer's. Marion's long-term memory had not been fully defeated before the cancer returned; on a good day, she could still recall the names of her husband, three children, and parents. But she regularly mistook her finger for a toothbrush, got lost moving from one room to another, and started sentence after sentence that she had little hope of completing because somewhere in the middle of the sentence, the beginning of it broke away. She would bravely try again, several times, before retreating in frightened confusion.

On New Year's Eve 1999, when Pam gave a party and everybody sang "Auld Lang Syne," Marion cried. She did not cry sentimentally, the way people do at that song, but out of frustration, dimly recognizing the words and melody, but not the occasion. "I don't understand! What are we *doing*?" she asked repeatedly. There was no place for their mother in the new century. Bush, Gore, and the contested election result completely passed her by. And when the Twin Towers collapsed on a television screen that was mounted neck-achingly high on the wall at the elderly day center, Marion was not paying attention. She was bent over an old-fashioned photo album opened on her lap. The pictures were small, with white borders and pinked edges, attached to little card corners. When skyscraper dust rolled like a giant tumbleweed, filling the television screen, Marion stared instead at a photograph of a wood-framed house, pressing it with her finger as though she could crush the house with her longing. "I used to play with that little boy there," she said to the care worker. "Oh—you played with a boy there?" the care worker returned, loudly and deliberately, as though they were in a foreign-language school. "Yes, I did," Marion said. "I used to play with that little boy there." And so the conversation went, even though the care worker was watching the television.

So, where was Kay during her mother's slow deterioration, during the incremental loss of language and order? In Los Angeles, where she had been living and working since 1980, the year she completed a doctorate in history and left Boston to visit a friend on the West Coast. This friend, a literary critic turned scriptwriter, had recently finished an adaptation of a Victorian novel for the screen. The production was just getting under way when Kay arrived. One poolside party led to another, and then she was invited to meetings, and before long, she was getting paid as historical advisor to the project.

The movie was a surprise hit, a relatively low-budget production that earned a sizeable profit. Her friend moved on to another project, another success, and brought Kay on board again. After that, the work kept coming. She didn't have anything better to do, so she stayed. Kay and her friend had an on-and-off relationship, and they made a living. By the time they broke up for good, Kay had enough contacts of her own and was never short of work as a script advisor, historical consultant, or both.

For a directionless, not exactly first-rate historian who had gone to ground in Hollywood, the eighties and nineties proved to be lucrative years. Patriotic blockbusters and award winners alternated with quiet little period pieces and literary adaptations. There were revisionist Westerns, baseball-saving-the-nation stories, feel-good films about slavery and the Holocaust. The movies, as always, made redemption look easy, fun, like something that happened to good-looking people.

By the mid-nineties, the recycling of both history and Hollywood genres had accelerated, bringing a new cohort of detectives and gangsters. There were remakes of classic films and television hits, or what the critics liked to call "*reworkings*," and a run of neo-noirs. Taken together, these productions helped to create, then proceeded to mooch off, a growing *fin de siècle* cultural moodiness, a kind of seasonal affective disorder writ large, a nonspecific collective anxiety. Kay was pretty open about it. She said she made money by stoking that anxiety, feeding and maintaining it, and then providing cheap, feature-length comfort before stoking it all over again. "If you really wanna know," she said, "the movies were *too* good to me."

Regularly employed, unmarried, and childless, Kay never spent the money she was busily amassing, never even bought a house. For over twenty years, she lived in one rented bungalow or another, still half believing a promise she had made herself in 1980, that this was a temporary venture. Even the men she dated were temporary, every one of them in the film business. Kay had become one of those people whose engines have stalled, who talk about leaving but stay, people whose claims of dissatisfaction are rarely believed by others. It's only by staring back on that time from after her mother's death and after the summer spent back home in Garden City that it is possible to understand Kay a little and see that her disappointment was real.

ONE MORNING, IN THE ROOM AT THE COMFORT INN, SHE SAT ON the edge of the bed, holding a pale green chiffon scarf that once belonged to Marion, one of the small items she had saved. She buried her face in the scarf, inhaled deeply, and nearly passed out trying to recover Marion's smell and breathe it in again, but it had gone. That was when she picked up the phone.

Joe lived only twenty minutes from Detroit Metro Airport, still in Garden City, where they had grown up together. He drove to the Comfort Inn, took one long look and a step toward Kay, as he always had done. He was alive. It was the first time Kay had seen him since Vietnam, but here was the proof, standing before her, of what she had heard but never fully grasped. Joe was not dead. The artery in his neck pulsed visibly beneath the open collar of a light cotton shirt, and there was a salty smell to his skin and mint on his breath. Coming from the sunny parking lot into the dimmed, air-conditioned room raised goose bumps on his sandy arms. He shivered, and Kay noticed that the tiny hairs of each forearm were already bleached for the summer, although it was only June. His sudden proximity and the tiny details and reminders of his body made her afraid. Of course she saw that Joe had changed. But his good looks had always been of the old, faintly unhappy variety. The high school varsity athlete never quite certain of the golden-boy tag, not quite living up to it. Back then, he sported the reticent handsomeness of a Heath Ledger; now it was rather more that of Gary Cooper in *Pride of the Yankees,* a little gaunt with dark shadows beneath his eyes. Kay saw too that he had grown cautious in his movements, perhaps favoring some stiffness in the joints or an old injury. She noticed these changes in a screen flicker before they passed away.

They stood opposite one another, self-conscious and struggling to maintain composure. But Kay knew then that Joe had not been taken by someone else, and she began to cry softly, wiping her eyes with the back of her hand, relieved. Any lingering doubts disappeared when he folded her in his arms and said she might come home with him. Kay's long sigh must have reeked with gratitude, but Joe never said so. He helped pack her bags, carried them down to the lobby, and stood by the entrance, watching as she checked out of the airport motel.

That night they slept fully clothed on top of Joe's bed. It reminded her of camping in the backyard, the way they used to do with her brother, Sidney, who was Joe's best friend. They always made a tent by stretching an old bed sheet from the ground to the top of the chain-link fence. They held it fast with clothes pegs and spread sleeping bags on the grass floor. One night, Sid and Joe, twelve years old, made scary faces with a flashlight, and Kay, just ten at the time, sang the songs from *West Side Story* until they chased her out. She ran crying to Marion, who dotted Kay's eyes with a Kleenex and found something for her to do in the kitchen. In the morning, Kay crept back into the sun-baked tent and dropped to her knees, watching the boys sleep, arms and legs akimbo. When Joe spooned her on his bed that first night in June 2003, it was all she could do to stop herself chanting *Okay by me in Amereeeka.*

The second night, they began to kiss and fondle one another like a couple of teenagers. It was as though they were fifteen and seventeen again, hiding behind the clubhouse at the lighted baseball diamond by the high school. Sid was with the other kids on the bleachers. Joe's breath tickled her neck and face, while his hand moved shyly from new breasts to the bony outline of her hips. He slid his finger into the belt loop of her jeans and pulled her against his young man's frame. They rubbed and panted and trembled, while the night game went on with cracking bats and the hum of spectators. Later, they both lied to Sid about where they had been. That way Sid did not have to lie to Marion.

The third night, Joe and Kay did things they had never done before, and the long, suspended years began to fall away. Then she imagined they were dead, thrown still young into an open grave with no need of a coffin. It was Parmalee Cemetery in Middleville, where Jake and Marion were, with Fred Gaillard and Ada, and Violet Parker. Joe and Kay rested there, coiled together in damp soil, while familiar faces from random times of life gazed at them from the earth's surface high above. They smiled, wrapped safely in the ground.

Kay had traveled to Michigan in a fever, like Fred Gaillard when he made his way across the state, looking for Ada. Why did Joe take her back, permit her to use him, make him the tool and repository of her disappointment and grief, her touch of madness? For all the solace in finding him alive, for all she had missed him and was sorry about things and meant well, she would soon set about killing him off. Almost from the start, they were in a muddle about what she was doing back there in Garden City. And although she never meant to, Kay treated Joe as though there were little difference between first love and dead mother, between first love and all the lost ancestors, beginning with Fred and Ada. Is this what we do to our impossible first loves? Reduce them to ciphers?

MAPLE COURT

OF COURSE, THEY WERE GOING TO FAIL. JOE AND KAY LONGED TO
live in reverse, but every cell in their bodies, like every blade of grass in
the yard outside Joe's little brick house, was living forward. They had
only to look out the window at the street and the town to see how far
out of sync they really were.

Garden City was part of the postwar suburban sprawl around Detroit. The identically designed houses seemed like the *little boxes made
of ticky-tacky* from the song; each consisted of 940 square feet of living
space set on lots 60 feet wide and 110 feet deep, the backyard plots demarcated by chain-link fencing.

Kay recalled the look of pride and anticipation on her father's face,
the day of the move to Maple Court. At the age of twenty-seven, he
had a business degree, a young family, an entry-level accountancy position at Ford Headquarters in Dearborn, a newly built suburban
house priced at 11,950 dollars, and a thirty-year mortgage at 4 percent
interest. The War was over. Wealth and corporate success lay ahead,
not yet visible, but coming. Then she remembered that day took place
in May 1952, two years and five months before her birth. She wasn't
there. The memory was a photograph, someone else's memory, relayed
to her. Jake and Marion Seger posed on the front yard, arm in arm; behind them, there was a newly planted, spindly plum tree. Blades of
grass peeped through the topsoil. Kay saw this as though she had held
the camera and snapped the scene herself.

On the street, which was typical of the other streets in Garden
City, everybody was white, with the majority of surnames suggesting
English, Irish, or German ancestry. There was a handful of Polish and
Italian names, some French. An Armenian family lived on the next

block. One or two residents had migrated from Appalachia, but the rest were from Michigan, either Detroit or the rural counties.

All the fathers were veterans. Many were blue-collar types, builders, truck drivers, and factory workers, like Joe's dad. These men made a permanent family home in Garden City. Then there were the men with college degrees; most of them, like Jake, had graduated to a sales position at a car dealership or to an administrative job with Ford, GM, or Chrysler. The men in this category were likely to be promoted by the company and therefore likely, eventually, to leave Garden City behind.

Jake and Marion rarely visited the old street after July 1970, when the family moved further out to the winding lanes with mock Tudor and Cape Cod houses and split-level, cool, modern ones set back from the road on wooded acre lots. At first, Marion missed the Maple Court wives, the coffee drinking, cup-of-sugar borrowing, everybody's children banging in and out through screen doors. But she claimed she was not sorry to leave behind some of the neighbors, especially Sally Benstone, who played country music records all day long, Mildred Harris, with her fifths of bourbon hidden about the house, and Mr. Wilson, who could be heard raging at his wife in the night. All the other parents on Maple Court knew he beat her, yet they did nothing but stand on their beds like kids, peering through the windows with the lights out, straining to hear the fight, only to talk about it in hushed asides the next day. Everybody was nervous around Mr. Wilson. Once, he forced his daughter Jodie to slap Kay in the face, chastising and shaming the girls in equal measure, after Kay said something mean and Jody went home crying instead of fighting back. This incident, a punishment ordered by the father and performed by one cowering child against another, created an odd, unspoken alliance, an affection between Jodie and Kay.

It was in February 1964, when a blizzard kept the children home from school, that the Wilsons' four-year-old son stopped speaking. The Maple Court kids were in Joe's backyard at the time, digging tunnels in the snowdrifts. Kevin picked his way over to them, awkwardly lifting one red-rubber-booted foot after another from nearly two feet of snow, a stunned expression on his face. When he reached the small group, he just stood there in his snowsuit, opening and closing his mouth, trying to push something out, but nothing came. He had become mute overnight. When the snow melted, Mrs. Wilson packed up the children and left Maple Court. Joe remembered that Mrs. Wilson visited the street many years later and stopped in to see his mother. That was how he found out that when Mr. Wilson could not get his wife back, he went home to the family farm in Muskegon County and hanged himself from a rafter in the barn. "I didn't go to the funeral," Mrs. Wilson said to Joe's mother.

When Kay returned after Marion's death, the Wilsons were gone, and so were most of the other old neighbors. Apart from Joe, only two or three of the original residents of Maple Court remained. Gone too was the uniform sense of everybody being at the same stage of life, the "we're all young families starting out together even if a few of us are oddballs" feeling that had given Maple Court its vibrancy and instilled a collective pride in the majority of its inhabitants. Now the neighbors had less to do with one another. Retired folks lived alongside single people and younger married couples. Like Joe, one or two people had inherited the family house and stayed on there. But the most striking change was the absence of young children. Joe and Kay counted four children on the entire block of eighteen houses, as compared to the forty-three kids they could still name from the first wave of residents.

In the fifties, the city funded school after school, state-of-the-art one-story facilities with flagpoles and large blackboards, slide projectors, gyms, hundreds of little chairs and desks, shiny lockers, and yellow-painted Ticonderoga pencils. Empire builders always make the mistake of assuming it will last forever. Now the entire project seemed a historical aberration, and an affecting silence had settled on the old classrooms and playgrounds. Most of the school buildings had fallen into disuse or, at best, been converted to storage or office space for the city. The baby boom was a distant memory, as long ago as tail fins and strap-on roller skates.

The outward appearance of Maple Court was also transformed. Large two-car garages had been built behind most of the houses, devouring backyard space and making the properties seem even smaller than before. Trees and shrubs planted in the 1950s had matured into pretty, if overly manicured greenery. A mania for garden figurines had seized the latest inhabitants. Nearly every walkway was dotted with plaster-cast rabbits and squirrels, in pastel pinks and blues. Grinning gnomes peeked from beneath rose and rhododendron bushes. After 9/11, dozens of shiny plastic American flags sprouted from flower beds and planted pots. Many householders no longer tended their own yards, employing local firms whose uniformed gardeners arrived in pickup trucks, unloaded lawn mowers, spades, and rakes, and set to work. There were two or three such businesses working Maple Court, and Joe regularly threw away the cards and flyers they left in his mailbox.

Mr. Chase—as Kay would always call Joe's father—had a heart attack and died in his sleep in 1985, a few months following his retirement from the tool and die department at the Ford River Rouge plant in Dearborn. To the other parents, he was known by his first name of Phil, when they chatted over the backyard fence, or at barbecues and block parties. Phil and Harriet. And their two boys, Joe and Lenny. Poor Lenny was killed in a car accident in 1976, full of liquor after leaving a friend's wedding reception across town. He was twenty-one at the time. Mr. and Mrs. Chase were nearly undone by the loss of their youngest son; it told on their faces, in their posture, the way they moved and did the yardwork. In a phone call to one of the other mothers, after the funeral, Mrs. Chase said it didn't make any sense to have one son come back from Vietnam without so much as a scratch, only to lose the other son just a few miles from home in a secondhand Chevy. She blamed herself for being worried sick for a whole year about Joe, exhausting her worry to the point where there was nothing left over for Lenny. Then she cried and recalled that her husband had always warned Lenny he'd have bad luck for making his first car a Chevy instead of a Ford. Anyway, the premature deaths of Lenny and his father meant that from 1985, Joe and his mother shared the small house on Maple Court until 1993, the year she died of cancer. After that, apart from the occasional short-stay girlfriend, Joe lived alone until Kay arrived.

Like his father, Joe worked for Ford. He had been a line worker for over twenty years, and after Kay moved back, he carried on as normal, going out every day to the Rouge plant, where he made Mustangs. Kay kept telling him he could quit his job and they'd live on her inheritance. In fact, Joe had savings of his own, because Mr. Chase had paid off his mortgage long before dying and left the house to his sole surviving child. But Kay was desperate to give her pot of money, once Marion's money, once Jake's executive earnings and life insurance and stocks and shares, to Joe and the reckless love affair. Why not use the dollars of a one-time Ford big shot to buy the freedom of a line worker? She said they could spend every day together, playing old Motown, Beatles, and Beach Boys records and driving around blue-collar suburban heaven. But Joe always said he'd go crazy if he didn't work and that *she'd* probably go crazy if he didn't work.

So he kept to his routines. At first, he simply let her back into his life as though the years had not intervened. He once remarked that he felt old most of the time, but never when he looked at Kay. When she fretted over her wrinkles and sags, Joe was genuinely incredulous. He simply could not see the signs of age pulling her down. As for him, there were pinches of gray in his whiskers and hair. His face was browned, toughened, and faintly lined; the corners of his mouth had settled into a slight frown. Yet his body retained the wiry slenderness of an end-of-career athlete.

None of the newer neighbors had known Joe when he was Phil and Harriet's boy, Lenny's big brother and Sid's best friend. They probably saw him as a loner, still living in his parents' house, one of those Vietnam vets who never quite "moved on." But to Kay, he was deeply familiar, positively shimmering with dozens of his younger selves. All his boyhood ages were still there, written into a man's face, chest, and limbs. She was powerless against so many Joes and found it hard to keep her hands off him. Beyond the physical warmth and seductive pull, there was trouble ahead, but that only made her want him more.

It must have been the fact of living on borrowed time that brought a brief rejuvenation in both of them. For a few weeks at least, maybe even the rest of June, they glowed; the rooms of the house glowed as they moved around inside it. Moreover, there was no practical reason why Kay should not stay in Michigan and live next door to her old house. If an objection had been raised, she would have dodged it, hidden behind Mrs. Chase's saggy old sofa.

She dared to hope this would be the kind of summer you look back on with relief and gratitude because it saved your sorry ass. She was in love with the person she had always loved. Back where she longed to be. But it was during July, yes, as early as July, when tiny fault lines began to appear. Once or twice, Joe arrived home from work and expressed surprise to find her there.

"I can't seem to get used to this," he would say, scratching his head.

Rather like an anxious doctor on rounds following a botched treatment of his patient, he began to check how she spent her days.

"So what did you get up to this afternoon? I hope you went out somewhere, took a walk or something. So *did* you . . . go out anywhere today?"

He tried to ask about her plans, apparently believing she *had* plans, that a resumption of adult life, away from him, must be imminent.

"How are you feeling? Have you been in touch with the people out in LA?"

"What people?"

"The people you work with. Aren't they expecting you back?"

If he didn't press much further than these few brief inquiries, and if Kay offered up few replies, it was perhaps because their affair was so retrograde, so childishly rebellious and secretive, so bulging with the pleasure once denied them by the arbitrary choices of parents and three-star generals. Neither possessed the will to move against it. Think of those songs and movies that made postwar teenagers believe they were separate and misunderstood, and you catch a glimpse of Joe and Kay and their belated insurgence. Think *Rebel without a Cause* or *A Summer Place*. Think the Ronettes belting out "Be My Baby" with unhealthy devotion or Tommy James and the Shondells, the illicit teen lust of "I Think We're Alone Now." Who wouldn't pretend to be young again, given half the chance?

Yet it seems clear now that where Kay was a defiantly starry-eyed runaway, Joe was already a little circumspect and anxious about his motives. He understood far better than she that their forced separation in adolescence had done more than pull them apart geographically; it had set them against one another. Let's face it: she had landed feather-like in a new bedroom with floral patterned wallpaper and a walk-in closet; he had woken up in the bush, having been brutally plucked from his home in the "big PX," as the troops liked to refer to the United States.

The day the Seger family moved out of Garden City was the last time Kay saw Joe before he was drafted. He waved goodbye, then put his hands in his jean pockets and stood staring down at the sidewalk as they drove away. She would attend a new high school in the fall, with two years to complete before graduation. Sid and Joe had just graduated, and her brother would soon leave for university. But Joe was undecided about college; his mother wanted him to enroll somewhere, if only to avoid the draft, while his father said it was high time he started working for a living. And if he got drafted, well, there was honor in that too. Joe hesitated, gravely weakened by the rift between his parents, the awful push and pull of his father's gruff authority and his mother's fears. At the time, Kay must have been dimly aware of the tensions in the Chase family concerning Joe's future. But she admitted later that she had never really believed he would leave Garden City for university, Vietnam, or any other place. Girlishly self-absorbed, Kay failed to imagine Joe anywhere but on Maple Court, waiting for her. And so she gave no help at all.

Joe phoned the Seger household twice during the first week or so after they moved. The first time Kay was out shopping with her mother. But the second time, she sat at the foot of the wide, plush-carpeted staircase, watching Sid as he stood in the front hall with the phone to his ear. She was miserable. It was the loneliness of moving to a new street where the houses were too far apart, having no friends there. The thought of Joe holding the phone in his house, his voice, his slender arms, Maple Court, the removal of it all. Fighting back tears, she clamped one hand over her mouth and listened to her brother's side of the phone call. They talked a little while, and she heard Sid tell Joe he was in danger of screwing himself.

"Look—register at community college. Get your name down. Do it by the end of the week," he said emphatically. "If you don't like it there, you can enroll somewhere else next year. The main thing now is to make sure you qualify for student deferment. Just don't get drafted."

Then she knew Joe had asked to speak to her. Sid glanced in his sister's direction and held out the phone. Kay shook her head, put her hand down, and mouthed *no, no,* tears starting to come. Sid guiltily explained that she couldn't come to the phone. Joe didn't ask for her again. The next she heard of him was that he had failed to register to study anywhere and would undoubtedly be drafted by Christmas. Kay started school and little by little joined clubs, made a few friends, even developed crushes on other boys. She thought less often about Joe and the old street.

So maybe, right from the moment Kay reappeared in his life, Joe sensed that the sharp divisions of the intervening years would weigh in sooner or later. Maybe he was a little vengeful when he kissed her and allowed her to stay. Maybe he thought, *what the hell—it's been long and lonely here*; or *I was the unlucky one*; or *she owes me*.

Then again, maybe he hoped they were bringing an interrupted, disabling romance to its long-overdue conclusion, discharging old promises and resentments and lingering obligations, squaring things so that each might cease to drag the other through life like a phantom limb. Nobody, including Kay, knew what Joe thought. Nobody asked him, and he didn't say. Kay, most deliberately, did not ask him. Really, it is striking how little they understood one another, how uncoupled they were, from the moment of her return.

TIGER STADIUM

ALTHOUGH KAY HAD NOT HEARD OF HOFER'S CONDITION AT THE time, it was during that month of July that she began, very tentatively, to allow that something was wrong. And it was Joe who inadvertently triggered what might be described as a Hofer's-like episode when he came in from work one evening, cracked open a beer, flopped down in front of the television, and switched on a Detroit Tigers baseball game.

It was the first time Kay seriously took note of the brash new Comerica Park. The sight of it on the screen and the reminder of the loss of the old Tiger Stadium were disturbing. She had been taken to Tiger Stadium regularly as a child; it was a foothold in Detroit. Her father went; her older sister, Pam, went with boyfriends; Sid and Joe went. When he grew too frail to be conveyed down there for a game, Fred Gaillard, her grandfather, fought for the stadium like a boy. Kay could still recall the summer her mother finally denied him tickets, gently explaining that it had become difficult to take him to the games. Tears starting and deep red flushing his face and neck, enraged by the loss of his powers, he told Marion *that* place, Tiger Stadium, was the nearest he ever got to home.

Now, Kay found she could not watch the game with Joe. She waited outside in the darkening yard, praying that the chorus of night insects might drown out the garrulous sports commentators, the static of the crowd, the infrequent pop and explosion of a base hit. She waited the nine long innings, listening for bugs, barking dogs, bickering neighbors, and humming car engines, anything to take her mind off the new stadium.

But she failed. That night, and for days afterward, she brooded about Tiger Stadium, about Fred, long deceased, and Marion, not so long deceased. She replayed their argument and wondered if her mother felt bad about it later. She wondered why the stadium was so important to her grandfather. She lay on the back lawn, staring at the sky and repeatedly whispering their names in thumping little couplets. *Marion Fred Marion. Fred Fred Marion.* Kay closed her eyes and could not help but see, in black and white, the downtown corner of Michigan Avenue and Trumbull where Tiger Stadium sat deserted. Her throat felt thick inside; it was the lump that forms when it might help to cry but tears don't come.

The thickness in Kay's throat didn't go away, and in the days that followed, she swallowed solid food with difficulty. She drank too much coffee, and it made her jittery. She suffered headaches and thought about movie headaches and how they always spelled bad news—terminal illness or a violent end. Jimmy Cagney in *White Heat*; Bette Davis seeing double and falling off her horse in *Dark Victory.* Alarmed and agitated, Kay followed Joe from room to room, fretting about the headaches, all the while talking about Fred Gaillard and the stadium. She told Joe that her grandfather was so long gone that barely a trace of him existed in the world. Shutting down the old ballpark seemed a final act of erasure. During the hours Joe spent at work, she sat in morose recollection, waiting for the sound of his car in the driveway and the bang of the screen door.

In the evenings, Kay tried to stop him watching the Tigers. While they cleared the kitchen table and did the supper dishes, she complained bitterly about her mother. Despite all the money and objects left behind, Marion had carried away the family gold. Whole houses and towns had disappeared with her. The look of a room or a yard, the grasp of a cut-glass doorknob—these were gone, blown away by death. So too, the sound of a front door in Middleville, clacking loosely as Marion ran in and out on skinny legs. On the day she ceased breathing, the timid, remembered voice of her first gentleman caller was finally extinguished. She took the last memory of antique window glass with its rippled effect, and the way a front step tilted and made a crooked seat. She took the wet shock of her dog's nose, the rush of diving from a raft into an icy river in 1928. By dying, Marion had pushed Fred and Ada, her own father and mother, and everything they remembered deeper into the previous century and even the century before that, leaving Kay stranded in the new one. The new century had started badly, and none of these people, snug in their graves at Parmalee Cemetery, could protect the ones left behind.

For several days, Joe indulged Kay, nodded his head, stared at the floor, and said little. He listened until his patience ran out, and finally he held up both hands, fingers spread open like stop signs.

"Why are you doing this? You are fighting a bunch of defenseless dead people. You're fighting *yourself* and making yourself miserable. You're making *me* miserable. And you're stopping me watchin' the games."

Then Joe paused, thinking to himself before he made a startling suggestion.

"I don't know, Kay. I mean *really*, what the hell do I know? But it seems to me you're like a hungry person trying to stick to the wrong diet. If you're not ready to leave these people and places behind, then *don't* just yet. Why not go back until you've had your fill? Drive down and look at the stadium. Go and rediscover your ancestors. You've got the training for it; you've got the skills, for Chrissake. Put 'em to good use. Who knows? Maybe there's a project here that'll lead you back to work, one way or another. But don't worry about that for now. Just do what you so obviously *want*."

So it was Joe, wise and undoubtedly with a few ghosts of his own, who encouraged Kay to go chasing dead people and the past. And when she looked at him, pathetically grateful, as if a doctor had ordered her to curl up with a dog-eared copy of *Little Women* or a stack of MGM musicals, Joe went further, offering up a big-hearted cause, offering *himself* as a big-hearted cause. Probably not a good thing to do.

"Find all you need to know," he said, warming to his idea. "Keep going until you're satisfied. Then . . . I don't know, maybe you could tell *me* your old family stories. What d'ya say? Lord knows—I could use some distraction. Yeah, I'll listen to your stories. It might even do me some good."

That was how Joe and Kay got their wires crossed. They struck a deal. Joe gave her something to do and a reason to stay in Michigan. And he looked momentarily relieved, although he was already ambivalent about her being there. He likely came up with the idea because he saw Kay's increasing distress and felt responsible for it because he had allowed her back into his life, his house, and Maple Court, where she so clearly did not belong anymore. But for all his undoubted care and concern, perhaps Joe also expected something in return, some resolution or final payback for the years she had ignored him.

Of course, neither of them knew about Hofer's condition at the time. Nor could they have known that Joe's proposal, which amounted to feeding the fever, was simultaneously the best and worst one you could make to a Hofer's sufferer. They were, each for entirely different reasons, trying to mend the past. Kay hoped to begin with 1896, the year they built Tiger Stadium, while Joe didn't mind where she started, as long as her account gave him some respite from his own bad memories and ended before 1970, the year he was drafted. "Just press the delete key on that year," he said grimly. "In fact, let's forget the whole fuckin' decade," he added, probably thinking of his brother, Lenny.

THEY SENT FOR THE LARGE CRATE OF FAMILY PAPERS, LETTERS, and photo albums that Marion had bequeathed, the terms of her will specifically mentioning "Kay, the historian in the family." Marion thought having a daughter with a stack of university diplomas was a big deal, and Kay never disabused her of it. Even Kay's sellout to Hollywood had failed to dent her mother's high opinion. But here was an opportunity to do something Marion had always wanted by organizing the Gaillard family archive, giving it some chronological coherence, and perhaps finally discovering how Fred Gaillard of Detroit came to find Ada Parker, a farm girl from way across state. Kay would pursue the messy past and missing pieces like a legitimate historian. But then she would plot history like a romance and pass it to Joe. *She* would help *him*. He would be a thankful, biddable listener, a passenger reclined in a small rowboat, allowing Kay to paddle them both downstream. *Joe's* need would give shape and direction to her disturbed searches and mask the mysterious symptoms of what ailed her.

So, while Joe made Mustangs at the Rouge factory, Kay spent her days examining every scrap of paper in that crate, marking relevant dates, names, and references. She sketched a timeline and a preliminary genealogy, started a list of topics to be researched, and opened a box file and computer file for each one. She ordered copies of birth, death, and marriage certificates and conducted Internet and library searches of city directories, cemetery lists, newspaper holdings. She read history books about Michigan and Detroit and produced summaries of them, tapping at the keyboard. She scanned her own memory for observations dropped over the years, for lowered voices in the kitchen late at night and half-formed remarks passed above a child's head, suspended in the air, waiting to be retrieved.

It was so compulsive, right from the beginning, this desire to compile, collect, inhale the dust, and above all, *never* reach an end. Kay was already taking far too much pleasure in drifting and getting lost in her makeshift repository. Each little "find" spiraled into further searches and a growing tendency to *historicize* everything around her. Not only Marion's box of papers, but the objects in Joe's house, furniture, teacups, items of clothing, even minor day-to-day remarks and occurrences. Of course, later she would realize that anybody can succumb to Hofer's condition, not just historians. In fact, Dr. Thisroy makes the compelling argument that historians may *not* be true sufferers. "A historian," says Thisroy, "is someone who has turned his symptoms to his advantage." *Humph. Unless of course he is a bad historian*, Kay thought when she read that. *Unless he is a bad, cheap historian who has defected to Hollywood.*

But at that point, she had not yet come across Thisroy and was thoroughly enjoying herself. Kay loved nothing better than a rampaging archive. The larger the archive, the longer she would be obliged to stay with Joe. It was perfect. She possessed a growing mountain of papers, books and clues, and the gift of time to create a rarefied, personal library. And of course, her larger preserve was the place itself. Garden City, the location of their own immediate history. Beyond Garden City, they had Detroit and the rural counties of western Michigan, the settings of various episodes in the deeper past. Joe liked driving around during his days off, and he was happy to take Kay wherever she wanted to go. Streets, houses, public records offices, libraries. Sometimes, he would visit places with her, but mostly he would wait in the car with a stack of newspapers and magazines, reading reports about the occupation of Iraq and sipping coffee from a Styrofoam cup.

In the evenings, they cooked and drank beer or wine. They raided Joe's parents' record collection, playing Sinatra and Nat King Cole on an old mahogany-veneer stereo console purchased in an era when record players and television sets were dark, aspirational pieces of living room furniture. Holding one another close, they danced in the kitchen to Harry James's "I've Heard That Song Before"; Joe didn't mind that she played it over and over again. After dinner, they might watch a movie or even a ballgame—Kay could handle Tigers baseball now that she was fighting the new stadium with the old one. Little by little, she began to tell Joe about the items she had discovered in the crate and her other searches. They cuddled together on the now-threadbare brown plaid family sofa, exchanging kisses and whispering, as if Mr. and Mrs. Chase were still asleep in the next room.

FRED

ONE NIGHT, KAY SHOWED JOE A PHOTOGRAPH AND HELD A FLASH-
light over it for added illumination. It was a somber picture, old and
brown, printed on thick card, but with a crease running along one side.
It showed a neat, sparsely furnished room, with a dark wood table
placed against the wall. Ada Gaillard, Kay's grandmother, had written
matter-of-factly on the back of the card: *McClellan Street, Detroit,
1919. Our daughter Marion was born in this room on March 20, 1917.*

"This picture," Kay said, "must have been taken before Fred and
Ada packed up and moved permanently to Middleville in western
Michigan, traveling in a Model T, probably one Fred had helped to
produce, as it passed down the assembly line."

Then she told Joe about Henry Ford's cranky declaration that the
city was doomed and the only solution was to leave the city behind.
"Some say this was the thinking behind the Model T," she said. "And
it's true that farmers and traveling salesmen fell in love with the
Model T.

"So there is little use looking for traces of my mother in Detroit.
Marion was moved out of the city in 1919, at the age of two, and did
not live there again. She grew up in the country, on the banks of the
Thornapple River, with no memory of the city. No one in our family
ever spoke much about the Detroit Gaillards. Until he died, Fred rep-
resented the sole person I might have asked, if only I had known back
then that I would care *later*. Once, when I was eight or nine, we were
shoveling snow together in Middleville. Fred made big mounds for me
to jump in. He told me then that I reminded him of his sister, Bell,
playing in the yard in Detroit, but I didn't take much notice of the remark at the time."

Joe handed the picture back and sank into the sofa, his eyes half closed.

"Keep talking," he murmured.

"When I knew him, my grandfather was already an old man, slightly built, with a handsome face, even as he aged. He was musical and could play the piano by ear. If he wasn't near a keyboard, he liked to take out his rhythm bones and click along to scratchy Louis Armstrong records. And sometimes when he sang popular songs, he cried, you know, the way people do. They choke on a particular line; tears stream down their cheeks to be wiped away by a shirt cuff. It's interesting to notice which songs get to a person. Me—I can't make it through the second verse of 'I'll Be Seeing You.' The first verse, no problem. But the second verse kills me every time.

"Fred had quite a few songs that killed him. But the one I remember best is 'Have Yourself a Merry Little Christmas.' In over twenty years of singing it, not once did Fred remain dry eyed past the opening lines. Thank goodness he never knew the original 1944 lyrics, discarded when Judy Garland demanded something less dismal to sing to little Margaret O'Brien in *Meet Me in St. Louis*."

"How do you *know* this stuff?" Joe asked.

"Oh . . . that's just Hollywood lore. Plus, I look things up."

And of course, Kay had looked up the original lines to the song and she sang them to him:

Have yourself a merry little Christmas; it may be your last.
Next year we may all be living in the past.
Have yourself a merry little Christmas, make the Yuletide gay.
Next year we may all be many miles away.
No good times like the olden days, happy golden days of yore.
Faithful friends who were dear to us will be near to us no more.
But at least we all will be together if the fates allow.
From now on we'll have to muddle through somehow.
So have yourself a merry little Christmas now.

"Jesus," Joe muttered. "Should I slit my wrists now or later?"

"There was nothing special about Fred," she continued. "Like anybody, he felt the movement of time and things changing and disappearing. You know. His eyes would mist, or he might choke up a little when he spoke about absent friends, taverns in Detroit, old baseball players, and Tiger Stadium, which he still referred to as 'Bennett Park' or sometimes 'The Corner.' I think he missed Detroit all his adult life. Whenever my grandparents came to visit us here in Garden City, even if the Tigers were playing away, Fred would try to organize a Sunday-afternoon drive downtown. But my father spent the working week commuting to Ford Motor Company offices in Detroit or Dearborn, and wasn't much interested in spending his weekends anywhere near those places.

"My final memories of Fred date from 1972, when he lived with us after Grandma Ada died. He was frail and frequently demented—"

"No," Joe interrupted her sternly. "Nothing after 1969."

"I can't cheat Fred Gaillard of his last years. I'm sorry."

Joe gave no reply, nor did he stand up and walk away. He closed his eyes tight, and the muscles in his face twitched; that was all. In fact, it would be Joe who, as the summer wore on, broke the "nothing after 1969" rule more often than Kay. He broke it to remind her that she had let him down.

"Anyway . . . so Fred came to live with us," she continued in softer voice. "And I remember that over his nightly martini, the last of a diminishing number of ritual pleasures, he watched the news, berating the anti-war protestors. He complained about the hippies and Yippies, who he said were taking over the country. He railed at a land in which he no longer recognized himself. I thought the future was mine and quarreled with him frequently. Sometimes, I played Donovan's 'Mellow Yellow' at top volume, just to annoy him. He loathed Donovan, called him the *ah-ah-ah* singer, on account of the vibrato in his voice."

"Yeah, I gotta agree with him on that," Joe said, relaxing a little.

"Physically, Fred had slowed to a crawl, and urine was always dribbling down his trousers because it took him too long to walk to the bathroom. His moods veered wildly. One day he was feisty and rambled about being a Frenchman. 'I'm movin' to Paris,' he announced from his armchair, addressing no one in particular. 'And I'll keep a bunch of lady friends there.' The next day, he was back in his armchair, morose and staring ahead in silence. My mom put her arm around his bony shoulder and asked, 'What's wrong, Dad?' And all he said was, 'It's hell to grow old.'

"Finally, my parents decided they could no longer care for him and found a place in a local nursing home. They moved him there after Christmas 1972, and he died within six months. He just stopped, like his old pocket watch he was always forgetting to wind."

Joe opened his eyes wide, the way listeners do when a story turns. Every look he gave Kay was composed of thousands of looks from the past, just as every one of their younger ages hung between them, refusing to die. They sat close, tenderly studying one another. It was such a long pause that she assumed the subject of her grandfather had come to a natural close.

"What do you want to do?" Joe asked, finally.

"You mean . . . do I want to go for an ice cream or get married?"

"I mean—what do you want to do about *Fred*," he said, with a rueful smile.

"Oh. About Fred."

She thought for a moment.

"I guess I'd like to go down to Detroit and see if he's still there. And *then* get married."

He reached over, took the photo from Kay's fingers, eased her slowly down onto the sofa, leaned over, stroked her lips and throat, and then moved his hand downward to unbutton her blouse.

FRENCHMAN

IN JANUARY 1896, SEVEN-YEAR-OLD FRED GAILLARD WOKE WITH A start when the downstairs door clicked shut. He listened for his father's footsteps, light at first, then a loud crunching noise in the snow outside the house, as they crossed the yard to the street and moved away. It was still dark outside and too cold to be out of bed, but Fred silently berated himself for not getting up to say goodbye. It would be his fault if something bad happened to his father.

Jacques Gaillard walked the two miles from their second-floor flat on Concord Street in Detroit to the downtown corner of Gratiot and Farmer. He was headed for J. L. Hudson's emporium, and he carried a letter of recommendation provided by his previous employer, who was friendly with the store manager. Having delivered the letter to one of the sales assistants, Jacques stayed outside the eight-story building. Just under an hour later, a second neatly dressed assistant returned to lead Jacques up seven flights to a paneled office. The manager, pink in complexion and embarrassingly young, stared from behind his desk at the Frenchman.

"Mr. Gaillard," he began. "I'm afraid there are no openings at present. Sales are down. As it is, I have a difficult time keeping the staff occupied."

Jacques remained there, wordless, as fresh snow flurries blew across the window behind the manager.

"Much as I would like to help you. . . ." the voice trailed off, then rallied. "We receive many requests such as yours, Mr. . . ."

"Gaillard."

"Yes. Mr. Gaillard. Sorry I cannot offer you anything at the moment."

There was further silence, after which the manager tried again. "We have a long list of applicants. And of course shopwork requires a certain demeanor, if you see what I mean . . . a manner . . . a *sociability.*"

Jacques stood, persistently polite and unable to leave, while the younger man grew flustered and talked aloud to the room.

"On the other hand, Mr. . . . Gaillard. I suppose there are small things that come up. Things that can't always be covered by the sales workers. I am afraid it would mean a good deal of waiting around, but I could use someone who doesn't mind doing odd jobs at short notice."

"I don't mind," Jacques returned quickly.

"And of course I cannot promise to have something for you every day. It would be payment strictly by the task."

"I don't mind," Jacques repeated.

This is how the manager talked himself into making a skilled typesetter and a man at least five years his senior an errand boy for Hudson's.

Throughout the early months of the year, from Monday to Saturday, as first light appeared in the sky, Jacques could be seen waiting at the back entrance of the Hudson building for his patron to arrive. He positioned himself carefully, not too close to the door, but not so far away as to be invisible. He had grasped that the trick was to appear as a permanent fixture, alert and ready to serve, without scaring anybody.

Each morning, the manager gave a nod as he passed the Frenchman. Jacques waited. Sometimes he waited minutes, sometimes hours. But most days, one of the assistants would come to the back door with a small job of some sort—a message to be delivered, a package to be dispatched, crates to be unloaded, or snow to be shoveled into the horse-drawn wagons that would carry it away to be dumped in the river. Jacques would complete each task and recommence waiting, shaking and rubbing his coat sleeves, shifting his weight from one foot to another, wriggling his toes against the numbing cold inside his boots. He stayed until after four o'clock each afternoon, and when there were no more jobs to be done, he would be handed an envelope with a small sum of money inside. As the winter sun lowered in the city sky, the former typesetter, a little gray for his thirty-six years, retraced the steps along Champlain Street toward Concord to put the day's earnings in his wife's hand.

EVEN IN THAT LEAN YEAR OF 1896, WHEN JACQUES WALKED HOME alone, face down in the cold, withdrawn in an oversized coat, he must have sensed the clamor and promise of a modern metropolis, of its two hundred thousand people. He might have loved that he belonged there, although his part in it was small and anonymous. Jacques had precious little knowledge of the chain of people and events that had set him down in this northern city, rather than anywhere else. He understood vaguely that his ancestors were old Detroiters, perhaps among the settlers of Fort Pontchartrain du Detroit, with its log houses, Jesuits, trappers, and fur traders. But the original French colony had long since disappeared, and anyway, the Gaillards had not been important. The surname did not appear on any of the early land grants, riverfront properties stretching a couple of miles inland, the so-called "ribbon farms" of French Detroit. Nor did Jacques realize that a handful of surviving French street names in the city—St. Aubin, Beaubien, St. Antoine, and Cadieux among others—derived from these farms or early landowners. The last houses of French Detroit had been wiped out in the fire of 1805, and only a few ruined gravestones or lost parish records might prove the old Gaillards had ever set foot in the place. It was a dislocated clan with no real legacy, and Jacques knew of only a handful of distant cousins still residing in the city.

This is not to say Jacques was without memory. Not at all. His *body* remembered, storing something of the dead generations. The ancestors inhabited his natural shape and gestures, the dark brown, already silver-flecked hair, the way his face weathered in the North American air, the tiniest inflections in his voice.

Ancestral memory colonized not only his flesh and frame, but something less corporeal that cast a shadow over his spirits and movements. For example, when passing various locations around the central and riverfront areas of Detroit, Jacques regularly suffered a strange sensation. It might be the pleasurable rush of butterfly stomach, pride and excitement in the place, or sometimes an alarming pang of cymbals clashing inside. And one day, walking along Jefferson Avenue, Jacques grew unaccountably tearful. He averted his eyes from passersby, ashamed to be discovered, a grown man crying on the street, overtaken by a sudden heartache for which he had no explanation.

Jacques was probably neither the first nor the last of a number of Gaillards across the generations who experienced their ancestry as a kind of affliction. Men who choked with pleasure when they sang and shivered when trains rattled across the city late at night. Men in whom lineal and place memory were so subtly registered that they could sense the trace of the dead in their earliest childhood room, and recall, decades later from their own deathbed in another house, the somber-hued texture of that first room. Men who might remember *forward* and so be seized by emotion for reasons they could not quite identify, though they felt certain that somehow, reasons would come to exist.

Jacques's wife, Clara, had grown accustomed to his brief fits of melancholy, comforting him or gently teasing him, bringing him back. In winter, it was hard to pull Jacques away from himself, but in summer, Clara could cheer him with a dose of mild air. A family outing to Belle Isle, just across the river from the end of their street, a cool drink under the late-afternoon sun, these devices worked powerfully on her husband's moods. Sometimes after the children were asleep, Clara took his hand and led him downstairs to the yard behind the house. There they might stand on parched summer weeds, laced together, watching the night sky.

CHARLIE BENNETT

JACQUES GAILLARD HAD PLAYED AND WATCHED BASEBALL SINCE childhood, and his closest friendships had been made in alleyway matches and in the bleachers. He could remember as far back as the Hollinger Nine, a local team formed in 1879 and disbanded after one season. Detroiters then switched their allegiance to the Wolverines, the city's first major league club. After five losing seasons, Jacques belonged to a dwindling but faithful band of enthusiasts finally rewarded with a winning stretch and a world championship in 1887. That year, the crowds returned to Recreation Park over on the east side to watch the likes of Dan Brouthers, Sam Thompson, and catcher Charlie Bennett take the team to victory.

In those days, Jacques was earning a good wage at one of the city's older, small presses, and could easily afford the fifty cents admission. He contributed to the collection made by supporters in honor of the crowd favorite Bennett and watched the presentation alongside workmates and boyhood friends in noisy stands along the first-base line. He grew hoarse with cheering when Bennett did the round of the bases, pushing his gift of a wheelbarrow loaded with 520 silver dollars and a floral horseshoe. Jacques had a clear view of the whole scene: Bennett and his wheelbarrow, the other players looking on, the carriages, horses, and lines of baseball fanatics that ringed the outfield, and the ramshackle wildcat stands, constructed by poorer spectators on the roofs of buildings just outside the park.

In 1888, the Wolverines returned to their bad-luck ways. Team injuries resulted in the loss of the franchise, and Jacques saw out the Wolverines' final matches in bleachers grown dolefully quiet. Charlie Bennett was picked up by the Boston Beaneaters, where he would play out his few remaining seasons. But in 1894, after a new Detroit franchise was formed to join the reorganized Western League, local supporters dared to hope the owners might persuade Bennett to come back to Detroit. Then news came of the catcher's tragic hunting trip to Kansas. Jacques wept openly like he'd lost a friend; he tried to imagine what went through Bennett's mind as he slipped under a moving train in a town called Wellsville and mangled both his legs beyond repair. The boys at the printworks took up a collection for him.

Originally called the Creams, the new team before long became popularly known as the Tigers. Nobody knew for sure where the name originated, but some thought it took hold after the players appeared wearing black and brown stockings. Whatever the reason, sometime after 1895, spectators and reporters began to refer to the team as the Tigers. The name stuck. At newspaper stands and in taverns around the city, people discussed their team with *the Tigers this and the Tigers that, how'd the Tigers do today, what's the Tigers' score,* and so on and so forth. Jacques latched onto it straightaway because his youngest son, Fred, liked the name.

The first years of Tigers baseball were also depression years, and a third of the laborers in Detroit were out of work as the city's heavy industries, the shipbuilders and railroad equipment manufacturers, were either shut or wound down. Already the target of local anti-immigrant sentiment and the first to lose their jobs, foreign-born, unskilled workers were among the worst affected. Detroit had highly demarcated ethnic neighborhoods, and in Corktown, Dutchtown, Polacktown, along Sauerkraut Row, and the small black quarter known as Kentucky, hunger and early death could be mapped room by room and street by street. After epidemics of diphtheria and smallpox, the gravediggers wrapped their heads in gauze, and marked doors could be seen throughout the city.

A skilled printer of good standing, Jacques held on to his job longer than many of his mates and even managed to attend opening day of 1895, when Charlie Bennett, now an amputee, caught the ceremonial pitch from Mayor Hazen Pingree. But by May of that year, Jacques feared the worst and began handing his ticket money over to Clara. By the end of July, he had lost his position. With the onset of cold weather in the fall, the baseball season came to an end, and there was little diversion to break the daily search for employment. In the dark winter evenings that followed, when the ballpark disappeared under snow and Jacques came back from Hudson's, carrying his envelope, Fred would race toward him, pull his sleeve, and demand to know about the team.

"Did the Tigers win, Dad? Did ya see the Tigers today?"

No matter how many times Jacques explained that the Tigers didn't play in winter, Fred, discomfited by the marks of anxiety and fatigue on his father's face, would pretend to forget by the next evening. When in town, Jacques listened out for a bit of team news, some rumor that he could impart to his son to keep the exchange going. Once he even lied to Fred that he had seen Charlie Bennett, hobbling on wooden legs along Woodward Avenue, smoking a cigar.

A DISEASE OF AN
AFFLICTED IMAGINATION

LATE ONE NIGHT, UNSURE IF JOE WAS ASLEEP, KAY SLIPPED QUIETLY out of bed, tiptoed to the fridge, poured a glass of iced tea, and carried it into the spare room, now a makeshift study.

Stacked with books and papers, the desk was lit pale yellow by a streetlight. There were some loose diary pages written by Fred's sister, Bell, along with a handful of letters exchanged between brother and sister after Fred left Detroit. There were also charts and lists pinned to a large bulletin board, but Kay's postings had spilled onto the surrounding walls. Various prints and photographs were held by blue tacks at crooked little angles, not just family pictures, but also early postcard scenes of Detroit, Belle Isle, and the Great Lakes. There were single pages torn from books, one showing Charlie Bennett and his championship team, another with photographs of Henry Ford and the Model T. The floor was covered in maps, a large, unfolded map of Detroit and next to it another one of Garden City, then a massive one of the whole of Michigan, also unfolded.

Each morning, holding a mug of coffee aloft, Kay walked across the map of Michigan to get to her desk. Or she stood there, bare feet on the middle of the Lower Peninsula, eating a piece of toast, dropping crumbs on towns and counties, as she planned her day. "Ha-ha. I'm covering a lotta ground," she said to herself one morning, looking down at her toes on the map. But in truth, much of Kay's daily movement, especially when Joe was at work, now took place within those four walls. After Marion's death, Kay had absconded from the present, gone AWOL, and that small, stuffy, increasingly cluttered room was her refuge, and the insular result of grief-stricken flight.

Like many people, Kay was interested in family history and the growing pile of available records. Documents, tinted photographs, mementos. The forlorn quest for ancestry, some sense of where she came from and something larger than her own place and life span. To cut loose from the houses and sidewalks, the rows of school lockers, the postwar decades that brought Silly Putty and electric toothbrushes to a generation with no identifiable claim to greatness. The baby boomers had exited their vitamin-fortified, comfortable childhoods to enter pill-popping, comfortable adulthoods. They found it hard to sleep. Those with cooperative doctors were taking state-of-the-art prescription drugs; everyone else stocked up on Benadryl and Tylenol PM, over-the-counter sledgehammers of sleeping remedies. *How'd you do last night? Pretty good, I took a PM. Just a little heady this morning though. Is the coffee on?* Kay fell into the last category, never having managed to persuade her doctor to write a scrip for more than five doses of anything interesting, even though she tried to tell him that she could not sleep for the most shameful of all possible reasons: she could not sleep because she had not done anything to tire herself out.

Yet not doing anything tiring, and not sleeping because of it, brought a different kind of fatigue, deep and chronic, as though each long day was like moving through snowdrifts. Kay knew plenty of people from college or work who, sometime during their adult years, began to drag and complain of feeling "tired all the time." If she stood outside their houses at three o'clock in the morning, she'd find some lights on. As a generation, they kept odd hours and were constantly scratching at nonexistent wounds, striving to invent a collective suffering or significance. But in the absence of hard evidence, as the years dragged on and they failed to come up with anything convincing, they turned to prescription and non-prescription aids, health foods and exercise, self-help books, therapy, shopping. And they looked backward for a personal history of some kind, using heirlooms, ritual, and ephemera, marking dates and locations, purchasing dozens of photo frames with little cutaway mounts for whole galleries of family pictures.

Like most people she knew, Kay often situated and described her own memories with reference to old songs, movies, and other ready-made cultural artifacts. Then she turned to more songs and movies in order to mediate her emotional responses to those same memories. The baby boomers were an exceedingly nostalgic bunch, insular, naive, and consequently a marketing man's dream. They could be relied upon to buy stuff they didn't need from catalogs, gift shops, and year-round Christmas stores. Nostalgia was a seduction of some complexity and deceit, an inescapable, addictive, and yes, quite agreeable part of most people's relation to the past and the workings of memory. Nearly every act of reminiscence was colored by it. The entire process was a stitch-up from start to finish. Wide awake in Joe's house in the middle of the night, Kay was dimly aware that it had achieved pathological proportions in her, and it was hard to imagine living otherwise.

She closed the study door, stepped as quietly as possible across the crackling map paper, found her chair, and switched on the computer. She sipped her iced tea while the screen flickered to life, then googled the word "nostalgia" and got a dizzying four and a half million hits.

After an hour or so spent scrolling through some of the web pages, Kay had found numerous swingin' sixties links and ones for every other decade up to and including the nineties. There was a Wild West screensavers site and another called Treasures of Nostalgia, which sold rock 'n' roll memorabilia and classic Hollywood posters. She took out a membership in that one, before moving on to links for baseball-card and comic-book collectors, big-band, vinyl, and jukebox junkies, even people with sentimental longings for yo-yos and Hula Hoops or cravings for cotton candy, Bazooka bubble gum, and snow cones. There were old coins, Civil War bullets, vintage dresses, souvenirs of gangsters and Prohibition.

She then tried another tactic, punching in different combinations, nostalgia and memory, nostalgia and the past, nostalgia and the present and future. With these terms, she found scholarly essays about postmodernity and the end of history. There was a political tract blaming nostalgia for the failure of revolutionary socialism. She even spotted an anti-nostalgia direct-action group that boasted over three hundred members, a newsletter, and an annual conference. Kay read until her concentration began to fail, after which she tried more random search terms—nostalgia and humans, nostalgia and men, women, then nostalgia and places—before lapsing into a hypnotic trail of free association: nostalgia and the sun, to moon, tides, water, lake, wishing well, *well*, sick, sickness, pathology. That was when the search broke wide open.

Kay happened upon a text wildly outside her time frame, yet eerily familiar and more intriguing than all the sites, links, words, and images seen thus far. In 1688, a Swiss physician named Johannes Hofer published his brief "Medical Dissertation on Nostalgia." In 1934, the piece was translated into English and published in the *Bulletin of the History of Medicine*. Having languished in the fusty back shelves of university libraries for much of the twentieth century, it now floated quietly in cyberspace, an unpolished gem among the thousands of web pages making mention of *nostalgia*. Hofer's dissertation was a brief but detailed investigation of a malady he characterized principally as "the sad mood originating from the desire to return to one's native land."

While allowing that notions of *homesickness*, the German word *heimweh* and the French *mal du pays*, went some way to defining what was in fact, a *disease*, Hofer argued that a medical name, an agreed set of symptoms and effective treatments were required. After briefly considering the terms *nosomania* and *philopatridomania*, Hofer settled on *nostalgia*—"Greek in origin and indeed composed of two sounds, the one of which is *Nosos*, return to the native land; the other, *Algos*, signifies suffering or grief."

According to Hofer, nostalgia was a disease of an "afflicted imagination" that regularly resulted in death. In its early stages, nostalgia manifested as a general melancholy accompanied by obsessive thoughts and recurrent images of one's homeland. This caused a "continuous vibration of animal spirits through those fibers of the middle brain in which impressed traces of ideas of the Fatherland still cling." The *increase* in activity through the nerve channels where memories of home were stored resulted in *decreased* blood flow to the other regions of the brain. So in a self-perpetuating process, the obsessive thoughts would worsen, while interest in one's own physical well-being and current surroundings would diminish. As the disease progressed, diagnostic signs included sadness and anxiety, "frequent sighs," disturbed sleep, loss of appetite, poor blood circulation, heart palpitations, and fevers. Finally, declared Hofer, "by consuming the spirits . . . it [nostalgia] hastens death."

Rattled by the chance discovery of a hidden history of nostalgia, Kay had no idea how the original meaning of Hofer's invented term had been lost. There was no reference to Hofer in the discussions of nostalgia she had tracked thus far. Although scholars now might present it as a collective cultural or political affliction, it was no longer considered an organic illness to be logged in medical manuals or even in the psychiatric casebooks. So it struck Kay as peculiar that she had wandered into the most obscure and distant domain of the kingdom of nostalgia, as if she had known it was there all along. In a flicker of projected light, she envisaged Dorothy standing at the portal to the Emerald City, desiring and dreading her first encounter with the Wizard.

Kay leaned over the keyboard and narrowed her search to Johannes Hofer and the history of medicine. There quickly appeared a handful of recent references to the Swiss physician: three genealogical links to Hofer family trees; a bibliographic citation in a book called *Mental Illness in Early Modern Europe*; and most promising of all, two separate articles by a Dr. Elmer Thisroy. The first, published in the *Baltimore Journal of the History of Medicine* in 1999, was entitled "Nostalgia Ain't What It Used to Be: Medical Discourse and a Lost Malady." The second piece appeared in December 2002, an entry in a psychiatric journal called *Case Notes*, under the title "Hofer's Condition: A New Pathology of Longing." Neither article was available online, so Kay made a note of the publication details. Dr. Thisroy would have to wait until she got to a library.

It was past three in the morning when she finally shut down the computer and left her desk. Somewhat reluctantly, she took a box file from the shelf, ready for later in the day. It contained papers and letters relating to Ada Parker, the Middleville girl Fred Gaillard would marry. Kay had delayed opening it, perhaps because she preferred to keep company with Fred, keep him young, keep him to herself for as long as possible.

As a child, Kay had never warmed to Ada naturally, the way she had to Fred. She certainly enjoyed her grandmother's energy and playfulness, the practical jokes she liked to pull. Ada was always game for a little harmless mischief, and that made her the most popular of the grandmothers who regularly came to visit the young families of Maple Court, back in the fifties and sixties. The kids on the street liked her; she was fun to be around. But within the family, tiny jealousies were sometimes roused by her arrival. Pam, Sid, and Kay knew that their grandmother had a great deal of influence over Marion, and their mother was less attentive to them when Ada visited. Ada was also more robust than Fred, bigger in physical size and build, and emotionally tougher. Kay never knew her grandmother to cry at a song or a memory; Ada wasn't one for reminiscing or keeping scrapbooks. The few times Kay asked her about growing up in Middleville, Ada answered somewhat forbiddingly, "Oh that's too long ago. I don't remember."

Kay decided to get a few hours rest before turning her attention to Ada and the next box file. She yawned and stretched, went into the living room, and looked out the front door, still vaguely trying to think of a reason to care more for her grandmother. There was a dank, uneven gleam over Garden City, a lonely place with its rows of houses and streetlights, dew-covered yards, redundant baby-boom schools and playgrounds, bowling alleys, used-car showrooms, and fast-food joints. The crickets and cicadas, so clamorous a few hours earlier, had quieted. She listened for a while, pressing her face into the screen door. Finally, she whispered her mother's name through the wire mesh, as if Marion had never disappeared from Maple Court, but was waiting on the other side of the door. Kay breathed her mother's name and could smell the name as it left her mouth and crossed the screen.

She wondered, then, if Marion heard or smelled or felt her, just as she wondered if *Ada* had felt *Marion,* calling out a few days before death. Marion's voice was weak by the end, and raspy, but the word "Mother" was audible and yes, it smelled, it smelled of cancer. Yet its meaning was as vital as a bell. At that precise moment, Marion turned away from her children and she was ready to die. She ceased to be an old woman or anyone's mother or wife; she was Ada's helpless child again.

48

ALLIE GREEN

HELD TOGETHER BY A PIECE OF WORN RIBBON, THE THREE LETTERS were addressed to Mrs. Violet Parker of Shaw Farm in Middleville. Kay transcribed them exactly as they were written.

Grand Rapids, Michigan
December 6, 1894

Dear Mrs. Parker,

I have become more than anxious to know how Baby Ada is. I hope she does not cry too much. My going away is postponed. When it came time to go I just could not, so it's postponed for a time and maybe for all time. Now you must write me on receat [sic] of this as it seems a lifetime since I heard from you. I hope Ada is getting along nicely and I long to see her.

I am working now, learning a trade, but will send some money in next letter. I am sorry I could not have sent before this. I have other things ready for you, but will keep my flannels and heavy night dresses now that I am staying here. One very much needs all the warm clothes they can get in this cold weather and it has been extremeley [sic] cold for about two weeks. I often wonder if the boys keep good fires these winter nights. How do they get along?

If you at anytime should grow tired of Ada, let me know at once. I think everything of her and it might be at some time I could do better by her than I can at present. As soon as I am able, I will go to see you, and the dear little Baby. I am sorry I could not have gone before this. Does she cry very much? I hope she is a good little girl.

49

Whenever I can do anything for you it would be a pleasure for me to do any good turn you may wish. You will always find me a true friend. You have certainly done an awful lot for me, and I appreciate it.

Hoping soon to hear from you, I close for this time. Kiss Baby for me, and please except [*sic*] my Love.

Allie Green

Grand Rapids
April 17, 1895

Dear Mrs. Parker,

Please don't let anyone but yourself read. Your note was received in good time and I am so glad Baby is better. I should like to see her sweet little face and hands and feet but I am afraid I never can. I must leave things to your judgment. I feel very bad to think I cannot have Her, but as it looks now I <u>cannot.</u> And I know if I were to see Her again it would drive me wild to think of giving Her away as she seems like a part of me. I love Her more than everything else on earth. And yet I cannot have Her. It does seem cruel, but I will say keep her yourself, or find good people who will want her.

I have had Him come to see me twice and have talked to him, but I don't think He will ever do my wish though He is sorry. I believe He worries over the trouble. That's why I have waited and tried to keep her with you, thinking possibly he could desid [*sic*] in the right way, but as yet he has not, and I don't quite expect He ever will. That's the way in this life. I often wish I were dead or I had money to take Baby and myself far away and act the widow, in some place where no one would know me. Then I would be happy and only then.

I am very sorry Baby seems to have throat trouble, and I feel more than greatful [*sic*] to you for the tender care you gave during Her sickness. Just be good to Baby while she is with you and I will pay you all I can. No one knows how badly I feel. It would be a blessing if she would die and a great comfort to me. As I always shall worry about Her. Girls do seem to have such a hard time in this world. I hope if she lives to grow up that she may be one of the fortunate ones.

Now I am going to change my address and don't know exactly what it will be. So I will tell you to wait till you hear from me again before answering. I am sending you a little express package, some things I think are to [*sic*] good to throw away. Maybe you can make use of them sometime. The tie is for you if you like it and the two picture cards I think will be nice to hang in your kitchen. I wish it was so that I could send something nice to my dear little girl. Sweet Baby, kiss Her for me. I am almost broken hearted to think my lot in life is such.

I am pleased you don't talk of me to any one. It's the right way to do. You make no mistake in doing for me all you can as I would give all the rest of my natural life to right all the errors. Never tell any of my People where I am if you please. They have no need to know and I wish to be forgotten by them, even if they ask you don't ever tell, and oblige yours truly.

Now I will close with love and many kisses for little Ada. And don't think strange of my saying I am going to change. I leave Grand Rapids tomorrow. You will hear from me when I get settled, which I expect in a week or ten days.

Yours very sincerely,
Allie

Chicago
November 27, 1895

Dear Mrs. Parker,

You will think me inhuman. I am sure, but please don't senture [*sic*] me too hard. You know, circumstance aulters [*sic*] all cases. I have so very often wished for news of my sweet little one, but as I have no chance of having Her, have thought it best not to know. But I cannot wait longer. I have not written a word in months. So excuse scribbling. Am I making a great many mistakes?

I will be here in Chicago a few days and will ask that you reply at once. Telling me how and where Baby is. If she is not with you, give me the address of the people where she is, write it plain so I will make no mistake.

I am just wild to hear of Her. Sometimes I have been nearly crazy and thought I never could live without knowing. Now will you please answer at once or have someone answer for you as I may not be heare [sic] long enough to get your letter if you don't reply at once.

I am staying at a hotel tonight but it's too high a price for me and I don't know just where to go, so cannot give street address. As it's not far from Post Office I will get mail there, General Delivery. I wish I could see you and talk to you. I imagine if Ada is alive she is walking by now. I must see Her before long, please do tell me just how she is my heart aches to know of her.

And now I ask you one favor more. Keep my letters safe. If for some reason I cannot write or go back, you must promise me if Ada lives to be sixteen, you will hand the letters to Her. I have not given names or spoken ill of anyone, you know it is so. Give her my letters, so she mighte [sic] understand things and the suffering it caused me to leave Her to you. If I never see her I may have the comfort of knowing that when she is grown, in the year 1910, she will have these few pages from me.

Now I close as time is precious and I trust you will write so I can get it before three o'clock Saturday, as I may not be able to stay in the city much longer.

Yours ever,
Allie Green

PS. Remember, General Delivery, Chicago, Illinois and promise to me

As far as Kay knew, there were just the three letters, spanning nearly a year, with several months separating each one. Hopelessly thin, rambling and evasive, they ended abruptly, at a terrible point. Crucial information, including the name of Ada's father, was withheld. Allie protected him, although he did not deserve it. In doing so, she colluded in a lie, a feeble lie that would not stand up over time. Yet, for all that, Allie Green's letters were among the few documents Kay possessed in which someone actually spoke from the past. And as ciphered material—ink marks on cream-colored stationery, words said or left unsaid, Allie's letters revealed much. They were a record of her poverty and exile, her gradual disintegration.

Kay showed the letters to Joe, and carefully disclosed who Allie was and her part in Ada's story. Joe would fall half in love with Allie Green; Kay knew that, and she proved to be right. He half loved Allie for the same reasons Kay half hated her. First, there was Allie's hesitancy and doubt, evident in the run-on sentences and random spelling errors made by a young woman who clearly had some education. Then there was her habit, like a ceding of power or a superstition, of capitalizing the pronouns referring to Ada: *She, Her.* And then, *Baby.* And the same for the unnamed father: *I have had Him come to see me.* The rushed handwriting in the original letters suggested distraction, time running out, blind alleys, hunger and fatigue, even the late risings and fallings of hope that people in deep trouble experience before the end.

Joe felt tenderness toward Allie and continued to wonder aloud about her after the letters had been put away. He talked about what he called her *ways.* The way she thanked Violet Parker repeatedly, described herself as "wild" and "crazy" to know of the baby. The way she changed her mind about leaving and then changed it back again, trapped herself in promises to write or visit, followed by resolutions *not* to write or visit, all in confused phrases that left her turning in circles without a compass. She even set down the fantasy that only her baby's death might bring comfort and release from worry, despite the fact that Ada (by Allie's own request) might read that fantasy one day. Yes, Kay saw that Joe would think about Allie and her ways long after the letters had been set aside. Allie Green was the kind of person he liked to think about.

The marks of Allie's misery, the very same marks that elicited Joe's tenderness, provoked resentment in Kay. Whatever happened could not be put right. It was too late. All the main players were dead and buried, and there was no undoing past injuries. Kay knew that. It was like being invited into a historical conspiracy, to do to Allie *again* what evidently had been done to her more than a century earlier: turn her into a secret, leave her out there, precise fate and whereabouts unknown.

SIXTEEN

"YOU DO LOOK BEAUTIFUL!" LON EXCLAIMED, GAZING UP AT HIS sister as she appeared at the top of the stairs.

Ada Parker smiled, brightening at the compliment. Just turned sixteen, she was celebrating two occasions in the same week: her birthday and her graduation from Middleville High School, class of 1910. Lon was accompanying Ada to the photographer's studio to have a portrait made, and she wore the cream satin dress made especially for the graduation ceremony. She carried her diploma, rolled and tied with a sky blue ribbon, and had pinned back her rich hair with a matching bow.

Beneath the satin, Ada was brown and strong-boned, with large hands and a square-shaped face. A tall and athletic girl, she normally turned stiff and awkward when forced into formal dress. But her slim handsomeness was thrown into relief by the straight, ankle-length gown, giving her a grace that surprised Lon and the others. Ada, too, was startled by her reflection in the hall mirror. Every day of the years now gone, she had caught a glimpse of her younger self, hurrying past the glass on the way outdoors, but change had concealed itself in the daily repetition of looking.

After the appointment with the photographer, they would all lunch at Aunt Lizzie's. There would be gifts and toasts from the cousins, and Ada had been promised her first taste of wine. A party was planned for the evening, and invitations had gone out to family, neighbors, and school friends. Mama and Ada had been cooking and cleaning for days, while the boys ran errands, hung Chinese lanterns on the porch, and pushed the furniture against the walls to make space for dancing.

Outside the white, wood-framed house, a warm breeze moved

through the leaves of the elm tree, causing sunlight to glitter like a thousand tiny shards of reflecting glass. In the forest at the edge of the fields, it was what Mama liked to call a "dappled" day, when light and shadow bobbed and danced together as old partners. The window shades, half drawn to keep the house cool, made soft sucking and flapping sounds when caught by the breeze. Touching her white-gloved hand to the banister, Ada stepped carefully down toward her eldest and favorite brother. The short sleeves of her dress were hemmed in a wide strip of satin, edged with a delicate fringe of tiny beads. The fringe hung loosely over the top of each fitted, elbow-length glove. On Ada's left wrist and set off by the white glove hung the pale gold bracelet Lon had given her as a graduation gift, a simple band finely engraved with her name and the year, 1910.

"You like?" she asked, holding out her arm so that Lon might admire the elegance of his choice.

He brushed his finger over the gold, studied it with a half smile, and then looked up. "I like," he answered, offering Ada his arm.

She was pleased and proud that Lon had been so determined to accompany her to the photographer. Clasping his elbow and tucking her other hand into the bend in his arm, Ada felt a wave of muscular force radiate right through his shirt sleeve and her glove, ending beneath her own skin in a sudden, low shudder.

"Oh! Somebody just walked on my grave," she said nervously.

"Don't say that," Lon replied.

Now aged thirty-five, Lon was a strongly built man, perhaps the most striking of Violet Parker's three grown sons. For as long as Ada could remember, he had lived away from home, in Grand Rapids, where he had worked his way up to well-paid foreman at Berkey and Gay Furniture Company. Her brother's return to Middleville every weekend was Ada's best part of the week. On Friday evenings in summer, sitting with her friends Helen and Betty on the front step, she would watch Lon make his way up the path, his straw hat pushed back on wavy hair and small leather traveling case tucked under his arm. Helen and Betty tittered and vied for his interest. But Lon reserved his attentions for his little sister. He winked and smiled and brought trinkets from town.

Every Friday after supper, Lon sat in the kitchen with his mother, talking over the events of the week and the things that needed doing around the house. Violet had been widowed for many years, and Lon helped her with household expenses and with the management of his younger brothers, or the *boys,* as Eugene and Merritt were still called. In fact, Eugene was thirty-two and thus far, the only Parker boy to settle down. As soon as the folks allowed it, he had married Mary Kendall, who lived across the fields at Parmalee Station. Eugene lived and worked on his wife's family farm, and the couple already had a son, Jack, eight years old, and a daughter, Agnes, who was six. Violet's grandchildren were regular visitors to the family house on Shaw Road.

Merritt Parker, now twenty-six, had been a high-spirited boy, playing truant from school and getting into fights. Recognizing his younger self in the unruly lad, Lon exercised a firm hand, and Merritt gradually settled down once his school days were behind him. He got a job at the town rail depot, proved a reasonably steady worker, and continued to live at home with Violet and Ada.

Despite his outward charm and the support he had given since his father's death, Lon had always been, and remained, Violet's most difficult son. The regimen he imposed on his youngest brother did not extend to his own conduct, and although he had lost some of the waywardness of his younger years, Lon, outside of work hours anyway, was restive and ungovernable. On Saturday evenings, he still went carousing or calling on one or two old friends not kept in by marriage, crawling home in the early hours of the morning, and only rising in time for Sunday lunch after the rest of the family had returned from church.

Violet felt sorry for any woman foolish enough to pin her hopes on Lon, as she was certain her eldest son never would marry. Lon's independence, like his impiety, was an immovable position, and the surest way to drive him away was to raise the subject of God or marriage. Each topic provoked the same response in Lon. "False beliefs and expectations make a person miserable," he would scoff before leaving the room. Violet suspected there might be a woman friend in the city, someone *without* false beliefs and expectations, but Lon never spoke of his life away from home, or of any alliances outside the family.

She recalled the years she had spent scratching at the surface of his good, if somewhat wild nature, trying to discover whether beneath it there was something that, as a mother, she ought to understand better, some flaw or childhood injury she had failed to recognize. Lon was eighteen when his father died, and as he passed from youth to manhood, Violet grieved and fretted about the late hours and drinking, the occasional rumor of rowdiness or of a girl left waiting for him. Violet followed her son around the house with anxious questions. At first, he patiently dealt with anything she asked, but nothing moved. Lon's outer line of defense was impenetrable, his affable answers designed to reveal nothing; her worries bounced off him like so many rubber tennis balls.

For a short period, Violet pressed her son more insistently, in a belated attempt to recover the veneer of parental authority that seemed to have disappeared with her husband. But Lon recoiled, became stubbornly withdrawn, and took to staying away for days, crawling home dog tired, and sleeping a few hours before disappearing again. This was an estrangement from her eldest son that no widow could afford, and so, finally, Violet accepted that she had never dictated the terms of the relationship and never would. Lon required a degree of autonomy that ran counter to her ingrained expectations, her unquestioned longing to care for him and be cared for in return. Therefore, she retrained herself. She began to push back the agitated words rising to her throat when he came home late. She stopped waiting up for him, tracking his movements, or reaching out to brush the hair away from his forehead. She imposed all sorts of bans on herself, until eventually the letting go of this son became almost natural. Motherhood was never the same for Violet after that. It was a regime overthrown, replaced by a lonelier, disappointed state, with no fixed laws or assured outcome. But Violet found this loosened her from the old ways of doing things, left her freer, because there was nothing more to try.

It was not long before Lon set Violet her toughest test. And so, during the central crisis of his emergent manhood, she kept close but silent, refusing finally to argue or take sides against him. In his down-to-earth and inscrutable way, Lon returned his mother's loyalty. There were things he would never say or give to her. But during the years that followed, she found she could rely on him to put money in her hand and kiss her cheek every Sunday after lunch, twirl Ada's braid in his fingers, remind his younger brothers of their chores, set off for the depot to catch the train to Grand Rapids, and be back the following Friday. Violet had released her first son, and to her great relief, he stayed. This was love.

Now Violet stood on the porch as he led Ada down the steps and along the front path to the livery rig hired for the day. She watched the two of them climb aboard, fuss over Ada's dress, laugh about something between them, wave back at the house, and trot away. Lon and Ada thought their mutual admiration was a private affair, but Violet had seen it unfold over the years. She was grateful that Lon had finally found one person whose claim to his care and protection required no fight. Ada had proved irresistible to him. But as they rode out of sight, Violet drew a sharp breath, her smile deserted her, and she stood, weary and alone, an old warhorse facing one last campaign.

The house, having been thoroughly cleaned and polished, was silent. There was no dust between Violet and her thoughts, and she suddenly felt unhappy, as though the old troubles had come out of their corners. She retreated upstairs to her room, where she sat for a long time on the edge of the bed, staring at the familiar branches of the elm tree outside the window. Then she carried a stool to where she could stand on it and reach the top of a tall wardrobe, a family piece that had once belonged to her mother and father. There was a thick molding that protruded above the wardrobe door and frame, behind which was a high flat space, out of view to anyone entering the room. Violet reached behind the molding, groped with her hand until she located a leather satchel, brought it down, and sighed with relief when she saw the layer of dust signifying that the satchel had remained undisturbed. It was the same relief that had washed over her a couple of times each year for a period of nearly sixteen years, when she stood on her stool, alone in the house because she had deliberately waited until every member of the family was out, lifted the satchel briefly, and wiped it with a dry cloth so that it could begin gathering dust for the next period. More rarely, she had looked inside to confirm that the letters were still there, held together with a piece of ribbon. Three dispatches, giving very little detail—there was so much more Allie might have written—but a powder keg nonetheless, one Violet had secreted away to her wardrobe cache from the time the last letter arrived in early December 1895.

Violet had not read Allie's letters since then, and she did not intend

59

to read them now. She feared losing her resolve and breaking her promise that when Ada turned sixteen, the letters would be handed over. Of course, Allie never confirmed that she had received Violet's last reply, the one containing the written promise, but what did that matter? A promise could not morph into something other than what it was. This particular promise had been carried through lightly falling snow to Middleville Depot, put on the train with all the other promises and transported to General Delivery in Chicago. There . . . who knew? Maybe Allie collected it, maybe not; maybe it sat there unclaimed until enough time had passed and it could be destroyed along with all the other unclaimed promises. Maybe it went missing. Maybe a young post office worker remembered Allie and searched for her; maybe he never found her, but kept the letter because he could not stop worrying about her. Maybe he did find her but it was too late, so he handed Violet's unopened reply over to the authorities, and it was buried with Allie in a pauper's grave. Maybe, maybe, maybe. None of that mattered because Allie had asked for the promise to be made and Violet had agreed to it because another *earlier* promise had *not* been made. Violet's promise existed; it was a fact, a ticking clock, and there was no release from it.

She reached for the letters, wondering how it would feel to hold them again. The girl's birthday had already passed. Violet would wait until after the party, but the fulfillment of her obligation could be postponed no longer. The letters seemed harmless now, retrieved from the satchel, lying there on her thin palm, a light packet, dry and crumbly at the edges. But it was a lonely, wretched, and regretful thing to have held them for so long, to have told a lie, to be the keeper of the last trace of a woman broken and gone.

Just thinking about Allie and the years of silence and wrongdoing and the grievous promise caused Violet to slump with age and tiredness. Sometimes, she thought she was nearly tired enough to die. She had dreamed of dying before this moment, thereby finding release and leaving Ada to live out her life in painless ignorance. But in fact, Violet had always been more afraid of dying than of *not* dying before the contracted day arrived. That, she knew, would be a cruel conclusion for truth and Allie Green.

CONCORD STREET

Jacques gaillard answered fred's questions about the Tigers before turning to his wife and handing her the envelope. He waited for her to reveal his earnings at Hudson's that day. Clara slit the envelope carefully and placed the wages on the table.

Each day was different—the pay varied and seemed to follow no rule that Jacques could fathom: thirty or fifty cents, sometimes as much as seventy-five cents. There was never a clue that certain tasks held greater value than others. The wages were mysteriously determined by the manager, by his mood, how his own daily business had gone, confused notions about work and charity. Whatever the amount, it was briefly there on the table for all the family to see, until Clara recorded the takings in a ledger, the way a bank teller officially counts and confirms sums already known to the customer.

"Seventy-five cents," she said.

Looking up from the ledger, she reached out and patted the thick sleeve of her husband's coat. Then, she placed the money in a coffee tin above the stove and set about making supper.

The three Gaillard children followed the transaction. Paul, the eldest at fifteen years, stood back, coolly observing both parents. He saw the gratitude and disappointment move across his mother's face and saw his father look away. But the son remained fixed and unblinking, as though committing the scene to memory. Perhaps he resented his father for giving her the money, resented him for not giving her more, or both.

For their part, Bell and Fred hovered close to where they might observe the envelope pulled from the pocket of his overcoat. The pocket was so deep that Jacques had to tilt sideways to reach its bottom, and a suspenseful time passed before his hand reappeared, holding the prize. Bell briefly broke the silence by clapping her hands nervously and startling herself, before returning to a timid scrutiny of her mother's expression. Fred remained still, gazing tenderly at his father's dry winter face, half expecting something large to be produced from the cavernous coat, something magical, a lamp or a lion or no, a *tiger*. His hopes were dashed when the flat cream envelope appeared, but he secretly told himself that no two days were ever the same. One day, it would be *this* moment that changed.

Preferring to think about things that had happened days before, or might happen tomorrow or next week, Fred was less rooted in the present than his brother and sister. Bell, three years older than Fred, fully inhabited the here and now, with little apparent desire to move on. She had no notion that the life they lived was one of paucity or that she ought to hope for bigger things from her father's overcoat pocket. She might cry over a sharp word or glance; her tears were genuine but short-lived. She neither brooded over past injuries nor projected hurt feelings onto the next day. Though Bell and Fred quarreled regularly in the course of their play or household chores, the girl kept faith with her mother's admonition, "Never let the sun set on your anger." Bell was always the first to say sorry, whereas Fred was prone to grudges and brooding. Physically resembling her dark-eyed Irish mother, her childish passions undiminished, Bell was all roundness and brimming affection. She loved to perch on Clara's lap or stand behind her father's chair after supper, her arms wrapped around his neck, her chin resting on his shoulder.

Paul's attachment to the present was of an altogether different order. First of all, he seemed to have escaped the affliction of nameless memory and passing melancholy that plagued his father. Dry-eyed to the point of inertia, Paul was committed to the present in all its hardness; if anything, he relished it. It was as though the predicament of family life confirmed something he had long suspected, and his handsome face wore a permanent *I told you so* expression that could chill a room, even in high summer. From an early age, he had shrugged off his mother's kisses, tightened under his father's hand on his shoulder and rejected Fred's brotherly admiration.

A terse and numerate youth, he had found work as an apprentice clerk for the Detroit Stove Company. Most days when his shift was finished, he took small jobs in the neighborhood, stacking wood, sweeping front steps, running to the shops for people who could not get out when the weather was bad. Paul never complained about the burden of apprenticing and menial jobbing, and in that, he could not be faulted. He took as much work as possible, dutifully handing over his small earnings to Clara and the coffee tin. If his parents found his morose silence and set jaw disturbing, they never said so aloud.

With both Jacques and Paul out of the house, and schools closed during the coldest weeks of the year, Fred spent the weekdays in the company of his mother and sister. In the mornings, Clara gave the two younger children small jobs around the house. They swept floors, made the beds, helped with the baking. On Thursdays, they accompanied her to the local grocer and butcher, both situated down on Jefferson Avenue, where she made a series of carefully planned purchases using the money from the coffee tin. In the afternoons, Clara drilled them on reading and writing, and then, weather permitting, the brother and sister might be allowed a short period outside in the snow.

The Gaillards lived on the block between Jefferson and Champlain. Along this stretch of Concord Street, there were fifteen or so red brick houses, most of which had been split into two or three flats of a few rooms each, or were run as small boardinghouses. Usually, other young children from the street came outdoors at the same time, and they congregated at a long strip of scrubland that ran behind the houses and privies. The neighborhood kids dug snow forts and igloos. They sculpted icy barricades, fashioned dead branches into swords and Springfield rifles, and played soldiers. They tunneled into the deepest drifts.

When the children played outside, Clara sometimes paid a visit to Mrs. Herbert, who lived in the downstairs flat. Mrs. Herbert was several years older than Clara, a widow with two grown sons, both married and living not far from Concord Street. After her husband's death, Mrs. Herbert had begun taking in sewing, and when the orders piled up, Clara would help out, for a tiny share of the earnings.

Mrs. Herbert also kept a series of lodgers, the most recent being Horace Ballantine, a stocky, copper-headed tram driver from Ohio. Ballantine worked the early shift and generally arrived home in time to sit with Mrs. Herbert and Clara. He always brought a cake for his landlady or a little bag of sweets for Bell and Fred. Clara was touched by these kindnesses and came to like the man whose extroverted manner had initially grated. And she couldn't help but notice that Mrs. Herbert had grown cheerier since his arrival. Sometimes in the evening, from her own flat upstairs, Clara overheard their voices, punctuated now and again by a burst of laughter or the whistle of the kettle. Once she asked Ballantine how he kept in such good spirits all the time, and he replied with a slap on his knee that if you didn't laugh, you'd cry. Then he fixed his grinning eyes on her.

"You should bring your husband down here some evening, and we'll see if we can't fix 'im up!"

Clara flushed deep red.

After an hour or so, Clara called Fred and Bell in from the cold and followed the children upstairs, where she helped them to remove their wet clothes. She quickly sponged and dried the two bright, shivering bodies before putting them into bedclothes for the rest of the day. As late afternoon shadows darkened the room, Fred and Bell sat near the low-burning stove next to the hanging clothes, chattering about their adventures and playmates. Clara made a pot of sugary tea to share with them and sat off to the side by the window, enjoying the comfort children's talk brings, its contained and secret universe, silvery young voices, words that are small and guileless and need not be studied closely. Sometimes her eyelids would begin to drop, only to start open at a sudden giggle from Bell or the scrape of Fred's chair on the wood floor.

If the clock had stopped at about three every afternoon, if the door stayed shut, the winter sun kept to its place low in the sky, and the deep, heavy snow outside never melted, Clara might have remained in that room forever, floating on the children's talk. She might dream that her husband and eldest son never returned home again. Jacques and Paul carried a sense of worldly injury into the house that was harmful to Bell and Fred, and Clara saw that lately, Fred had become anxiously watchful of his father.

She knew that Jacques was ashamed of losing his job at the printing press. She could manage the shortages, the rationing of supplies, the patching and repatching of thinning shirts. Her husband's funny turns never bothered her either, for she understood that Jacques might produce his tender smile and warm affection only if he sometimes indulged his melancholy. Clara was not given to tearfulness, and frequently it was in comforting her husband that she found some release of her own.

They had been a boy and girl together, meeting and marrying young, and their union retained a heat and a conspiratorial playfulness even after the birth of the children. They whispered and stroked one another beneath the bedcovers. He was a giving husband and a patient father. But lately, as the weeks and months of hardship and uncertainty accumulated, there had been a slow tiring of the gaze between husband and wife, until both were forced to look just past one another. The loss of regular employment brought a daily repetition of failure that was, for Jacques, an altogether different affliction. It could not be spoken about or kissed away.

Clara showed no resentment; there was only a steady draining of intimacy, a physical heaviness and lethargy that began to seize her in Jacques's presence. After the onset of winter, she regularly went to bed at the same time as the two little ones, leaving Paul bent over a book at one end of the table and Jacques wordlessly leaning on his elbows at the other. Hours later, Jacques would stand over his wife, watching her sleep.

On more than one occasion, he left her alone, crept into the children's room, and spent the night at the foot of the bed on which Fred and Bell slept, half upright, his back against the wall, his big overcoat serving as a cover. The quick, easy breathing of the children steadied his rhythms, enabling rest to come. Bell never knew her father had been so near, for she was a sound and guiltless sleeper, and Jacques rose early. But the two boys knew. Having sat at the table until very late, Paul would finally slide into his own bed and lie on his side, watching the dark shape of his father until he could no longer hold his eyes open. Fred might waken once or twice in the night to find his father there, and each time, he lay as still as possible so as not to disturb him. He feared that if he moved, Jacques would stir and remember his unhappiness or return to his own bed. Fred wanted to keep him near. When moonlight fell through the frosted windowpanes and turned everything blue, he studied his father's face with the unblinking stare one normally fixes on the dead.

There was a strong likeness between father and youngest son. Fred had the same slight build, pale olive complexion, and delicate good looks that could turn girls' heads from an early age. He also shared his father's love of tools and fixing things, and his pleasure in singing. Fred learned the Irish songs his father had first heard as a child, growing up in Detroit's Corktown neighborhood. His son's voice was as yet unformed, but Jacques noted the boy's excellent ear and memory that enabled him to pick up a tune quickly.

On Sundays, when Jacques did repairs around the house, Fred was his apprentice. Little by little, the boy was given access to the contents of the toolbox. While they worked, they talked about the Tigers or about old ballplayers. Jacques recalled the Hollinger Nine and the Wolverines and the players on the 1887 championship team. He told Fred how Charlie Bennett's hands used to be covered in cuts and bruises at the end of every game and how he had once seen Bennett catch with one hand wrapped in blood-soaked bandages.

Fred heard with pride people's frequent remarks that he was the spitting image of his father. The one exception was when Mrs. Herbert's lodger, Mr. Ballantine, would loudly ask "how's the little French fellow today" whenever Fred returned something Clara had borrowed. "Been to *Paree* lately?" the man would chant in his red, husky voice, winking at his landlady. Fred shrank from the tram driver's greetings and his bags of sweets because he disliked the man. He disliked him stubbornly and for no reason that he could find or say out loud, when Clara questioned him about his sullen responses to the lodger. It was the inexplicable, intuitive antipathy that can sometimes be exhibited by normally affectionate puppies and the sweetest of children.

THE CORNER OF
MICHIGAN AND TRUMBULL

ON THE LAST SUNDAY OF JULY, THEY DROVE DOWNTOWN. JOE WAS AT home in his used Ford, on the highway, within the magnetic field of the big city, a Detroit station playing on the car radio. But Kay felt uncomfortable, like the fraudulent Wizard in his hot air balloon, drifting away from Kansas and about to land in the wrong place. Also, she was wishing they had one of those heyday automobiles with the wide, continuous front seat, the kind you could slide across, squeeze close to your boyfriend, nuzzle his neck, and place your cigarette between his lips while he drove.

"Do you remember the rumors that went around after the '67 riot?" she asked.

"Oh yeah. Loads. Black guys were gonna come out to the suburbs and shoot one white kid on every block. Then, they were mining the freeways to blow up all the commuters. You mean those rumors?"

"Did you believe them?"

"Hell no. But they stirred things up for a while. Gave us something to talk about at the dinner table. And I remember all those white housewives buying guns and signing up for target practice. Now, *that's* scary."

They laughed.

"I'll tell you another thing," Joe said. "There were just as many black rumors about white people."

"How do you know?"

"There was a guy at boot camp, came from Detroit. We used to talk sometimes. He told me some crazy stories. Down around Twelfth Street, everybody thought armed white people from the suburbs were coming with the police to invade the city. There were secret plans to turn the whole downtown into a concentration camp holding black people."

"You're kidding."

"God's truth," Joe replied.

Kay looked out the car window as they moved through the "trenches"—a local name for those sections of the freeway sided by high concrete walls that cut a rapid swathe to downtown Detroit. The trenches masked whole sections of the city, and reduced the sensory experience of the commuter, confining him to the car, the road, the art of monotonous motoring. Her father had driven through them every-day in the late 1970s, to his new office in the Renaissance Center, De-troit's post-riot, glistening, cylindrical towers, a last hurrah from cor-porate leaders led by Henry Ford II. Out of the trenches, phoenix from the ashes and all that. But the building owed more to dreams of Los Angeles and the Bonaventure Hotel than it did to a Rust Belt city past its prime. The men in designer suits were already stealing glances at their wristwatches, gazing from windows on the upper floors, calculat-ing when they might quit the dying party without seeming impolite. In 1979, Kay's father took her on a tour of the RenCen, pointing out that a man's office location matched his salary grade. Floor 15 trumped floor 14, a window on 15 was a half grade higher than an internal cubi-cle on the same level. Jake Seger was high up, a short elevator ride from the executive boardroom, with a large window overlooking the river and views of the Ambassador Bridge. Passing through the inner cubicles on one of the lower floors, he pointed to a brightly colored sign tacked to the bulletin board above one of the desks. It read: *I'd rather be fishing.* "That guy'll never get a window," Jake had remarked.

Staring now at the cement sidings of the freeway, straining to glimpse the neighborhoods racing by above their heads, Kay asked Joe if he ever felt nervous downtown.

"Nervous? Not really. *Conspicuous,* more like. And maybe a little disappointed, because nobody down here is remotely interested in my white ass. Why should they be? Our parents walked away from Detroit. Literally abandoned it. Okay, if the Tigers make it to the playoffs or one of the neighbors buys a Japanese car, everybody in Garden City turns into an overnight Detroiter. But the rest of the time, nobody gives a damn. This town doesn't belong to us. Not anymore. But no, to answer your question, I'm not nervous in Detroit . . . Mostly I think of it as a question of density. People per square mile. Everybody downtown is packed in, trying to do the same thing you and I are doing on our nice patch of green in the 'burbs."

"And what's that?"

Joe smiled, keeping his eyes on the lane of traffic. "Good question," he replied. "What do *you* think we're doing?"

He paused and then offered reassurance. "Fred Gaillard left footstep traces in Detroit. That should make you feel more at home. What's the line you gave me the other day? Geography is nothing but history in space?"

"Élisée Reclus said something like that."

"*Who?*"

"Élisée Reclus. A French geographer. He's long dead now."

Joe said nothing, still smiling as he drove. He liked that Kay was pretty well versed in obscure geographers and historians and their forgotten observations. But he was the smart one. Whatever had happened to him during the years they spent apart, it had made him smart. Scarily so, at times. Kay regularly had the sensation that he was about to drop a bucket of cold water on her head, deliver with vague hostility some piece of wisdom for which her expensive education left her utterly unprepared. But on this occasion at least, Joe's intelligence came as a relief. His voice, his opinions, relaxed Kay. The tightness in her chest eased. Then, as if they possessed all the time in the world, he took one hand off the steering wheel, reached across, and touched her face. Long afterward, Kay could still feel the dry, grainy texture of his fingertips on her cheek.

Thinking about Fred Gaillard did help. Joe accompanied her to various locations identified by her family archive searches. They got out of the car and walked around, often the only pedestrians in sight. At Grand Circus Park, a lone taxi driver sat in his car in front of the derelict Statler Hotel, eating a sandwich. He watched with a wry smile while Kay photographed the hotel, the Adams Theatre, and the statue of Hazen Pingree, Detroit's great populist mayor from Fred's era. They paused to read the monument, dedicated in 1904 and describing the famously eccentric Pingree as a "gallant soldier" and prophetically, in light of Detroit's late decline, as the "first to warn the people of the great danger threatened by powerful private corporations." In Fred's day, Grand Circus Park would have been teeming with people. As late as the Seger family New Year's Eve outings to Detroit in the 1950s, it crackled with the noise and commotion of holiday crowds. Now, Joe and Kay found it eerily quiet as they walked around the corner to find Comerica Park, replacement for the old Tiger Stadium.

It was much closer to Grand Circus than Kay had anticipated, a massive bulldozer of a creation, loud and cartoonish, with a fifteen-foot figure of a tiger at the entry gate. Joe nudged her and teasingly played devil's advocate.

"*Some* fans, even ones who campaigned to save Tiger Stadium, claim it's pretty good inside," Joe said. "Let's get tickets for a home game. It's about time I went to see for myself."

"Let's not and say we did," she replied like a sardonic teenager. "It's named after a *bank,* for Chrissake."

"Yeah well, if ya got it, flaunt it. Comerica paid sixty-six million bucks for the privilege."

Kay did allow that Comerica Park must bring lively baseball crowds, if also a new kind of corporate presence, to Grand Circus and Hazen Pingree's little spot. But the day they visited, the Tigers were playing away, and the old mayor seemed quite alone.

Joe grew animated when they reached the old Ford plants at Piquette Avenue and Highland Park. Working at the Rouge in Dearborn had given him an interest in Ford history and an odd, belated sense of belonging to the automotive dream. At first they had trouble finding the Highland Park factory, partially hidden by a large shopping center, the Model T Plaza. But then they saw it, nearly a hundred years old, magnificent and deserted, a gem of Gilded Age industrial architecture and the site of the first moving assembly line. Big as a town, row upon row of wide glass windows, many of them broken but sparkling under sunlight. Joe said that at the height of production, a thousand Model Ts a day rolled out of Highland Park and that Fred would have heard dozens of languages spoken there, as immigrant workers from around the world made their way to Detroit.

Joe had been more excited than Kay to discover that 1896, the crisis year in Fred's young life, was when the horseless carriage first appeared on the streets of Detroit. On March 6 of that year, in the middle of the night, Paul Brady King drove out from his machine shop on St. Antoine. And on June 4, Henry Ford spent the early morning hours driving his buggy along Grand River and Washington Boulevard. In between those two signal moments, Fred's life would change forever.

At the corner of Michigan and Trumbull, Tiger Stadium stood locked and empty, shut down for good since 1999. There wasn't much to see anymore, and again, Joe and Kay had the place to themselves, although Joe said it was crowded with a hundred-year measure of ghostly Tiger fans, so thick on the ground you couldn't help but step on them. He rattled the padlocked entry gate and read a commemorative plaque dedicated to Ty Cobb. The souvenir and snack stalls built into the outer wall of the stadium and on the surrounding streets were closed behind metal shutters. A low-built building opposite the site retained an old advertisement. Painted on its long, red-brick exterior was a fifties-style comic-strip figure of a Tigers player with a Flintstone smile. And next to the figure, faded blue wording on an orange background: *Baseball Souvenirs: Caps, Jackets, Buttons, Cards, Pennants, Jerseys. Enter on Michigan Avenue.* A blue arrow pointed the way to a boarded and dilapidated shop front.

Joe wanted to stroll over to nearby Plum Street, once a short stretch of craft shops and coffeehouses, and Detroit's modest equivalent to Haight-Ashbury during the late sixties. He remembered going down to Plum Street a few times after his return from Vietnam. Kay suggested he walk over there without her; she would take a few more photos of Tiger Stadium and then join him. Joe occasionally worried about separations, but she was feeling comfortable near the old ballpark, and assured him it would be fine. He set off reluctantly.

The crossing of Michigan and Trumbull was wide and desolate, with sections of road still laid with red brick. In order to photograph the entire stadium site, Kay picked her way through light traffic and managed to take up a spot at the center of the intersection. A few drivers cast side glances as they drove past. Away from the shelter of the buildings, her hair and clothes were caught by a gust of warm wind, and before she could lift the camera, a piece of grit struck her eye. She stood momentarily wounded and disoriented, one hand cupped over the watery eye. The grit soon washed away, but for reasons Kay could not quite fathom, both eyes were now brimming. It was as if the wind had carried a grain of original soil from the ballpark, reinflicting an old injury or irreparable fracture.

Fred had spent hours and hours of his life at the stadium. In later years, he never spoke of it with anything but affection. He remembered every team roster, winning seasons and losing seasons. He knew the best seats and the cheap seats and the names of the hot dog vendors. He had vanished, but now, in this of all places, some shard of his trouble had shot through time. And it finally hit Kay that right here at the big ballpark, the one place a boy should be guaranteed happiness, Fred had been deeply unhappy.

She couldn't be sure how many minutes had passed, but as she stood blinded and dazed, traffic whirring by, she began to register Joe's muffled, distant voice, anxiously calling from across the road. Yet when Kay managed to wipe clear her eyes, he was in front of her.

"Why wouldn't you let me take your hand? I thought you were going to pass out. You pushed me away," he said.

"I never knew you were here," she replied, shaken and still disoriented.

Joe took her by the shoulder and steered her to the pavement, but once they stepped onto the curb, he let go, withdrew coldly, and walked away. Kay stared at his back as he headed for the car. They had planned to drive over to Concord Street and Belle Isle, but Joe had apparently changed his mind. As soon as her seatbelt clicked into place, he started the engine and pulled onto Michigan Avenue. Heading west toward Dearborn and Garden City, she watched the downtown skyline recede in the side mirror. Joe's intense anger was plain in his set expression, his white grip on the steering wheel, the way he swung the car from one lane to another. Kay should have kept quiet, let it pass. Joe could be moody; she knew that before she spoke.

"What's wrong?"

He refused to talk to her.

"*Please*, Joe. Tell me what's upset you."

After that, she let it go. She was impatient to tell him about the incident outside the stadium, but instead she turned away and leaned out the car window, closing her eyes and gulping hot, rubbery freeway air. They arrived home quickly. Joe pulled into the driveway, but left the engine running. Neither of them moved.

"Don't leave things this way," Kay said.

"I'm telling you, Kay. Don't press me right now."

His voice was pinched and very sharp, as though he had tightened a screw on his anger.

"Please don't speak to me that way, Joe. It's not you."

That tore the screw off. "What? It's *not me*?"

He let out a moan of low rage, followed by bitter laughter, then pressed his head against the steering wheel and kept it there. His chest and shoulders convulsed as he clutched the wheel, burying his face into it. After a few minutes, Joe lifted his head and spoke, staring forward through the front windscreen, as though he were afraid of losing his voice if he looked at Kay.

"Listen, I guess we're having a great time together, playing house. But let's be honest—we are hanging around our hometown pretending shit did *not* happen. Why do you think I like hearing your stories about Fred Gaillard? Because he is somebody else; he's far in the past, and just maybe, he's a way to feel close to you again. But the fact is, you were not around during the most important years of my life. I mean, where *were* you when I got drafted? In that nice new house out there. I never even saw that house. Where were you when I came home? When my brother Lenny smashed his car up? I guess by then you were havin' a good time in Boston with a bunch of guys who got a student fucking deferment. If you knew—" he stopped, then tried again—"if you knew, I don't think you'd be staying with me now."

"I want to know, Joe. I do."

"No. Believe me, you *don't*. And you cannot understand what it takes for me to be with you, with *anybody*. What it takes out of me. I gotta control the bad shit in my head. *All* the time. *Constantly*. I gotta keep everything safe, keep *you* safe, even though you never did that for me. You disappeared. Except for my mother, the only person who tried to stop me going was Sid. But now, you've walked back into my shit little world, and so I have to keep you safe. We're out somewhere and you tell me to go on ahead without you? I'm *panicking*. Right away, I'm panicking. If you're not safe, I'll wind up hating you—"

"I'm safe, Joe."

"You don't get it." He laughed again, but quieter and sadder than before, and finally turned to look at her. "This time, it really doesn't matter what you think, Kay. It's about what *I* think. I fucked up once, *more* than once, and it wasn't safe. You are never gonna get it. Don't even try."

He paused, but now Kay waited; she could find nothing to say, and she knew Joe had not finished.

"Listen, what happened today was my fault. I don't know what made me want to go over to Plum Street. It's not a particularly good memory. I scored pot down there a few times, after Vietnam. Some guy who looked like John Sinclair would sell me a dollar bag and ask me how it felt to napalm women and children."

A dark silence finally crawled inside the car. Sitting there, stationary in the driveway, should be like heaven. A used Ford with warm vinyl upholstery, keys dangling from the ignition, thick windscreen and dashboard, the sticky sweet whiff of gasoline on a summer day. Kay could hear the little boy from two doors down, shrieking hysterically as he ran through the yard sprinkler, wearing his swimming trunks. He had a lazy eye and always seemed to be playing on his own. From a couple of blocks away, the tinkling tune of the ice cream van was just audible. With so few kids on these streets now, she wondered how the ice cream man kept going.

In the 1950s and 1960s, there were armies of children. Kay could remember when every block was a nation of leaders and followers, soldiers on shiny bikes with plastic streamers that sparkled and whooshed in the wind when they raced up and down. There were boundary squabbles, raids, and secret societies. With the men at work and the mothers drinking coffee in each other's kitchens, kids governed the suburban streets. Now Joe and Kay were older than the Maple Court fathers were when they made down payments of one thousand dollars on these hopeful little houses back in 1952. The parents all rode into town on the GI Bill. Decades later, here were two of their babies, beyond grown up, sitting in the driveway in a second-hand car, completely at a loss.

Kay wished she might reach across the front seat to hold him and be held.

"I'm sorry, Joe."

"What for?" he said stiffly. "I'm doing better than quite a few people I can think of right now."

CIRCLE

ONE AFTERNOON, THE CHILDREN ON CONCORD STREET AMUSED themselves by leaping from the back porch of one of the houses into deep, drifted snow. They tumbled on top of one another, spluttering and shrieking and making messy indentations in the white crest until it collapsed, flattened, and the frozen earth beneath it began to reappear. When Fred landed on rock-hard ground, pressed under the weight of two other boys, he failed to get up again. He had slammed his forehead, and after a sharp, dizzy sensation, passed out face down. The other boys stood up, brushing themselves and casting alarmed glances toward Bell, who stood on the porch waiting to jump. Bell leapt down next to her brother, pressed the side of her face against the frozen ground in order to look into Fred's, sat back up, and felt her throat tighten with fear. Bell did not hear her own scream, but Clara, sitting in Mrs. Herbert's kitchen, was pierced by it. Within minutes the two women were in the yard, followed by Ballantine. The burly tram driver scooped Fred into his arms and carried him into Mrs. Herbert's.

Fred came round quickly to the dazed vision of his mother's pale, anxious face and the sound of Bell sobbing behind her. The adults asked him what day it was, did he know where he was, what happened? Everyone examined the bump on his forehead, pronounced on it, said *what on earth were those children doing jumping on top of each other like that* and so on. Fred basked in the attention right there in Mrs. Herbert's kitchen, like an outlaw in a Wild West story, after a gunfight. They sat him up and gave him warm, sweetened tea, eventually deciding that he should be put to bed and closely watched, but hopefully they need not send for a doctor. It was only when Ballantine made ready to carry him upstairs that Fred stiffened and resisted. As the big man reached for him, Fred kicked and turned his face away.

"Fred, stop that now. What's the matter with you? I'm so sorry, Horace."

Clara was flustered and embarrassed. But Fred would not be cajoled, sensing something disagreeable in his mother's use of the man's Christian name. Ballantine only laughed, gathered the struggling lad in his strong arms, and took him up to his bed.

"Nothing wrong with your boy, Clara! I might need the doctor though."

Ballantine stood joking, his hands on his hips, next to Clara at the foot of the bed. Fred tightened his jaw and fought the hot tears beginning to sting his eyes.

The incident caused an estrangement between mother and son. After Ballantine returned downstairs, Clara nursed Fred with a morose proficiency that alarmed him. He made himself as uncomplaining and docile as he could be, while Bell, hushed and watchful, sat cross-legged on the bed next to him. Fred cast anxious glances at his mother's set face, expecting her to relent, but the remainder of the afternoon passed in bitter silence. Mrs. Herbert brought up some cake for the children, but even she sensed the danger in her neighbor's house and kept her visit short. Paul came home and stood in the doorway, asking what had happened to Fred.

"He's been a very stupid boy, gone and bumped his head, and now he's making extra work for everyone. He's lucky we didn't have to send for a doctor. Lord knows that would be the end of this week's food money."

Paul started at Clara's reply, unaccustomed to any severity in his mother. He glanced around the room, a quizzical half smile crossing his face, before deciding to go back out into the winter evening, roll a cigarette, and have a smoke behind the house. Fred pulled the bedcovers up to his chin and squeezed his eyes shut, trying to conjure the image of his father. An hour later, he woke to find Jacques at the side of the bed, leaning close, peering at the bumped forehead through watery eyes. His father carried the chill evening air on his clothes and in his whiskers, and there was a slight catch in his voice that made Fred reach for his rough, cold hand.

"I didn't know what to think when I came through the door and no-body asked me about the Tigers. The world was gone wrong!"

Jacques stayed with the boy, talking to him and stroking his hair. At suppertime, he carried Fred to the table and let him eat sitting on his knee. That night, a circle closed around the father and his youngest son.

YELLOW BRICK HOUSE

"I NEED TO GET OUT OF HERE FOR A FEW HOURS," JOE SAID finally.

Kay climbed from the car and walked toward the front door. He waited until she was safely inside the house, then reversed out of the driveway and drove away.

"Our first fight," she said to herself, knowing full well that phrase could not capture what had happened between them during the visit to Detroit. It was a phrase for young lovers, people wearing class rings and varsity sweaters with big numbers on the sleeve; it required two-and-a-half-minute love songs and jealousies, breaking up and making up. It was for the *back* seat of the car, not the front seat, where the two of them had been sitting in silence for some minutes. Pitiful as it may seem, Kay had been clinging to girlish pictures of her love affair. But after the trip to Detroit—after they sat in the driveway, the car engine idling, Joe slumped over the steering wheel—after that, she would have to work much harder to summon those pictures.

The day had turned humid. Maple Court baked under thick, hazy sunlight. Even the little boy two doors down had stopped running through the sprinkler and retreated inside. Kay stood at the front window staring at the empty street, praying for Joe's return, until anxious fidgets got the better of her and she began walking in and out of the small rooms: kitchen, living room, three box bedrooms, and bathroom. The cramped proportions and floor plan of the Chases' red-brick house made a rabbit run that she knew only too well. She might be living in the house next door, but it was *her* old house, *yellow* brick but with an identical floor plan, that lived in Kay, coursed through her limbs and pricked her senses. These were the binding angles and dimensions she carried into every space she would ever occupy. There was no getting out of Munchkinland. The family house on Maple Court had permanently limited her.

From Joe's place next door, decades later, she could still recapture every line and surface, having explored them from the day she began to crawl. In dreams, she ran her child finger along the neat moldings. She straightened and pressed her back against the height marks penciled on the plywood closet door beneath the cellar stairs. She crouched, heart pounding, in Marion's bedroom closet behind the big garment bag where the winter coats were stored, while Sid counted down from fifty, his voice muffled and far away. Sometimes in Joe's bed, when a dream kicked her awake, Kay sat up in the dark as a child, waiting for Marion to come and hold her. It would take a moment to remember she was in Joe's house and her mother was gone.

Beyond the house, Kay found a more public familiarity. It seemed that the brick facades, the cracks and tiny remembered imperfections in the cement sidewalk, and Maple Court's large central telephone pole were the last simple reminders of the old neighborhood. The pole had once served as "home" for street games; if the kids touched it during various versions of tag or hide-and-seek, they were in a free zone. They started again, fresh, with no points against them, no past. Joe and Kay continued, superstitiously, to tap the pole whenever they walked by it, but it had lost its power, just as the street and town had moved on and stopped waiting for them long ago.

At times, Kay felt the dull eyes of the lawn figurines on her back. Joe didn't have much to do with the newer neighbors, and from behind the front doors and windows, Kay sensed a mild, unwelcoming curiosity at her arrival. As for the few old friends still living in and around Garden City, there wasn't much contact. When Joe and Kay bumped into former neighbors at the supermarket, exchanges were friendly, but brief and a little embarrassing. Members of their own families stayed away, perhaps expecting the affair to end before anybody felt obliged to take it seriously. The only relation still living in Garden City was Joe's aunt Della, and he visited her once a week, on his own, as he had done since his mother died. He probably never even mentioned Kay to his aunt.

"Just let people be. It's their business. We won't be needing their approval anyway," Joe said tersely, using an ominous verb construction, when Kay pressed him into a discussion following a particularly awkward encounter with an old school acquaintance.

Once in a while, Kay and her sister met for lunch in a Mexican restaurant on Telegraph Road, a spot midway between Garden City and Pam's workshop in Pontiac. Pam still owned the sign-painting business she had started after art school, although it was an ailing enterprise. She used some of her share of the inheritance to keep the small team of workers in pay, while waiting on some outstanding contracts. Her few extravagances after the money came through included an ankle tattoo, a new set of art supplies, and finally, a Harley Davidson. Her ex-husband drove a Harley, and Pam said she would never be a biker chick again. "From now on, I'll drive my own damned bike," she announced, sitting across from Kay in the restaurant booth. Then, raising a glass of margarita to the parking lot, shrubs, and cloudless summer sky beyond the window, her eyes welling with tears, she thanked Jake and Marion. "Cheers, Mom and Dad! Miss you!"

"I'm not gonna judge you for moving in with Joe," she told Kay. "Look at me, for Chrissake. I've made plenty of mistakes. Anyway, it's your life. I love you, and I want you to be happy. But I don't really like coming back to Garden City, so don't take it personal if you don't see me too often. When you get sick of romance, run over to Pontiac, and I'll take you for a ride on my Harley."

After that, Pam never asked much about the relationship, just enough to reassure herself that her little sister was okay. She accepted the situation without fuss, but continued to avoid Garden City, the site of her painful adolescence. In any case, Pam was too busy working, painting, and motoring around with her biker friends to spend much time with Kay. They talked on the phone every couple of days and always said they loved each other. *Love you! Love you too!* It was a family mantra, especially on the female side, repeated so often that it meant everything and nothing. Yet coming from Pam, perhaps more than anyone else, it was a trustworthy declaration. Kay never knew anybody with cleaner, no-strings-attached love to offer than her sister.

So Joe and Kay managed their families separately. The sole exception to this was Sid, who was of course not only Kay's brother but Joe's earliest friend. In the summer of 1972, when Joe came home from Vietnam, Sid was on vacation from university. They hung around Garden City together, looked up old schoolmates, and drove downtown to see the Tigers play.

Sitting in the car outside the drugstore, or lying side by side on the high school football field, they embarked on a summer-long conversation that effectively put their shared past to rest. In the seemingly harmless, mundane reminiscences of "before Vietnam," when Joe returned obsessively to old teachers and classroom pranks, neighborhood scrapes, little league games, the senior prom, Sid sensed the damage. There was volatility, an anger that had not been in Joe before. They rolled out their boyhoods from opposite sides of the wreckage of Joe's year in the army. Joe talked himself ragged, before finally collapsing in bitter exhaustion and sleeping for two days. At the end of that summer, one friend returned to college, while the other stayed behind and looked for a job.

By the early eighties, Sid had finished his studies, moved to Chicago, and was working for a corporate investment firm. Joe remained in Michigan taking factory jobs. In 1982, Sid married and started a family. They had less and less to talk about, but Sid stayed loyal, making regular phone calls to Joe. For his part, Joe was less reliable. He went through periods of heavy drinking, and those tended to be the times he contacted Sid and a few other old friends.

Perhaps because he knew them both too well, Kay's brother was extremely uncomfortable with the relationship. In separate phone calls to Kay and Joe, he tried, gently at first, to talk them out of it. Most likely, Sid feared being forced eventually to side with one against the other. But when pressed, he issued vague mutterings about water under the bridge, nothing in common between them, no future. He warned that they would end by losing each other completely and that would be a sad conclusion to a long friendship.

"He's jealous! Can't handle his sister and best buddy being together without him," Kay shouted tearfully, slamming down the phone.

Joe sat at the kitchen table, staring ahead, his chin resting on his hand.

"He's only trying to help."

"How can you say that?"

"He knows so much more than you do, Kay. I understand why Sid would see this as a bad idea. For a few years after I got back, and even later, if I was drinking, I used to phone him in the night and say things about you. Not always nice things. I guess I was still crazy about you. But crazy *at* you, too. I got crazy at everybody at one time or another. But nobody more than you. Sometimes, I think I was quite aggressive with Sid and demanded your address or phone number. I don't know— I could never remember what I'd said the next day. But your brother, very wisely I now realize, kept you and me apart. I was in no shape to see you. And you had moved on.

"All the same, every so often I would bother Sid about you. *Where is she now? What's she doing? Who's she with?* Finally, he sent me a snapshot taken of you in Boston, sitting on the grass among a group of students. I remember the picture fell out of a short letter from Sid. It fell on the floor, and when I reached down to pick it up, I saw it was you, barely recognizable and wearing one of those peasant dresses. All beads and peace symbols you were. Long, straight hair, parted in the middle. Your hair fell over the sides of your face because you were bent over a pouch of tobacco, holding a cigarette paper between your fingers. But I could just make out your expression, and I still knew it. I stared at you for a long time. Then I imagined you looking back at me, right out from that picture, surprised at first and then sizing me up, before turning away in disgust. I could almost hear you laughing with your friends, the other people in the picture, with *their* beads and peace symbols. I can still remember how my face and neck boiled with shame before that picture. And right then, I hated you."

"Joe! I never stopped thinking about you. And never, *never*—would I have laughed at you or turned away."

"You're a little late, honey."

He smiled unhappily. "Look, I know I can't blame you for moving away and going to college and living your life. Let's be honest—things were always heading that way for us. But as far I can tell, there were two people who waited for me and stuck with me over the years. My mother and your brother. She's gone. But Sid—well, put it this way, Kay. I won't hear a word said against him."

After that, Kay's brother stopped phoning, and there was no doubt that the loss of his confidence was a blow to Joe. They couldn't talk about Sid anymore. They couldn't say much about their families or childhood friends. The few people they saw socially were a couple of Joe's mates from work and their wives. None of these people had known them before.

In a very short time, it had become a brittle and detached existence there in Joe's house, but Kay had dug in; she wanted nothing more than to stay put. She would close her eyes and ears, if necessary. She would refuse to care what Sid, Joe's aunt, the neighbors, or anybody else thought.

But pacing the rooms that late afternoon following their visit to Detroit, Kay's confidence was shaken. The threat would not come from outside the house, from other people, but from Joe, the two of them together. Right now, Joe was out driving around or just sitting in his car somewhere, trying to shake off anger and things he could not tell her. She knew before it happened that he would come home after midnight, drop onto the sofa, and sleep alone, fully clothed. Sometime in the early morning hours, he might wake and crawl into bed beside her. There would be no explanations or excuses, but they might hold each other again. It was a picture as sad as a Hank Williams song.

CHARLIE BENNETT'S PARK

IN LATER YEARS, FRED LIKED TO THINK HE HAD GROWN UP WITH the Tigers. He and Jacques and their baseball team came before the first horseless carriage made its way along Detroit's muddy streets, even before *The Great Train Robbery* played at the Wonderland Theater down on Woodward Avenue.

Several weeks after Fred thumped his head in the yard, and the snow began to melt, people were once again speculating about the coming baseball season. One Sunday in early March, Jacques took Fred aside after breakfast. "Dress warmly, two layers. I want to show you something on the other side of town."

Father and son set off in an icy wind, a last reminder of the harsh season still being beaten away by the city. It was a long trek for Fred's skinny legs, so Jacques paid the three cents for a streetcar run to Cadillac Square, where they changed to another line heading west along Michigan Avenue.

Fred had never been on a streetcar, never been so far from the house on Concord Street, and for the first time, he glimpsed something of the scale of Detroit. He pressed his face against the glass, counting the stops while his father pointed out important crossroads, shop fronts, and the top of the Hammond Building. Jacques sat close to his son, smiling and withholding the name of their destination. Even on a cold Sunday, people strolled along the downtown streets, one scene replacing another as the streetcar made its way along the line. Jacques watched his son grow wide-eyed and pink with curiosity, and the weight of his own worries and disappointments temporarily lifted.

They trundled further westward, away from downtown. The dis-

84

tance between stops grew longer. The packed city blocks and large buildings were behind them now. As the crowds on the street thinned, Fred began to wonder why he had been chosen for this mysterious outing. How had his mother and Paul and Bell fallen away recently, setting him apart with such a fragile man? Fred feared that if he did not love him enough, his father might weaken and die; then sometimes he feared that if he loved him any harder, Jacques would shatter into pieces. Now, the boy experienced a similar wave of dread, a vague premonition of disaster. Gazing from the tram window, his father's breath tickling the back of his neck, his spirits dropped as rapidly and perceptibly as a stone tossed into a stream. Keeping watch over his child's wavering moods, Jacques tapped the boy's shoulder.

"Not long now, we're nearly there," he urged in a low voice.

They set down at the old Haymarket, on the northwest corner of Michigan and Trumbull, into a din of tapping hammers and a chilly afternoon that smelled of freshly cut wood. A twelve-foot-high fence was being erected around a vast open area with a main entry gate at the corner itself. Jacques took his son's hand and led him through a gap in the fence, where they joined a dozen or so curiosity seekers picking their away around the site. Inside the fence, teams of wagons delivered loam to spread over the cobblestones of the Haymarket. Off to one side, men were cutting felled trees into lumber. At the far left end of the field, Fred counted five magnificent elm and oak trees still standing. An L-shaped grandstand was already in place, and carpenters were beginning work on a separate set of bleachers opposite.

Jacques leaned towards his son and whispered, "This is the Tigers' new home."

"Hey, Frenchman!"

Fred saw his father break into a wide grin as they approached a small group of men who stood bunched together in the cold, pointing and discussing the field. One of the men embraced Jacques and addressed the child.

"Who is this young fella then? Chip off the old block there, Gaillard. Hope you give 'im an American name at least! What ya called, son?"

Drawing courage from his father's evident pleasure in this company, Fred replied in his clearest voice, "Fred. I'm Fred Gaillard."

"Fred! I remember now. I'm Tommy. He's your youngest, eh, Jacques? How old are ya, Freddie?"

"Almost eight," Fred answered.

"*Almost* eight—*not* seven then. Good lad!"

"Don't grow up too fast, Fred," Jacques said. He pulled his son closer to his side.

"Well, little man," laughed Tommy. "I've known your dad since before you were born. We went through a few battles together, him and me. And some good times too! Did your dad tell ya we were there in '87 when we won it all? Anyhow . . . listen to me ramblin' as usual. I used to hear about you back in the time when your dad and I were still at the press. I remember your pretty mama too. She and I were old Corktown neighbors, and I knew her people. Are ya comin' to see the Tigers on opening day, Freddie?"

"Are we, Dad?"

"What do *you* think?"

Jacques released the tender look reserved for his youngest child, and again Fred suffered a flutter of unnamed anxiety. It was with some relief that he saw his father turn back to Tommy and engage in a long conversation about their days in the printworks. They talked over mates they had seen and those who had disappeared since the layoffs. They speculated about whether the press might start hiring again now that things seemed to be picking up. Tommy escorted father and son around the field, pointing out the future locations of home plate and the base lines.

"Did ya hear the owners are discussin' what to call this place? That is if they have it ready for opening day. But it's Charlie Bennett's park if it belongs to anybody."

"Charlie Bennett's park . . ." Jacques tried out the words. "That's it! Fred, we're coming to Bennett's park on opening day, and if we're lucky the ole man'll hobble out on wooden legs and take the first pitch."

The two men laughed there in the middle of the mud-soaked field, while horses and wagons and construction workers moved back and forth. Rubble was carried away from the outfield. Loam was carted in. Meanwhile the sawing and hammering around the fence and bleachers went at a feverish pace, and March winds tore freely across the site.

After Tommy left, Jacques stood in silence, watching his friend's back grow distant and finally disappear. Then he turned very slowly on the spot, taking private measure of the vast space where players would soon field the hits and run the bases. For a moment, he let go of Fred's hand. In later years, long after Jacques was gone, Fred could recall losing the touch of his father's hand in Bennett Park.

SPRING

JACQUES BEGAN TO THINK THAT BETTER TIMES LAY AHEAD. WARMER weather brought people out of doors, and he regularly ran into friends and former workmates downtown. They loitered on street corners, discussing job prospects, exchanging leads, speculating about the coming baseball season and the progress of the new ballpark. Most days, after leaving Hudson's, Jacques walked to his old workplace or another of Detroit's presses to see if they were hiring. Nothing had materialized as yet, but he was now regularly encouraged to "keep asking." He dared to hope that by the 28th of April, the Tigers' opening day, there might be something more to celebrate than a victory over the visiting team from Columbus.

At home, Jacques maintained a cautious silence, dutifully handing over the daily envelope containing the small but regular amounts of pay. He gave Clara no reason to expect good news, partly because he did not want to disappoint her, partly because the estrangement between them had become habitual. Over the winter, husband and wife had perfected a simple way of running the household without talking to one other. There really wasn't much to talk *about*. Clara was earning a bit of money for helping Mrs. Herbert, and Jacques and Paul made their deposits in the coffee container. These collective earnings were scarcely sufficient for a tightly fixed weekly budget. Anything left over was put toward the rent arrears that had accumulated since the layoffs began. As there were no real choices to be made, and no comfort in remembering old times, conversation had become redundant. It belonged to another life.

Privately, both Jacques and Clara feared that unless Jacques was rehired soon, the Gaillard household would not last the summer. If her husband could no longer provide for them, Clara would be forced to take the children to her father's house over in Corktown. This was the prospect that neither husband nor wife dared mention, the leaden fact that finally secured the silence between them.

Only Fred noticed the flickering changes in his father's mood. Their plans for opening day gave Jacques a hook on which to hang his recently recovered sense of anticipation. Now, when the father came through the door each evening, the boy asked how many days until the game. Jacques kept count for him, taught him the names of the players and their positions, and put tiny amounts of money aside for the outing.

Clara made no complaint about this diversion of funds. If anything, she experienced the alliance between Jacques and their youngest son as a personal release. Both needed her less. Her eldest son didn't *want* her, and Bell had always been an undemanding child. An unprecedented space had opened for Clara, and slowly, she began to fill it. She looked outward, lost some of her habitual shyness, paused to chat with neighbors and acquaintances. She visited Mrs. Herbert each afternoon, whether or not the older woman had any work for her. And on warmer days, the two women sat on the front step, waiting for Horace Ballantine to return from work.

The pleasure of Ballantine's company, in contrast to the sad, distracted presence of her husband, was undeniable. Like a thief, the tram driver shone a light on Clara that made her giddy. He knew how to address his attentions to his landlady, even as he shot furtive arrows at the younger woman. In the mild, unspoken rivalry between the two women for Ballantine's favor, Mrs. Herbert might be the lines of the letter, but Clara was *between* the lines.

Ballantine's daily return had changed the shape of the days, but in truth, that was all Clara really wanted of him. She could not help but notice that her spirits were highest minutes before the tram driver appeared, then disappointingly low, even guilt stricken, minutes after. Her satisfaction lay in the lightness of the afternoon prior to his arrival and the continuous deferral of desire. Clara no longer wished to sit alone in her kitchen, halting time, but nor was she certain of what she hoped time might deliver.

Late afternoon on the 12th of April, just a couple of weeks before opening day at the new ballpark, as Clara looked up to see Ballantine's approach, Jacques stood in his usual place outside Hudson's. Having completed a number of errands, he waited for his envelope to be delivered. The sun dropped, and shadows advanced from the opposite pavement, crossing the street toward his spot at the foot of the building. Closing time came and went. Jacques watched the sales assistants emerge from the building, small knotted groups, conversing and walking together to the corner, where they lingered a few minutes before heading off in their separate directions. The clock at City Hall chimed six-thirty, seven-thirty, and then eight. The night watchman had arrived and stood chatting with the floor supervisor just inside the doors. Jacques rubbed his whiskers, kept an eye on the scene, and waited. The supervisor stepped out, and Jacques approached him. A glimmer of irritation showed on the younger man's face, and he glanced up the darkening street, as if calculating his chances of avoiding an encounter with the Frenchman. Then he spoke first.

"The manager's gone for the day. He had a meeting with the accountant, and they went out by the main door."

Jacques felt his body begin to tremble, but he looked straight into the other man's eyes. "Did he leave anything for me?"

"No, nothing today. Sorry."

"Will he be coming back?"

"No, like I said, he's gone for the day."

That was as long as Jacques could hold eye contact with the younger man. He turned his head to the side, fixing his gaze for a moment on the near-empty street, then walked away, commanding his feet toward Shelby, where the printing press was located. Electric light towers over a hundred feet in height dotted the downtown area, but most Detroiters complained that they were mounted so high they lit the sky rather than the ground. Crossing Cadillac Square, Jacques joined the evening crowd, hurrying along in the gloom beneath the tall streetlights. By the time he got to the press, there was no one to speak to, no one with the authority to hire.

Jacques stood for over an hour in the dark street outside his old workplace, staring without expression, the fingertips of his left hand searching the lining of his pocket, casting about for the habitual feel of the Hudson's envelope. He had stopped thinking, and so, when he finally began moving again, it was without conscious effort. His brain had moved to his feet, and they took the only course that offered itself. They proceeded from Shelby to Fort Street, then across Griswold, Cadillac Square, Brush, Beaubien, and St. Antoine. Jacques had paused on these corners thousands of times, felt the tilt of them. His curious, solitary spells of elation and melancholy had left traces along this route, changed the city and made it his place in the world. But now, Detroit was a flat plane of forgetting, an abstraction, its streets little more than lines on a map, and Jacques a dumb horse heading for the stable, for lack of a better idea. He barely slowed his pace or noticed his surroundings until he came to a halt, partially hidden by an elm tree, across from the house on Concord Street.

Jacques looked up, and there was Clara moving about in the dim gas-lit room on the second floor, casting an occasional glance from the window. She appeared to be keeping watch, waiting his return. Just as the sensation of falling in a dream sometimes caused him to wake with a start, sit upright, and call out in the dark, the sight of his wife brought his mind careering back. Had she begun to worry? Was she lost forever?

For the first time in many weeks, he craved the taste and smell of her, and wondered what her secrets were. Momentarily, Jacques forgot his empty pocket, and stood in the deepening night, replaying his earliest memories of Clara, her dark gaze, her grandmother's locket resting in the little dip at the bottom of her throat where the collarbones meet, and the way the color used to rise to her cheek when they talked. He saw, as though it were yesterday, her agitated, impatient expression as she opened the front door to him in Corktown. Whispering in the hallway, their hands on one another. He pictured himself pulling the flannel nightdress away from her pale, soft skin, that first time, in her father's house. Jacques recalled the deep shudder that tore into him, when she wrapped herself around his thighs and lower back. Trembling now, he stepped into the street just as someone spoke behind him.

"Lovely, ain't she? You're a lucky man, Gaillard."

It was Mrs. Herbert's lodger, who had strolled up behind Jacques and now stood alongside him, looking up at the window. There was a faint smell of beer and cigar smoke on the tram driver, but his gait was steady.

"You goin' home tonight? Or ya got other plans?" he asked.

Caught off guard, Jacques found no reply. He could not read the question or the questioner. Ballantine's tone was playful, as though the two men belonged to the same club, but the expression on his face suggested some other meaning, something less friendly. After an awkward silence, Ballantine laughed good-naturedly and punched the Frenchman's arm. Jacques glanced up to see Clara draw back from the window.

"Well, I've had a brew and I'd best turn in. Some of us gotta work tomorrow. Mind you don't turn to stone out here. The nights are still cold, and she'll be needing company."

The tram driver lumbered across the street, up the steps, and into the house. Clara had disappeared from view, but tiny changes in the light from the window could be perceived as she moved about the room. She would be settling the children now or clearing the table. The encounter with Ballantine left Jacques swaying, as though his blood had drained away. He needed time to recover, so he decided to go behind the house and have a smoke before going in. There he found Paul, perched on the back step, just recognizable in the gloom, his cigarette making a fiery pinprick in the night. Jacques hesitated, and then dropped down next to his eldest son. They sat for some minutes in silence, smoking and flicking ash onto the damp ground. Jacques was surprised and embarrassed by Paul's body, thicker than his own, manly. Waiting his turn.

"You oughta go in, ya know. She'll be getting worried."

The sound of his son's voice, so rarely heard, was startling too, richer than Jacques remembered.

"How late am I?"

"Late enough. That kid of yours is wandering around with a look of panic on his face."

"Fred?"

"Who do you think?"

"And Bell?"

"Bell's fine."

"What about you?"

There was a pause before Paul tossed his cigarette end to the ground and stood to his feet. "Me? I'm just glad I'm not Fred. You keep it up, and you'll turn the kid into a freak."

"Keep *what* up? What do you mean?" Jacques asked, pulling himself upright, a frightened, pleading note creeping into his voice. His son shifted his weight from one leg to the other, and glanced toward the street.

"Nothing. I don't mean nothing. I'm goin' out. I'll see you later."

Paul walked to the corner of the house and then slowed, sighed, and turned around to his father.

"Look. I don't know why you're late, and I don't care. Just do what you're supposed to do. Go inside and give her the envelope. You got the envelope, right? Give it to her. Answer the kid's questions about the Tigers."

"Paul."

"Yeah?"

"Is it my fault?"

"Is *what* your fault?"

"I'm not sure . . . You. *Everything.*"

There was a pause in the darkness. Jacques could no longer make out his son's face.

"I don't know," came the unseen reply.

And he was gone. Jacques stood squinting at the night, waiting until his son's footsteps could no longer be heard. Then, without looking back up at the house, he set off down Concord Street toward Jefferson Avenue.

It had been a day of puncturing his routine invisibility, catching himself in the eyes of others: the store supervisor at Hudson's, Ballantine, Clara, and finally Paul. As he walked, Jacques replayed his son's words over and over again, until they began to assume a particular shape in his mind. It seemed that the eldest child had come of age, and under his unforgiving gaze, the father stood finally revealed, weak and pathetic, envelopeless, worthless. Jacques had been waiting a long time for this moment. All along the streets of Detroit, it had haunted him; that he should be brought to it by Paul made it complete. Exposure brought a wave of relief, a pleasant numbing, as after bathing in cold water.

Clicking alongside him on the pavement, Jacques heard—what was it—a voice or a thought. *Don't let Fred see.* He looked around, startled, but the street was empty. The voice came from no one but himself, and it continued now, in condensed, typewriter bursts, racing faster than the beat of his step. *Fred. Clara—Bell—Paul. FredFredFred—Ibreak - yourheart. Everytimeyoulookatme. Ibreakyourheart. Iseethelookonyour- face. Fred. Iamsorry.* These were the fitful thoughts that came and went. On another day, entirely different thoughts might have oc- curred, with an entirely different outcome. But it was not another day. Jacques rubbed his eyes. Words fell fast and uncontrollably, as if torn from a book, scraps of white paper, dropped from a tall city and flut- tering like snow around him. He was clawing the air, finally snatching the missing pieces to a long and difficult phrase.

Gathering pace, oblivious to the chill and the streets, Jacques was pasting the words together, gaining a sense of what to do next and what he wanted, what they all wanted. He experienced a pleasant surge of force and impatience in his limbs. Clara would think it was another one of his funny turns. She could not be more wrong. The cold air coming off the river pierced him into contented wakefulness. Her hold over him was gone. There were no grasping memories of their marriage. Only the bitter relief of an immediate solution, a shat- tering remorse about Fred, and the final certainty that at least one son would never stand weeping on a street corner.

He did not know it until then, but he had already calculated where to place himself and how to climb the railing to the best spot. Since its opening in 1889, the Belle Isle Bridge had been the scene of numerous and regular suicide leaps. Jacques had read about them in the news- papers. He was certain that if the accelerating fall didn't kill him, the cold waters would. And if his ribs broke with the impact and tore into his internal organs, ripping his heart apart, he wouldn't feel a thing. He was not afraid.

It was not until he stood high on the bridge, face forward into the light wind, poised to drop, his body weaving slightly, that the clicking in his head subsided and the words came more gently. It occurred to him that he might have explained things in a letter. Left instructions for Paul, released his wife and children. Or that he might be making a mistake. He was about to fail in a way that no previous failure could touch. It was a selfish ending to a life that had not been selfishly lived. He wondered how many people changed their minds at the last moment, when it was too late.

Then, as Jacques hurtled downward for a full six seconds, gathering speed, toppling, blood rushing, he thought—not in words but in a picture-like flash—that for Fred's sake, he might have waited until after opening day.

Fred.

The sharp fist of an icy river that had brought the first Gaillards to Detroit reached up and took one of them back.

THE RAGGED MOUND
OF HISTORY

OPENING DAY CAME AND WENT. CLARA ASKED PAUL TO TAKE HIS brother to the baseball game, but Fred refused to go. It would be several years before he returned to Bennett Park. He stopped looking forward to things promised in the future. Nor, in his bitterness, would Fred look back to the past, for he did not wish to find his father.

When Clara, some ten months after Jacques's death, nervously announced that she had agreed to marry Mrs. Herbert's lodger, Paul moved out and cut his ties with the family. He had given up his apprenticeship at the Stove Company and taken a job at the docks, and with some help from Clara's father, he had kept the family from going under. But he calculated that his mother's remarriage released him from further obligation.

Bell silently grieved the loss of her father and older brother, but resigned herself to the new regime. Outwardly, she remained amiable and loyal to her mother. But she lost forever the simple attachment to the present she had held when Jacques was alive. In fact, she became a secret hoarder of memories. On the way to school each morning or in bed at night, she composed an exhaustive, mental record of things said and done in the family before her father's death changed everything. In this way, Bell divided the world into a history of before and after, invoking a golden age that came to an abrupt end on April 12, 1896.

She held imaginary conversations with her father, promising him that nothing would ever be as good as it had once been. Spelling out words in her head, Bell compiled dispatches of family and neighborhood news, so that he wouldn't feel left out, carefully withholding the fact of her mother's remarriage and Ballantine's reliable wage. She made lists of her likes and dislikes, favorite colors and seasons, gave him school reports, things a father ought to know. In this way, Fred's sister learned to comfort herself.

In later years, Bell worked in the county clerk's office, filing birth, marriage, and death certificates, ideal employment for a compulsive archivist. And when she died in 1959, her daughter Katherine found a cardboard box containing a series of lined notebooks, each one filled with letters addressed to Jacques. They were short missives, rather like diary entries, three or four each week. They began in December 1899, became less frequent from 1909, with the last one appearing in early 1912, a year after Bell married. It seemed that Bell had made a decision, just before the turn of the new century, to put her communications to her father in writing. Katherine moved to California not long after her mother died, and the notebooks disappeared with her. But she sent numerous loose pages to Fred, entries she thought he might care to read. He kept them, and after he died in 1973, Marion kept them.

To Clara's surprise, Fred accepted her marriage to Ballantine without a fight. He had never liked the man, and never would. But he was too young to leave home or strike out on his own. Moreover, he was determined to punish his father by forgetting him, and the presence of the big tram driver was like a stick with which to beat away his father's ghost. After Ballantine moved in with them, Fred grew quiet and watchful, and grimly confined his efforts to the monotonous repetitions of the present. Rise at dawn. School. Chores. Bedtime. He wore the set frown of a disappointed old man on a boy's coltish body.

It was as though Bell and Fred had changed places; she retreated and fastened onto thoughts of Jacques, while Fred obstinately fixed on the everydayness of a life without him. But both brother and sister lived in the unstoppable city of Detroit. By the end of the century, Ransom Olds was turning out gas-powered Oldsmobiles from his factory on Jefferson, near Belle Isle Bridge. At the bottom of Woodward Avenue, a burned sugary smell hung over Vernor's ginger ale plant. In 1900, the Tigers joined the American League, and the following year, Detroit celebrated its bicentenary with pageants and floral parades.

Hazen Pingree went down with peritonitis and died just before the celebrations got under way. Even as Detroiters mourned the loss of the old populist politician, the sounds of ragtime could be heard in a few taverns, and passersby hummed along to the "Maple Leaf Rag." The new music caught Fred's attention, and for the first time since his father stopped singing, he lifted his head to listen.

Bigger and stronger, he began to have the run of the city. On winter days, the boys hitched ladders to the backs of streetcars for rides along the snowy avenues. In summer, they pooled their pennies for an ice cream soda at Sanders on Woodward. Fred was outside Sanders on a bright September day in 1901, not long after his twelfth birthday, when he heard of President McKinley's death. He was sharing a string of licorice with his friend Ralph, and together, they watched the excited crowds gathered around the newsstands. Glancing up and down the street, Fred saw people in clusters, buzzing, gesturing, and shaking their heads. The president had been pronounced dead eight days after being shot by Leon Czolgosz, a former factory hand turned anarchist.

Ralph's cousin Harry was a newspaper peddler, and the two boys lingered late in town, hoping for a free copy. When Harry finished work, he strode across the street, pulled a folded paper from his jacket, and handed it to Ralph.

"You boys are lucky I saved you one. Folks in this town sure do love bad news."

"Aw, I bet it's the same everywhere," Fred remarked.

"Maybe so. But Czolgosz was a Detroit boy, and that makes him pretty famous around here. Most of my customers reckon he's brought shame on our town. One man said it done no good to force foreigners to sign an oath promising they weren't anarchists. They would just lie about it and we shouldn't let any more of 'em in. I spoke up and reminded him Czolgosz was born right here, but he said what kind of a name is that? That's no American name. Then another fella said if they weren't anarchists when they left the old country, they sure would be after livin' here a time, and that no matter *where* he come from, Czolgosz done a good thing. That was a customer that had to run off before bein' strung from the nearest tree."

Harry adjusted his cap and said he'd better get home. He ordered his cousin Ralph to start moving too, and the three boys walked along together. Harry and Ralph discussed McKinley and his assassin, recounting rumors that over on Benton Street, people remembered Czolgosz and claimed that even as a child, he showed a bad character. Then Harry lectured the two younger boys about anarchists, ascribing all kinds of perversions to them.

Fred was only half listening. Instead, he was noticing that lately, whenever something big happened, something like the murder of the president, it made him lonely. It didn't seem to make any difference whether it was good news or bad news. The effect was the same. The more life got cluttered with events and facts, the lonelier he felt. Jacques was disappearing behind the ragged mound of history. Fred had set out to forget his father, but he had not bargained on how well the world would pile up and do that for him.

SPIDER HUFF

October 10, 1901

Dear Dad,

I write you from the heart of our city, where the spluttering of the automobile engine has joined the familiar racket of trams, pushcarts, manure wagons, and market vendors. Fred is something of a street boy now. He crosses the downtown avenues wherever he wants, dodges traffic according to his own rules, and regularly gathers with his friends in the middle of the road. But don't worry, Dad. Fred is blessed in some way I cannot quite explain. Danger may brush him in life, but it will not knock him down. He is a quiet fellow, who draws the loyalty and affection of nearly all who cross his path. Anyway, I haven't told you much about him lately, and I will try to write more soon. In the meantime, you mustn't think Fred has forgotten you. Just the other day, he cleaned your toolbox and mended Ralph's bicycle. And I have heard him humming one of your old Irish tunes, though he stopped when he noticed me. Be patient, Dad. His heart was truly broken.

Today, as I write this, Fred and his pals are hiking way out of town to watch an automobile race that is being held there. I do believe these boys, in their baggy wool trousers and flat caps, will be the last to remember Detroit before horseless carriages. We still depend on our trams and rigs, but Fred assures me that automobiles are the way of the future.

Your loving daughter,
Bell

A month after the death of President McKinley, Fred, Ralph, and some other boys walked to Grosse Pointe, east of Detroit, on Lake St. Clair. Grosse Pointe was a seasonal resort for wealthy Detroiters, old money and new money, propertied men and industrialists, who owned mansions in town. Fred had never been that far outside the city before, and he was buoyed by the air coming off the lake and the bright fall sunshine. A handful of summer villas sat on tended lawns, and along the shore, residents could be seen beaching their pleasure boats for the end of the season.

The boys were high-spirited trespassers, teasing and jostling one another as they fell in behind a stream of people headed for the mile-circuit racetrack. As they approached the site, Fred saw teams of workmen building up the corners of the course with soil, creating speed banks. Away from the track, the usual scene of jockeys, owners, and horses had been replaced by grease-stained drivers and mechanics busily cleaning and tuning their automobiles. Poised with wrenches in hand, they conferred in low tones and cast side glances at the competition. Spectators milled around the area, mostly men in suits topped by straw boater hats. They lit large cigars and conversed, occasionally leaning back to laugh at something said between them.

Automobile races were a new attraction and a means for ambitious inventors and manufacturers without capital to attract wealthy investors. At Grosse Pointe that day, there was a former farm boy from Dearborn. Back in 1891, he had landed himself a job as a mechanic-engineer with the Edison Illuminating Company and moved his reluctant wife to Bagley Avenue in Detroit. It was easy employment at Edison, involving routine maintenance tasks, and Henry Ford had a knack for devising shortcuts, gadgets to speed the work and impress the bosses. He was soon rewarded with pay increases and promotions.

Ford found a corner of the Edison power station in which to indulge his new fascination with the gasoline engine. In his spare time, he built a trial engine from scrap and, in the process, gathered a small group of enthusiasts from the plant workforce. One of them, Edward "Spider" Huff, later helped design and make the Quadricycle, Ford's first horseless carriage, the one he had tested in June of 1896.

Fred had never seen the spindly Quadricycle, but reports of it at the time, coming so soon after Jacques's death, left a scratch on his memory. Local people had joked about the eccentric Ford and his contraption. But Fred, raw with nightmares and visions of pallid, waterlogged bodies, coffins, gravestones, and his mother's silent grief, heard the wisecracks with grim satisfaction. He guessed that Ford and his buggy, however amusing, prefigured a wind change. Whether a good or bad thing in itself, the advent of the automobile would be a further punishment meted out to his father—something in the future that Jacques would never witness, just as he would never see the Tigers win a championship.

After the Quadricycle, Henry continued to work closely with Spider Huff and another talented young mechanic, Oliver "Otto" Barthel. This was the team that had spent a year designing and building the racing car they named Sweepstakes and brought to Grosse Pointe on October 10, 1901. Its ash-wood frame was reinforced with steel, and the engine was placed under the seat. The fuel tank held five gallons of gasoline fed to the engine by gravity. Huff and Barthel were responsible for the brilliant one-off ignition system, a forerunner of the spark plug, in which the coil was insulated by porcelain. Barthel had recruited his dentist to make the porcelain casing. The result was a hotter and more reliable ignition system than any car racing that day.

With its two cylinders giving twenty-six horsepower, Sweepstakes was impressive. But it was not favored to win. Ford was up against Alexander Winton, an automobile manufacturer from Cleveland, who had already achieved racing success, most notably beating the competition over a fifty-mile run in Chicago the previous year. It was Winton the spectators had come to see. He had announced his intention to break the world mile-speed record in Grosse Pointe, so the promoters were assured of nationwide reporting of their event.

Fred pulled Ralph away from their gang.

"Let's go see Ford and his buggy."

But Ralph wanted to look for the Winton camp. The boys ducked in between groups of men to gaze at Bullet, Winton's forty-horsepower prizewinner. They overheard one of the race organizers going over the program for the day, five laps for the steam engines, then the electric cars. Next, Winton would have his chance to break the mile record held by Henri Fournier, a French racing driver. Winton, and Detroit, would have their world title. And the final event would be the twenty-five-mile race, featuring Winton and all comers. Of the twenty-plus original entrants, several had pulled out. But it was an exhibition race for the champion. He would take home a thousand dollars and the trophy—a cut-glass punch bowl requested in advance by Winton in anticipation of victory.

As the program got under way, Fred and Ralph wandered along the uneven line of automobile fanatics with their entry vehicles. There was an atmosphere of mild, but good-natured panic at each camp, as drivers and mechanics made ready for the various exhibitions. Fred finally found Ford and Huff bent over their engine, fiddling and talking rapidly. Sweepstakes was a beauty, low and elegant, encased in large wheels with shiny bicycle spokes. Its crouched, horizontal lines promised speed, while the neat steering wheel projected upward like a trumpet shout.

Fred looked from the car to its driver and his mechanic. From their leather boots, sensible wool suits, and bow ties, Ford and Huff could just about pass for a couple of clerks. But from the shirt collar up, they resembled two schoolboys playing truant, in hot pursuit of a newfangled hobby. Each man sported a baggy racing cap with a small, smart leather visor at the front. Ford's cap sat neatly on the top of his head, revealing an expanse of forehead and ears that stuck outward. Huff wore his hat pulled down over his brow, accentuating his round eyes and a sandy handlebar moustache.

"Ford'll never outrun Winton," Ralph said authoritatively, repeating an opinion the boys had overheard several times that day.

"You wait and see," Fred returned. "If I had any money, I'd put it on Ford and Huff."

"Well, what *do* ya got? I'll bet the Civil War bullet my grandfather gave me."

Ralph always carried the dented .38-caliber bullet in his pocket so he could pull it out at any time and impress the other boys.

"You'll get grief for giving that away."

"Naw. It's mine. He gave it to me. I can do what I like with it. Anyway, I ain't riskin' nothing. Winton's a clean winner."

Fred stuck his hands in his pockets, kicked at the dirt with his toe, and closed his eyes as he tried to think of something he owned.

"Here you are, lad."

Fred opened his eyes to a dollar bit lying on a large, greasy palm. Spider Huff stood over him, a wide grin stretching his face.

"Take it," Huff said. "Never hold back on a good bet. And when we win, I'll have that Civil War bullet. You come to work for Mr. Ford, and you can buy it back out of your wages."

Fred was struck dumb, but Ralph stepped forward.

"Mister, he can't go working for Mr. Ford or anybody else. He's at school. And anyway, this is *my* bet."

Huff laughed, delighted by Ralph's bluster. Then he looked back at Fred.

"You heard my offer. Take it or leave it."

"I'm takin' it, Ralph," Fred said, bravely holding Huff's gaze. "If you're so sure of Winton, what do you care where your winnings come from?"

Fred picked up the dollar from the outstretched palm and stood holding it as if it would crumble.

"You boys come see me after the race."

And Huff was gone. Fred stood for a moment, watching him tell Henry Ford about the bet. Ford gave him a short glance and a nod, then turned back to his engine.

Some eight thousand spectators witnessed the outcome of Fred's gamble that day. Winton got his mile-speed record, but it was Henry Ford who won the twenty-five-mile race and carried the punch bowl home to his wife. Spider Huff took the Civil War bullet, while Fred went home with a dollar piece and a bloody nose after a thump in the face from Ralph.

GEORGE MINNIVER

BOTTOM OF THE FIFTH, TIE GAME, TWO OUT, RAMÓN SANTIAGO ON second, Craig Monroe at bat, full count. Kay glanced up from her book for the next pitch, a strike which ended the inning. Joe cursed the team, although he could never stay mad at the Tigers for long, even in that disastrous 2003 season. She was thumbing through a history of Detroit street names, how they had originated and evolved. How people argued about names. How the addresses on a street one hundred years ago might not correspond to the same addresses now. Now, you might go looking for an address and find an empty lot between two derelict properties. Numbers moved, street names changed, buildings fell into disuse or were torn down. And half the time, nobody could remember the reason why. *That house? Disappeared years ago. We don't remember what happened to it.* You might look for an important spot, the location of some historic event, and be off by half a mile or more. Nothing was certain, least of all the event itself.

"Whenever I think of the man lying on the road, at the intersection of Brooklyn Avenue and Lysander Street in Detroit, all I can see is George Minniver."

"What man on the road? And who's George Minniver?" Joe asked, keeping his eyes on the game, not yet sure whether he was receptive to this particular story. He disliked openings that teased. He disliked switched identities.

"George Minniver. . . . from *The Magnificent Ambersons.* Didn't you ever see that film of the old Booth Tarkington novel? George Minniver is the spoiled son of Isabel Amberson Minniver, and all through the movie, the people in the town talk of how they are waiting for the day that George gets his 'comeuppance.' But when that day finally arrives, and later, when George is run over by an automobile, there is no one left to witness his bad luck. The town has disappeared, and so have most of the people in it.

"Anyway, it wasn't George Minniver, but George *Bissell,* a real person, not a character in a film. He was wealthy, described variously as a local businessman, a lumberman, and a capitalist. Some said he had made and lost a few fortunes during his eighty-one years. But nowadays, if he is remembered at all, it is as Detroit's first recorded auto fatality. On the morning of September 2, 1902, Bissell was out driving his carriage when a passing automobile frightened his team of horses, throwing him to the ground and fracturing his skull. My grandfather was thirteen years old at the time; I suppose he was in school when the accident happened.

"I've been looking for a picture of Bissell, but can't seem to find one. So, whenever I try to imagine him, he ends up looking like George Minniver after his comeuppance."

Joe was more interested in the game.

WITNESSES

FRED ARRIVED A FEW MINUTES *after* THE EVENT, TOO LATE TO BE an eyewitness. He thought about this, thought it was something that happened to him regularly. He was always a little late and forced to rely on other people's untrustworthy accounts.

After Mr. George Bissell was carried off to Harper's Hospital, where his death was formally announced, the crowd took some time to disperse. There was a lively debate about whether to blame the automobile or the horses. Passersby were shown the patch of road, and the accident was told and retold. Even the people who claimed to have seen it with their own eyes could not agree on what had happened. It was an object lesson in how an incident becomes a story, how it passes along a chain of retelling, until the story becomes the incident and nobody cares about the difference. Nevertheless, Fred lingered there some time; he would be late for school, but he calculated that a fateful encounter between a team of horses and an automobile, even if he had only arrived for the aftermath, was a token of things to come. Maybe in twenty years' time, it would be judged as a historic occasion, as significant as anything his teacher might say that morning in the classroom. And then wouldn't he kick himself for having slouched along to school?

It was only eleven months since he had backed Henry Ford at the Grosse Pointe race, winning both his bet against Ralph and the promise of a future job from Spider Huff. Over the next few years, a number of auto plants opened in the city, including Ford's Mack Avenue plant. Fred followed the fortunes of the various cranks, inventors, and carmakers, some of whose products came and went overnight, automobiles with fanciful names like the Oxford, the Oriental, the Dearborn, the Wolverine. But mostly, with Spider Huff's words still ringing in his ears, he paid attention to the fledgling Ford company. Ralph said Huff would never remember him, or the promise, but Fred thought otherwise.

On July 15, 1903, a Chicago dentist named E. Pfennig became the first buyer of a Ford automobile, the Model A. Mr. Pfennig paid $850, and the company made a profit of about $150. Modest beginnings, but Pfennig had punched a hole in the dam, for within a year, a further 658 cars were sold, at a total profit of $98,851. As sales continued to grow, Ford's small group of investors got their money back with interest, and the Mack Avenue plant was quickly outgrown. It was not long before the Ford Motor Company stockholders held a meeting to approve the relocation of the Ford factory to a larger site.

In 1904, one year before Ty Cobb joined the Tigers, Fred turned fifteen, left school, and went looking for Spider Huff. It took several days of watching and waiting outside on Mack Avenue before Fred was able to approach Ford's top mechanic. Huff, though brusque in manner, remembered Fred and his bet on the Ford racer.

"You've got timing," Huff told Fred. "We're getting ready to move to a bigger plant over on Piquette Avenue. I don't know . . . you're a skinny fellow, ain't ya? How old are you, son?"

"Almost sixteen," Fred replied, pulling himself up as tall as he could.

Huff laughed and placed his hand on Fred's shoulder. Fred stood still, unsure whether to laugh along or show his serious intent. He opted for the latter and waited.

"*Almost* sixteen," Huff said. "So, you're not really fifteen. That much we can agree on." He was smiling widely now and looking Fred up and down, as if trying to guess his height and weight.

Fred paled at the mechanic's last remark, momentarily startled because it recalled some childhood scene that he could not immediately place. Then it came to him. He remembered the day his father took him to see Bennett Park, before it opened. They had met a man who asked Fred his age, and Fred had *stretched* it in the same way, claiming to be "almost eight." His father had smiled too, but differently than Huff, and told Fred not to grow up too fast.

"Well, a promise is a promise," Huff continued. "I can offer this:

you help with the move, and if you're a fast and reliable worker, I'll get you apprenticed in engine assembly at the new place. After that, it's up to you."

The new factory, on the northern side of the city, at the corner of two old French-named streets, Piquette and Beaubien, was a three-story brick building, over four hundred feet long. Within months of the move, sales had increased fivefold, and Fred was still at Ford. One of the youngest of three hundred employees, collectively producing some twenty-five cars a day in the years just before Ford introduced the moving assembly line, Fred soon knew pretty well how an automobile was made. He rarely saw Spider Huff after that, but once in a while, he might spot the mechanic at a distance, conferring with one of the supervisors or surveying the factory floor. Fred was looking for an opportunity to raise the matter of the Civil War bullet. Ralph never mentioned the bullet, nor would he have expected Fred to spend his hard-earned money buying it back. But Fred wanted to surprise Ralph by returning it and, at the same time, prove to his skeptical friend that Huff was made of honorable stuff.

Finally, Huff noticed Fred Gaillard on the factory floor, walked over, and stood for a moment, observing Fred and his team as they worked on a partially built engine. He moved in closer and patted Fred on the back.

"Looks like you found your calling," Huff said.

"Yes sir, I guess so," Fred replied.

Then he mustered his courage. "Say, Mr. Huff. I'm wondering about that Civil War bullet."

But when Fred looked up, Spider Huff was gone.

And that was it. In an instant, Fred knew the man was unlikely to acknowledge or speak to him again. And as he watched his erstwhile benefactor walk away, Fred finally understood his location in Huff's universe. The older man had taken a passing liking to a boy and later helped him to get a start with Ford. Huff kept no memory of other things said or half promises made on the day of the race in Grosse Pointe. Why on earth would he? At last, Fred grasped that the one who holds the upper hand rarely remembers such encounters with the same layered detail as those beneath him. It was not Huff's fault, but rather a mark of his position, that he attached little importance to a larkish incident in the past, forgetting his offer to sell Ralph's bullet back to Fred. He could not have imagined that Fred, like a jilted lover, would store up every word said that day. No, there was no one to blame. Huff had done a good turn in hiring a young fellow and was pleased about it. But it ended there. And so Fred let it go, but he always felt sorry about the Civil War bullet.

He stayed on at Ford, although there were regular layoffs with no guarantee of being rehired, whenever the company ran short of materials or orders. When the factory shut down at Christmas, Fred waited with everybody else for the sound of the factory siren to recall the workers. It was a precarious living, and most of his wages went to his mother and stepfather and the old coffee tin above the stove. Nonetheless, Fred finally had a little money in his pocket and with it a growing desire to stay away from the house on Concord Street. And after his last brief exchange with Spider Huff, Fred finally began, almost in spite of himself, to look for traces of his father in the city.

For a few months, he sought the company of his older brother. He knew the house where Paul boarded and the tavern on Chene Street where he passed the evening hours after work, playing long hands of cards, before returning to his room to sleep. But Paul retained his habitual coldness toward Fred. He inquired about Clara and Bell, and seemed satisfied to know that the new husband kept food on the table. Fred said that Ballantine liked his beer and whiskey and sometimes came home a little worse for it. Paul eyed his brother and replied that if the man ever raised a hand to Bell or their mother, Fred was to come to him straight away. Beyond that, Paul showed little curiosity about his family, and no inclination to spend time with his younger brother.

It was a hard task to give up on Paul, just as it had been throughout Fred's boyhood. Fred tried to keep away, but there were days when he craved the blood relation, craved being together in the same room, breathing the same air. Failing that, he often went down to Chene Street and positioned himself where he could not be seen, in order to watch Paul shuffle home after a drink. Paul was easy to follow, because he never looked right, left, or behind. He usually exited the tavern alone; there appeared to be few regular companions outside the nightly card game. Fred kept a short distance from his brother, squinting in the dark, searching for movements or gestures that might remind him of their father. But through the eyes of the younger son, following ten paces behind the elder son, longing for signs that were not there, Jacques Gaillard was a man as lost in death as he had been in life, apparently leaving the faintest of imprints on the world. Of course, if anyone carried his father's gestures, it was Fred, but he could not stand outside himself to see them.

He had a large gang of friends, mainly boys he had known from childhood. Most of them were in jobs now, though they still congregated on Saturday nights or Sunday afternoons; weeknights too. But Fred also noticed that some things he preferred to do alone. Now and then, he needed the quiet of his own company. Maybe this was true of everyone, something that happened naturally, just a part of growing up. Or it was a character trait in him, a flaw, more marked after the death of his father. But certainly, no one was with Fred when he left school and mustered his courage to go looking for Spider Huff. No one saw him shadow Paul home at night. And no one noticed when, in his few free hours, Fred took to loitering around one of Detroit's downtown theaters, befriending the piano player who accompanied the films.

The musician was a jovial, heavyset man with a deep laugh, but he was a light touch on the keyboard. He soon recognized Fred's natural ability and in no time at all had taught him the generic musical phrases to accompany chase scenes and duels, unruly mobs, villains, and parting lovers. When the studio began sending out cue sheets with each film, imposing greater standardization on his craft, the piano player complained and talked of finding a different job, but Fred taught himself how to read the enclosed notation. After that, he needed little instruction. Fred had only to hear a popular tune once or twice before he could sit at the keyboard, work out the melody, and play it for himself.

In one of her notebooks, her little missives to Jacques, Bell later recorded her surprise and delight the first time she heard Fred play. They were attending a wedding party in Corktown. Seated at an upright piano, with rolled-up sleeves and a shy, proud smile, Fred played a new, jaunty tune, surrounded by a group of lads, all lustily singing: *Katie Casey was baseball mad, had the fever and had it bad. Just to root for the home town crew, ev'ry sou, Katie blew.*

It was not until after Bell died and Fred received the pages from her notebooks that he learned at least one person had taken note of his modest achievements. Bell told how Fred hiked out to Grosse Pointe to see the race, how he became a Ford worker with a good wage, how he could repair an internal combustion engine with impressive speed, and how well he took care of their father's toolbox. Whenever she heard Fred at the piano, or singing or humming, she wrote about it in glowing terms, because she knew his love of music would have pleased their father. And in a brief entry, dated June 3, 1907, more than ten years after Jacques's death, she wrote: *Dear Dad, This afternoon, Fred attended his first Tigers baseball match at Bennett Park. Yours, Bell.* She stated it simply, as a piece of news long expected.

He became a regular Tigers enthusiast again and remained so to the end of his life. Nearly every week, at least until he moved to Middleville in 1919, packed high in the bleachers, in the rowdy roaring crowd, even in his own hollering at the players and the prodding and jokes with Ralph and the others, Fred kept watch over a private spot in that grand place. A tiny patch on what was now the infield, not far from second base. It was where he had stood with his father the day they visited the new ballpark together, and at least once during every game he attended, Fred's eye rested on that spot, and the noise of the occasion momentarily dropped away.

Finding his way forward in the city, moving on, had been one thing. Finding his way *back*, that took longer. But eventually, Fred grew into his father's shirts and even wore one or two of them. He sat on the back stoop at Concord Street, smoking and thinking about the first trolley ride to Bennett Park. He remembered how long the hours were when he was a boy waiting for Jacques to come home and patiently answer his questions, the same, repeated questions about the Tigers, day after day. No one had ever entered their house the way his father did, in that oversized coat, smelling of winter, nor would anyone again. Fred recovered the old tunes and taught himself to play them on the piano, and finally, he yelled for the Tigers. While still a young man in Detroit, Fred forgave his father.

HEAT WAVE

KAY AND JOE HAD PLANNED A ROAD TRIP TO WESTERN MICHIGAN, where they hoped to spend a few days exploring Ada's hometown of Middleville, in Barry County. They were put off, in part, by the weather. There was a heat wave during the last two weeks of August, pushing daytime temperatures to the high nineties.

Garden City was a ghost town, its sidewalks deserted by the residents of every street as they took shelter behind canvas window awnings and blinds. Only the concentrated whirring of fans and air-conditioners broke the still of Maple Court. At Westland and Wonderland, the local shopping malls, indoor fountains sprayed against a soundtrack of pop classics piped in to soothe customers coming in from the baking parking lot for the end-of-season sales. In Kroger's supermarket, shoppers lingered in the frozen food sections. But most people simply disappeared inside their climate-controlled offices and houses.

Some of the neighbors spent their time belowground, in cool basements that had been "finished"—as people used to say—probably some time in the sixties or early seventies. That was the era of cellar paneling, to be followed by an era of building "additions" or extensions onto the little bungalows, creating spaces that came to be known as family rooms or recreation rooms. Jake and Marion never built an addition onto the Maple Court house, but in 1961, they redecorated the living room and, at the same time, finished the basement, paneled its walls in oak veneer, and laid red linoleum tiles over the concrete floor. Then, they hung ceiling-to-floor bamboo curtains in order to divide the large room into two spaces and functions.

On one side of the bamboo—the side Kay thought of, in those Cold

War years, as East Berlin—Marion had her washer and dryer and a huge, deep, casket-shaped food freezer. The furnace that made Sid and Kay jump when it roared into action was also on that side. They both feared being sent downstairs to fetch a package of frozen beef or pork chops. Having steeled their nerves to cross the bamboo curtain, they needed added muster to lift the heavy freezer lid and reach inside the compartment. They came out in goose bumps as frosty light escaped from a bed of hard, ice-crusted provisions, illuminating the cobwebs on the ceiling and causing the hunched furnace to gleam in its shadowy corner.

On the friendly side of the bamboo curtain, West Berlin, Marion made a sitting area, cosily arranging an old sofa and chair, a candy-striped throw rug, and the Segers' first TV set, items demoted when Jake and Marion purchased a new television and more elegant furniture for the living room upstairs. But not long after, events conspired to make Kay as uneasy in West Berlin as on the other side. It was there, in August 1962, at the age of eight, that she watched the newscast of Marilyn Monroe's overdose, tried to imagine the star's puffy flesh in death, and overheard the adults commenting that it came as no surprise, as though there were something about Marilyn that had predetermined such an end. It was there, too, that they followed the Cuban Missile Crisis, certain Detroit was a target. Pam said Maple Court might be blown away by Thanksgiving, and Marion told Pam off for scaring the little ones.

In November of 1963, the entire family retreated to the basement to watch coverage of the Kennedy assassination: the convulsions of Friday afternoon and on Saturday interviews with bystanders in Dallas, footage of the Kennedys sailing at Hyannis cut with photos of Jackie's bloodstained spray of flowers abandoned in the back of the limousine; on Sunday, Jack Ruby's casual shooting of Oswald live before the cameras, and then back to the public display of grief on Monday. Afterward, particular terms entered the lexicon never to ring innocently again: motorcade, grassy knoll, book depository, Elm Street, for godsake. It was said that everyone retained a precise memory—what nowadays would be described as a flashbulb memory—of where they were and what they were doing when they first heard the news.

And two or three years later, Kay was curled beneath Marion's

Christmas quilt, safe and warm on the sofa in West Berlin, when she saw her first truly disturbing film, *Vertigo,* broadcast on the normally innocuous *Million Dollar Movie* program the family tuned into every week. These were their earliest experiences of watching movies on network television, rather than going out to the cinema or drive-in. After *Vertigo,* Kay went to bed with a picture of Kim Novak on the inside of her eyelids. Every time she shut her eyes, there was Novak, her cool, severe beauty, menacingly white hair, black eyebrows, and tight, tailored suits. Kay sat upright in bed, in the dark, rigid with thoughts of obsession, duplicity, spiral staircases, staring down from high places, falling—threats that in the movie had been embodied by Kim Novak, but now seemed to be floating freely above the bed. Kay had already decided she did not believe in God, as there was no visible evidence of him in the nondenominational church the family occasionally attended, nobody could actually point him out to her, but after *Vertigo,* Kay thanked him nervously, just in case he did exist, for not setting them down next to a lighthouse or bell tower.

It was during the hours upon hours spent sitting cross-legged on that cast-off sofa in West Berlin, after these various public events and after *Vertigo,* that Kay began to allow for the wider possibilities of deception and delusion, to have doubts about a number of things, not just God, the presumed happiness of a Hollywood blond, or the lone gunman theory, but matters closer to home, her parents and their histories and the things they purported to believe, and Garden City itself. What kind of place was it where the sun always shone on the yard?

Yet as late as 2003, the summer following Marion's death, with the scent of sun-baked, cut grass hanging over Joe's lawn and her old lawn next door, Kay closed her eyes and wished she were only *playing* at Joe's house and she could have it all back. Any minute, there'd be a fight with Sid and she would run home crying, Jake would pull into the driveway in his shiny, company car, and Marion would call them in for supper. Sid would kick Kay beneath the dining table. Pam would be sent to her room until she took "that rat's nest" out of her hair and removed the heavy black eyeliner. Soon Jake would shout at her to turn down the racket coming from her record player. Elvis Presley and Chuck Berry, Eddie Cochran, "Summertime Blues." Pam was crazy about that song.

Even the radio deejays of 2003, feeling the loss of their Eddies, Buddies, and Elvises, seemed to be searching for a hole in time, hyping their hourly weather reports with expressions like *sizzling and soaring* and playing all the old summer standards. Michigan was deep into its lazy, hazy dog days, and the radio encouraged everybody to remember when they were mildly rebellious kids on school vacation. But the heat, especially humid heat, had a detrimental effect on Joe. It made him jumpy and irritable. In a rare direct reference to Vietnam, he said he would never again long for the season every kid cherishes and every adult looks back on with sweet regret; the jungle had destroyed summer forever.

"The heat over there made us nauseous, dehydrated us until our brains got slow and cloudy," Joe said. "Most of us slept with our boots and socks off to avoid getting jungle rot, but we had to check in the morning in case a black scorpion had crawled inside a boot during the night. We got jungle rot anyway. Our clothes stank with sweat and stuck to the skin, but it was hard to undress and stand naked with the VC nearby. Sometimes, out on patrol, I thought about how I used to take my shirt off when my dad made me mow the lawn, to keep cool, get a tan, get the girls. But out there, removing a shirt was like removing a last layer of care and protection, like forsaking your own mother. But guys did it, they stripped off, the heat was that bad. *I* did it. Sometimes we stood around, shirtless, joking and acting tough when *really*, we were hugging our scared little tits, expecting to be found by a stray bullet. Now, every time I mow the fuckin' lawn, I think about that."

Although he found the heat oppressive, Joe obstinately refused air-conditioning because, he said, air-conditioning hid the weather, and weather was important. You needed to know what the weather was, he said. So instead of an air-conditioner, he brought out a couple of large window fans and positioned them, during the afternoon, to suck thickened air out of the oven-like rooms. At sunset, he turned the fans around to draw fresher night air inside. While waiting for the house to cool at the end of each day, they cooked on a barbecue grill and ate at the picnic table in the backyard, an insect-repellent candle between them. They took showers before bed in order to start the night dry and comfortable. Then Joe lay next to Kay, on his back, unfolded, one arm propping his head, the other lightly touching her thigh.

It usually took him a long time to get to sleep. By then, Kay knew that he had regular nightmares, but the onset of the heat wave seemed to make them more frequent and intense. Several muggy nights in a row, usually a couple of hours before dawn, he woke drenched in sweat, shouting or groaning, refusing comfort from Kay, even pushing her away. Sometimes he dropped to the bedroom floor in fear; other times, he went into the living room and began pacing up and down, muttering incoherently and gasping for breath. This might go on for up to an hour, during which he would not allow Kay near. If she approached him, he shouted and gestured at her to leave. Later, she might find him crouched in the corner of the bathroom, his head in his hands. As long as she did not ask about the content of his dream, Kay could eventually coax him back to bed, where he lay trembling until exhaustion finally carried him back to fitful sleep. In the morning, her tentative questions were rebuked or met with bewilderment, as if Joe had no memory of a bad night.

There was nothing Kay could do about the nightmares, but she did try to help Joe unwind in the evenings. After the sun went down, they took walks around the school playgrounds, stopping for a turn on the swings. Up and down, they soared past one another for a long time, stirring up a small breeze, clasping the thick chains and enjoying butterfly stomachs. Then they slowed themselves by scuffing their shoes in the gravelly dirt trough beneath each swing, tracks gouged by generations of kids in their sneakers and by the teenagers and grownups who trespassed in the night. When they came to a stop and idled, they laughed at how the narrow seats pinched their adult behinds. Joe might go and perch on the monkey bars while Kay stretched out on the slide and gazed at the stars.

She did not know if his brief outburst about the heat in Vietnam would be followed by other more disturbing ones, or if his nightmares might lead to some kind of collapse, traumatic memory, or confession. Joe clearly did not wish to reveal things to her, but how much control did he really have, especially when frayed by lack of rest? In truth, Kay was ambivalent about whether she wanted him to talk about the war. She feared her own cloying curiosity, and equally feared his divulging some piece of information that, once out, could never be put back, something that might come between them. Increasingly, Joe and Kay were changing positions, engaged in a series of maneuvers to do with disclosure and withholding, a long game in which their loyalty to one another would be tested. She had not told him about Johannes Hofer and the lost disease of nostalgia because she knew he would find her interest in it worrisome. It follows then that she also neglected to mention Dr. Elmer Thisroy, whose essays she had ordered.

Kay had to navigate these rocky waters, try not to see her lover as an adversary or sinking man, and try to keep her own head above the surface. She waited for a change in the weather and in their moods, and took care not to pressure Joe into unwanted conversation. They had always enjoyed knocking around together in silence, but during the late August heat wave, when they whiled away an evening at the playground or strolled home beneath the streetlights, Kay developed a habit of singing to herself. It was her way of interrupting, or drowning out, the questions and anxieties already producing a low, constant static in the back of her mind. She began with songs from their early years on Maple Court, sweet, painful ones about surfing and cars, then Motown tunes. Seeing that it brought Joe pleasure, she sang more boldly and moved on to songs their parents knew, ones she remembered easily because Marion, with her warm, grainy voice, used to sing them all the time. "Paper Moon," "These Foolish Things," "Where or When," "Happiness Is a Thing Called Joe." Dozens of songs by Yip Harburg, Harold Arlen, Rogers and Hart, Cole Porter, and others.

Together, they recalled old folk ballads: *I been working on the railroad all the livelong day . . . did you ever hear tell of Sweet Betsy from Pike who crossed the wide prairie with her husband Ike . . . I've got a mule and her name is Sal, fifteen miles on the Erie Canal.* Joe knew the words to all of these and prompted Kay when she got them wrong. "No not *that* way, it's *this* way," he would say, supplying some small correction. He asked for more and more, tiring her and usually ending with Bob Dylan songs about rain on the Great Lakes, iron mines, Duluth, love gone wrong, gamblers and pretenders and time running out. Songs to last a hundred heat waves and to sing walking back in the dark from the playground and find the way home, where a melody or lyric might give way to kisses and whispered words and short, cautious phrases, or to reminiscing through the small hours. Moving back and back. Looking for a time before nightmares.

ONCE IN A WHILE, JOE ASKED ABOUT ALLIE GREEN, BUT KAY WAS
already learning to do without her. She had resisted for a time, forcing
herself to read and reread Allie's letters in a belated effort to project
the story beyond that desperate, hurried script. Repeatedly frustrated,
Kay tried to trace Allie by searching the Illinois and Michigan census
returns, Chicago city directories, death notices in both states, anything with the remotest possible connection. She could have gone on,
perhaps looking for Allie in some other place, living under an assumed
name or married. Or she could have stuck to Chicago, looking for
charity records or a pauper's grave somewhere in Cook County. In fact,
Kay preferred these searches to the tortuous, disorganized letters, the
final dispatches of someone increasingly beyond clear thinking and
planning. But the searches were set to fail because Allie's letters fore-
told her final defeat in terms Kay could never match. Allie Green, raising her own words as a shield, blocked any attempt Kay might make to
imagine the outcome or put flesh on the bones of the story.

There was little point in pursuing Allie any longer, but there would
be every reason to learn about Violet Parker and Ada. Kay knew the
only option was to defend the letters zealously and try, finally, to determine what happened after Violet handed them over. So, in what might
be considered Allie Green's small but enduring triumph as a vanished
mother, Kay preserved the letters and thought about Ada and what to
do next. In the end, it was Allie who overcame Kay's resistance and
made her care for Ada.

Now, if Joe brought up the subject of Allie Green, Kay sought to
pull the story more definitively toward Ada, Violet, and the history of
Shaw Farm. She showed him a bracelet, a simple gold band that had
belonged to Ada, before being handed down to Marion. She also found
an early photograph, evidently taken when Ada graduated from high
school; mounted on heavy card and damaged, it looked as though the
top right corner had been deliberately trimmed. In the picture, Ada
wore a long, cream-colored dress and held her diploma. It was Joe who
spotted the same gold bracelet, pushed halfway up her gloved forearm.
After that, Kay took to wearing the bracelet, turning it over in the light
to read the prettily engraved name, *Ada*, and year, *1910*.

In addition to the bracelet and the few family papers and photographs from the period, Kay located an early, undated map of the

land platting, indicating the site of Shaw Farm. She brought out Jake and Marion's Kodachrome pictures of family picnics in and around Middleville in the 1940s and 1950s. And she supplemented these various pieces by ordering books and maps and using the Internet. However, Kay decided to delay the visit to Barry County until an unspecified date. She told Joe it was too soon, that she needed more time to research the place before going. In truth, Kay knew he was in no mood for a road trip, while she was a little jangled herself and waiting, with curious, growing apprehensiveness, for the library to track down Dr. Thisroy's articles about nostalgia.

Anyway, it was too hot to travel, and Joe's used car had no air-conditioning to be capriciously switched on and off, while the two of them bickered about the best way to keep cool in a heat wave.

YANKEES

"SO TELL ME ABOUT BARRY COUNTY—IS IT ALL CORNFIELDS OVER there, or what?" Joe said after they came in from a walk one night. He opened a beer and flopped down on the sofa.

"Yeah, right," Kay called from the bathroom, where she stood splashing her face and neck with cool water. "Complete with talking scarecrows and ghosts of misunderstood, dead baseball players."

"No, seriously. I've never been to the western part of the state. What's it like?"

"I hardly know anymore." She returned to the living room, settled onto the sofa beside him, and took a sip of his beer. "As children, we used to go often to visit Fred and Ada. But the grandparents died. We all grew up and left home. You know how it is.

"The last time I spent there was during the final months of my mother's life, after she demanded to be moved to a care home in Middleville. It was a peculiar demand, because Marion barely knew *where* she was by then, but she was insistent. 'I want to go home,' she said over and over. 'To Plymouth?' we asked. 'No.' 'Garden City?' 'No.' 'Dearborn?' 'No. *No.*' We worked our way backwards through the locations in Marion's life, already guessing what she wanted but trying to get her to fix on one of the other, later locations, all of which were closer to Detroit and Pontiac, where Pam lived."

"That's cruel," Joe said.

"I know, I know. It *was* cruel. But we honestly believed we'd be better able to visit and care for her if she stayed in the Detroit area, or near Pam. But in any case, my mother dug her heels in and found the name herself. '*Middleville*,' she said emphatically. 'I want to go to Middleville. *Right now.*' It was her last request, I suppose.

"There can't be more than about three thousand people living in Middleville, and it still has the look and feel of a small town. After we moved Marion there, I took occasional walks. Even Main Street was quiet; very few shops, very few pedestrians, not many more cars. Of course, an outsider, having no local friends to visit or talk to, tends to revert to his or her own emptiness and project it onto a place. Nonetheless, it was hard to escape the feeling that Middleville was a town left behind, probably sometime in the thirties or forties. And it struck me that if you grew up there, you might be quick to leave it behind yourself, only to discover much later that you had not really got very far. I guessed that was what drove Marion back to this place, so late in life.

"But one evening before sunset, having spent several hours at my mother's bedside, I walked into town and followed Main Street to where it crosses the Thornapple River. I stopped on the bridge at one end of the street, overlooking a dam and a small sandy bank. There were a couple of boys, fifteen or sixteen years old, standing at the river's edge, throwing a stick in the water for a dog and sneaking a smoke. They saw me watching them, shared a private joke, and cast a cool, defiant glance in my direction before moving further along the riverside path and disappearing into the trees. I closed my eyes.

"Marion, and Ada before her, used to paddle in the water and picnic at this spot, and various other locations along the river. I tried to imagine Ada crossing to the opposite bank, barefooted beneath a loose, ankle-length cotton dress and pinafore, leaping from one stone to another, and then Marion, wearing a thirties-style tank suit or swimming skirt, diving from a homemade raft into the deepest part of the river. Performing underwater somersaults. My mother and grandmother once had springs in their arms and legs; they had a daring-do, curvaceous vitality.

"Standing on the bridge and listening to the river below, I saw that brash and joyous physicality as a gift from this place, rather than something in their genes. Finally, it struck me that my mother had come back for the remembered fearlessness of the body without bounds, limbs that could carry her for miles down the Thornapple trails, strong lungs that gave her the pluck and stamina to swim right under a raft and hide there. My mother's short-term memory was shot to hell, but Middleville was hardwired, more persistent than all her snuffed memories put together. I'm glad we finally listened and took her back home to die.

"I've managed to find maps and land records for Middleville and Barry County, as far back as the mid-nineteenth century. These show the names of the first landowners and roads. On the maps, you can see where the river flowed through the town and out to the surrounding farmland. Running from Middleville in a northward direction, you can find the road that would become known as Shaw Road. You can see what was once the family homestead, where Violet Shaw Parker spent her childhood, and after her, Ada. And after Ada, Marion. My mother was the last to be raised there.

"Shaw Road was named for the Shaw brothers—including Violet's father, Alonzo Shaw—who were early settlers in the area. The road is still dotted with the spare, but pretty, wood-framed houses built by these first successful farmers. Just north of the original homestead, Shaw Road meets Parmalee Road, leading straight to the tiny, wooded Parmalee Cemetery, where nearly all of my Barry County ancestors are buried. The day of Marion's funeral, when we drove out of town to Parmalee, I was surprised to see how little had changed. Shaw Road was still unpaved, and the gravel made crackly sounds beneath the slow-moving line of mourners' cars trailing the hearse."

"Was it a long line?" Joe asked.

"Very short. Three or four cars, I believe. Marion used to know a lot of people, especially around Middleville. But most of them were dead or gone. It seemed my mother's time had come, and I hoped she wouldn't mind so much, because the others were dead too. And it's funny. As we drove out on Shaw Road, crossing the fields, I remember thinking, 'I could just stay here.' It wasn't that I wanted to *live* there. It wasn't *my home*. Maybe I wanted the Thornapple Valley to make *me* brave too. Or maybe I just wanted to go with my mother. It would be a comfort to be small again, give into land and blood ties, let go of other plans. Sometimes retreat can be so pleasant, such a relief. Anyway, of course the feeling passed. After the funeral, I packed up and left with everyone else.

"I don't know. I never had a realistic idea of that part of the world. I imagined western Michigan as a picture book of red barns and old-fashioned farmhouses with porch swings and cut-glass doorknobs. *And* cornfields. Beyond Shaw Road and Parmalee, there were roadside stands selling blueberry preserves in advance of summer and fall, when there would be stocks of plump, brightly colored farm and garden produce: ears of corn by the dozen, watermelon, tomatoes, apples, squashes, and pumpkins. And everywhere lakes and rivers. Waters with evocative names like Gun Lake, Chief Noon-Day Lake, Algonquin and Sugarbush lakes, Yankee Springs, and of course the Thorn - apple River."

"Sounds like a list of winners and losers," Joe remarked.

Kay nodded.

"Violet descended from Yankees, the winners, as you say. Her father was a son of New Englanders who had migrated from Massachusetts to Genesee County in upstate New York, sometime after the War for Independence. Alonzo Shaw was a young man in 1836, when he caught the 'Michigan Fever' then sweeping the East. Along with three brothers, one sister, and two other family groups, Alonzo left New York, traveling in a party of seventeen adults and six children.

"Barry County had been constituted by act of the Territorial Legislature in 1829, following over twenty years of a piecemeal takeover of Indian territories across the region, mainly achieved by treaties and land grabs. There was already a system in place for the distribution of lands. They were to be surveyed and divided into townships of six square miles, with each township subdivided into thirty-six numbered sections of one square mile each. In Michigan, as elsewhere, every section was charted with precision, had clear boundaries, ended in right angles, and would sooner or later be occupied by expansionist, ambitious farmers from the East. Like many new arrivals, Alonzo Shaw was a squatter; he occupied his initial lot of eighty acres, raised a basic log cabin, began to clear the land, and then applied to buy the lot at the minimum government price of $1.25 per acre.

"Of course, the local Pottawatomie and Ottawa peoples never considered land as property in any European sense of the word. Ownership, the grid survey and its declaration of spatial order, the partitioning of land into plots to buy and sell, these would have been alien ideas. Even where tribal groups tried to negotiate in terms that might be understood by the white authorities, the odds were against any lasting accommodation. Federal policies of 'restriction and removal' had been pursued since at least 1825, and by 1840, the majority of the Pottawatomie had been forcibly removed to Kansas. The Ottawa would eventually negotiate a series of land cessions that prevented their complete removal and later resulted in the creation of Ottawa reservations north of the Muskegon River."

Kay paused, expecting an acerbic comment from Joe at this point, but he said nothing. She saw that he was listening intently and his expression had hardened. Not for the first time, and with a pang of anxiety, it occurred to Kay that the family stories might not be a distraction for Joe, but a rather more dangerous form of entertainment. Perhaps he was fastening them to his own experience, taking them into dark corners of his own. What if these same stories, instead of joining them to the past and one another, threatened to break them apart?

Joe noticed that she had stopped talking, and he nudged her with impatience.

"Are you okay?" she asked hesitantly.

"Yeah. I'm interested." He sounded fine, if a little irritated by her concern.

Kay went into the study and returned with a large map of the northeastern states, sat close to Joe, and spread the map across their knees.

"The Erie Canal opened in 1825 and radically sped movement to the Old Northwest—what you and I now call the Midwest—by linking the Hudson River with Lake Erie. The population of Michigan was nearly 32,000 in 1830, but by 1840, after a single decade of rampant land speculation, it was more than 212,000. People traveled any way they could manage: by water or land, in mail coaches, flatboats, covered wagons. I believe Alonzo Shaw's group followed an overland stage route that passed via Buffalo and the southern shore of Lake Erie, up through the Black Swamp in Ohio, toward Detroit. That was the most affordable way for a large party of migrants to move the livestock and wagons loaded with provisions and belongings."

Kay traced the route on the map as she spoke.

"The hardiest among the group probably walked a good part of the way, while ox teams pulled the wagons. From Detroit, they would have traveled the Chicago Road to Ypsilanti, where they joined the Territorial Road that would take them westward into Calhoun County, finally turning northward up the Thornapple River Valley to Barry County, following a series of oak openings into fertile and heavily timbered land.

"Not long after their arrival in Michigan, some of the younger members of the migrant group married one another. Alonzo married Hannah Richardson, the sister of his boyhood friend Thomas Richardson, and Thomas married Alonzo's sister, Ellen. Alonzo's three brothers courted the daughters of neighboring settlers, and a kinship network of adjoining fields took root.

"Progress to market agriculture was slow, but the extended family shared labor, farm equipment, and livestock to the mutual benefit of everyone. It was rolling country, but with fertile soil and large sections of level land for planting. Grain farming and dairy production were supplemented by market gardening and fruit orchards. Within ten or fifteen years, Alonzo and his brothers had sizeable holdings of rich farmland all along Shaw Road, less than a mile from the center of Middleville village.

"Alonzo and Hannah had five children, a son and four daughters. Of these, all but the third daughter lived to adulthood, including Violet, the youngest child, born in 1850. Violet's brother, Lansing, was nineteen years old at the start of the Civil War. He enlisted as a private and on September 4, 1862, was mustered into Company C of the Michigan Twenty-first Infantry. Eight days later, the regiment was given orders to report at Cincinnati, and from there, sent to support forces already fighting in Kentucky. Lansing Shaw was killed in action at Perryville, Kentucky, on October 8, 1862. His Civil War service had lasted all of thirty-four days.

"Three years later, twenty-one-year-old James Parker, a private in the same company and one of Lansing's fellow recruits, was mustered out of the Union Army. Returning to his home in Freeport, northeast of Middleville on the county line, he worked for a local ironmonger for a few years before being hired as a live-in laborer at Alonzo's farm."

"Had James Parker *known* Lansing Shaw? Is that why they hired him?" Joe asked.

"I don't know how they found James, or how he found them. Certainly, they would have needed a young farmer to replace Lansing. Why James Parker and not another—who's to say? Maybe James *had* known Lansing and later came looking for the family. Maybe he had something to tell them about their son, some message or personal effect to deliver. Or perhaps the two soldiers had not known each other at all, but the simple fact of James Parker's proximity to Lansing on the battlefield assured the hiring. Alonzo and Hannah superstitiously believed that here was a young man capable of returning something of what was lost to them at Perryville.

"But that is pure speculation. The only thing I can say with certainty is this: James came to work and live on the farm, and he married Violet in 1873. Their first child, a son, was born in 1875. They named him Alonzo, after Violet's father, but from the beginning, the boy was known as Lon. There were two more sons to follow, Eugene and Merritt, and a daughter, Caroline. The three boys were healthy and robust, but Caroline died of pneumonia in 1890, at the age of seven.

"Caroline's death was the beginning of a devastating period of loss for Violet. Her father, by then the last surviving Shaw brother, died in January of 1892, and Hannah followed him in less than six months. Undoubtedly, Violet's parents had believed the farm to be secure in the hands of James Parker and their youngest daughter, but James died suddenly, sometime in late summer 1893. So far, I have not been able to locate the exact date. I have no idea what calamity removed James from the picture, but our family stories tell that Violet, already bereaved three times in succession, was so devastated by this fourth death that she never spoke of it. This *may* account for the lack of information we have about James, but I suspect there was something else at play. Ada was born the following June, and as you know, by then Violet had a few secrets to keep."

"Ada's parentage?"

"Yes."

"Are you suggesting that Violet was trying to pass Ada off as her own? As a last child, conceived before her husband died?" Joe looked incredulous.

"It's what I'm thinking."

"And the dates didn't match."

"That's right. But it was *close*—a matter of a month or two."

"Who would believe it?"

"Probably nobody except a child—Ada, up to the age of sixteen. I think Ada was the only person Violet *needed* to believe it. If Ada could be given a family and sixteen years of innocence before receiving the letters, then some good would have come from a bad situation. Allie Green was gone; the father had refused her. Other people *knew* of course, but Violet must have calculated, rightly I believe, that there was no one who had any interest in bringing this history to light. No, I think this was a deception created for Ada's benefit."

"So . . . it was best not to dwell on the timing of James Parker's death in relation to the date of Ada's birth."

"Right."

"I'm sorry, Kay, but that has got to be one of the least convincing deceptions I have ever heard told!"

"That's what makes it so interesting."

"Have you found Ada's real father?"

"Yes, I think so. But I'm not quite ready to tell you about him."

"Something about this is not right. I can't follow Violet's motives. There's something missing."

"Maybe."

Joe rubbed his chin stubble and stared a long time at the map, still opened on their laps. Finally, and with a note of disapproval, he remarked, "One secret generally leads to another."

"I . . . guess so."

And there they were. Nearing the end of a long story, but suddenly locked in an awkward silence.

For a moment, Kay wondered if Joe had guessed—correctly, it has to be said—that she was deliberately slowing her searches in order to prolong their arrangement. Or maybe he had been through her papers, discovered that she was running a covert line of inquiry into nostalgia, making detailed notes of symptoms and ordering journal articles. Then it struck her that Joe might be mulling over his own secrets, that neither of them had a specific charge to make against the other, yet they were *both* guilty. Information, knowledge, and thoughts, too often withheld by Joe as much as by Kay, had settled like invisible toxic dust on their skin and on the furniture and floors of the little house on Maple Court. But Joe had a more legitimate reason for withholding things; his inability to share his experiences in Vietnam was at least understandable. Kay felt this difference in their positions now, like an unspoken accusation. It lasted only a matter of seconds, a ripple, but it deflated her.

"You like Violet," Joe said finally.

"Yes," she replied, relieved to hear his voice. "I like Violet."

"Even though she lied for so many years? And her lie was so *lame*—everyone except Ada must have known, or guessed the truth. Everyone in the family and the town."

"Maybe I like Violet *because* she lied. And because her lie was so ineffectual, so lame, as you say. I don't know. Her choices were cruel and limited. It had been left to her to decide who got hurt and when; loyalty to one person meant injury to another. But she took her decision and didn't try to blame anybody else. For sixteen years, for all that time Violet raised Ada as her own, *Allie* was the injured party. Even though Violet had helped Allie by keeping the baby, both women knew Allie had been . . . *denied*. I guess I like Violet because from the day Ada was put into her arms, the situation was an impossible one. Yet Violet threw in her lot and lived with the consequences."

Joe looked unconvinced and a little unhappy, but said nothing. He simply waited for Kay to recover the storyline. He did not help her because he was still thinking about Allie. Kay tried to steer his interest back to Shaw Farm.

"So, to pick up where we were . . ." she began again, her voice wavering slightly, "the farm never recovered from the loss of James Parker. Some of the larger family holdings had already diminished following the deaths of Alonzo's brothers, and like a number of his cousins, young Alonzo Parker, or Lon, as he was known, had found factory work in Grand Rapids. By then, Violet's eldest son was disinclined to return to a life of farming."

"How do ya keep 'em down on the farm after they've seen Grand Rapids?" Joe cracked, a touch of warmth returning to his voice.

"Something like that, I suppose. Lon had become a city boy, and his two younger brothers, Eugene and Merritt, were neither capable nor old enough to take over the farm. Even Violet's sisters were gone, having married into clans in nearby townships. To Violet, her family utterly depleted, the sad truth was that the value of the Shaw land now resided in its speculative worth—the dollars per acre it could fetch—rather than the crops it might yield. Fortunately, her father and mother were not there to see the youngest daughter commit the sin of 'spoiling the whole' by selling off Alonzo's fields in small parcels to neighboring landowners, even if many of them were related by the Shaw brothers' marriages.

"Violet maintained the boys and Ada on the proceeds of the land she sold. She managed to hold onto the house and three acres of the lot on which it stood. Alone, she raised the boys, each son in turn, edging past the age of the father when Violet first met him. She probably marked every child's birthday with regret, as mothers sometimes do, and as James receded and diminished in importance. And she took care of Ada. She must have been made of strong stuff, because she outlived her husband by more than two decades. I think she outlived him because she had to. There was nobody else."

Kay had finally talked herself dry. Having listened intently, Joe put his head back and closed his eyes. Of all the old stories, this one had made him work hardest, perhaps because he was less credulous than before, less willing to stand and gaze at the surface of what she told him.

"You look tired," she said.

"I am a little."

They stayed quiet for what seemed many long minutes, fingers resting lightly on the large map still spread clumsily across their laps, knees, and upper legs. Joe's hip and thigh touched hers, unseen, somewhere beneath the Erie Canal, the old Chicago Road, the big lakes and the fields.

Kay wanted him, but she was apprehensive. Nothing was straight between them. Answers to simple questions; looks and gestures; passing in the hall or bathroom; eating together at the table. Nothing was straight, and they both knew it. They knew it in a thousand tiny, daily ways, including when they brushed against one another in bed. The wonderful, clumsy impatience of their early lovemaking, of excitation so many years deferred, racing and panting, the delightful, muffed performances during the initial rush to make up for lost time, like kids again; then the slow tumbling *through* time, an astonishing transition from fast to slow as they learned to hold back, delay and please one another, all of this had diminished. Kay tried to put it down to the heat, Joe's nightmares and broken sleep, her own nagging grief, but the truth was that she had no idea where their desire was heading or whether they could follow it there.

She held her breath, slipped one hand beneath the opened map, and tentatively began to touch him. She saw Joe tighten with surprise and uncertainty as he thought about what she was doing. She saw him battle to want her, to strip away reason and let go of thinking. Kay began to wonder if she should withdraw her hand when he was caught, finally, by a small gasp of pleasure. He sighed and relaxed slightly.

"What are you doing?" he said, eyes still closed.

"Nothing."

He opened his eyes and turned to look at her.

"Joe," she whispered. "Is it okay if I just stay here, doing nothing?"

"It's okay."

MORNING

LATE MORNING SUN COVERED THE HOUSE. IT WARMED THE GRASS and dandelions, dried the dew from each blade and stem, until a sweet, green smell hung over the yard and drifted indoors. Light pushed against Ada's lowered window shade, turning her room into a slow oven, coating the walls and furniture in amber. Downstairs and beyond the house, in the town, people were moving. Voices stirred, barely audible in Ada's room, but familiar, like the creaks in the house.

Stretching her limbs, eyelids heavy, Ada let the voices coax her out of sleep. She blinked, rolled onto her back, and lazily began to replay the scenes of the previous day. The rooms polished and rearranged for guests, pictures on the walls, even the summer light falling on the yard. She remembered dressing for the photographer, carefully fitting herself into the graduation gown, fixing the bow to her hair, sliding the gold bracelet over the long white glove, and finally emerging from her room. She saw herself poised at the top of the stairs, Lon waiting below. Then, wincing as though she had pricked a finger on a sewing needle, Ada opened her eyes wide. Lon. At the foot of the stairs, leaning on the banister. She hadn't quite seen it yesterday, but in retrospect, the expression on Lon's face was unmistakable. He had been shocked by her.

Turning to face the window, Ada told herself that after a special occasion or party, in the light of the following morning, it was possible see things strangely, experience feelings of doubt. It was inevitable, after such anticipation and excitement, to find remembered impressions unreliable. *Did* my guests enjoy themselves? *Was* I pretty and amusing, or did the attention and the dancing and laughing crowd make me believe so? But this was a questioning of a different order. And mostly, it centered on Lon. Every conversation of the previous day, every exchange between them, seemed like the lines of a play now, or part of a parallel life, from which she had exited during the night. It was like falling asleep on one train and waking up on another, without remembering the change or being able to prove it, because all the fittings remained as they were in the first train and even the scenery outside the window was the same.

She recalled Lon pulling her wrist toward him in order to examine the bracelet, how she stiffened and turned red, because he controlled the movement of her arm and this made her momentarily angry. Then as Lon lowered his head to read the engraving, Ada noticed that his hair was thinning on top and she tried to look away. Now, on this new train, it struck her that Lon had never stooped before her, never bowed his head in her presence. He was losing ground. No one, not even Lon Parker, could run around town forever, stay muscular and handsome and make her girlfriends skittish.

Then there was Mama, waving from the porch and worrying about something, as they rode away in the rig. Mama's quiet, private manner of worrying. But Lon swung quickly back into view, in a new scene. He had positioned himself, arms folded across his broad chest, just behind and to the left of the photographer. A look of surprise still marked his face, but fainter than the first shock he had registered at the bottom of the stairs. Now he was startled, discomfited, but gaining control over the startling thing itself. Ada held herself nervously, constrained by the dress, as she posed in front of a backdrop painted with stone columns and a hanging tapestry, trying to stay still and gaze toward the camera eye, as instructed. She fought to conceal a wave of nausea brought on by the heavy odor of chemicals in the studio. The photographer came out from behind his camera, adjusted the fine tilt of her head, and demonstrated how to hold the diploma gracefully in her gloved hands. He called out impatiently when once again Ada's eyes shifted to her brother. Later, as they walked from the studio back to the carriage, Lon placed his large hand on her back.

And finally the party, already a pastel blur. The girls in their best frocks embraced Ada, one by one, as they climbed the front steps to the door. The gangly lads in twos and threes, hands in pockets, followed the girls and stepped awkwardly into the house. Music and dances. Lon leaned against the wall, chatting with one of his cousins, casting an occasional glance at his sister. He rolled up his shirt-sleeves to stay cool and rubbed a hand across his chin and the back of his neck, the way men do when they are idle. He smiled his approval each time Ada caught his eye, until eventually he stopped looking for her among the other girls. She thought he must be bored. Between the moving dancers, the skirts and raised arms and bobbing heads, she caught one last glimpse of Lon as he strode from the room toward the front door. Then he was gone.

Ada went into the kitchen for more punch. Mama was sitting with Aunt Lizzie. They stopped talking. "Mama, where did Lon go?" Ada knew Violet sometimes disliked this fretfulness about her brother, but the question would not be suppressed.

"Oh, you know Lon and his ways. Don't worry about him. Go and enjoy your company, and he'll be along later."

Ada managed to overcome her disappointment. She joined in the party games. She amused herself with "friends of her own age," as Mama liked to put it.

It was late when Lon reappeared. The guests were getting ready to leave. Someone, who was it, played the final tunes of the night on the piano. There were a few girls still singing and dancing together. As Ada stood watching, someone approached from behind, took her by the waist, and drew her into the cluster of twirling girls. It was Lon, perspiring and unsteady; Ada could smell his body and gin breath. He pulled her in, but then swung her back out, too hard and fast, hurling her into the other dancers. The girls shrieked and laughed, nervous and coquettish in the presence of Ada's handsome, worldly brother. "*Careful,* Lon," she begged, laughing too, in order to cover her embarrassment. It was a gentle chiding, but Ada flushed bright pink and her voice trembled. She had never reproached Lon before, never secretly wished he had not come home.

Lon caught the look on her face, stopped dancing, and froze for a moment, feet planted and arms at his side. Misery passed between them, as though it were the only possible future. Then Lon pulled Ada very close. Holding her angrily, tight against him, he put his lips next to her ear and started to whisper something, then appeared to change his mind. She heard nothing. His breath was a hot blast, and then it was gone. Lon turned away, weaving slightly, and left the room. Oblivious to the last strains of party music and the swaying skirts, Ada watched him go.

SHE SAT UP IN BED, TERRIFIED THAT SHE HAD HURT LON. SHE MUST see him before he left for Grand Rapids, put things right. Maybe he would not remember. Maybe it had not happened the way she now imagined it. He would laugh at her fears, pat her hair as usual, and she could go back to being a child. But as Ada plotted a return to life before the party, the sounds coming from downstairs had grown sharper and louder—short, heated bursts, back and forth between one deep voice and one higher voice. Ada remained upright in her bed, rigid and straining to hear. It was impossible to make out the words, but the voices belonged to Mama and Lon. Mama's tones grew more pleading and placatory, doing the work. Lon's replies remained low and abrupt, each one a stone wall to something that Mama wanted. Ada was paralyzed, wretched and filled with dread. And without any idea of what they were fighting about, she knew it was to do with her.

The argument subsided within minutes, but the voices carried on for longer, lowered and grave. Ada waited, seated on the edge of her bed, still unable to dress or venture downstairs. Finally, the kitchen door opened and closed, and Lon's heavy step could be heard on the stairs. Ada listened to the muffled noises coming from his room, as he gathered his things, quick and determined. His door clicked shut; he thumped down the hall past her room, paused, and then moved downstairs, out of the house and away.

Ada had never lived anywhere but in this solid frame house, the old Shaw Farm, and as long as she could remember, important conversations were held in the kitchen. Violet and Lon had been together in the kitchen minutes earlier, but when Ada ventured downstairs, she found Violet alone at the table, a small packet of letters in front of her. Ada sat down opposite and waited. Finally, after what seemed an unbearably long time, her fear and impatience got the better of her.

"What's wrong, Mama?" she asked.

In a low, drained voice, Violet began to speak. Deliberating over each phrase, she told Ada of a young woman from the city who gave birth to a baby girl she could not keep. The young mother had no savings, no means of caring for the child, no offers of help from her own family. The father of the baby was unwilling—or perhaps unable—to marry. Violet paused to study the girl's face. Ada's solemn expression told her that she had already said enough, and that it was perfectly possible for a person, even a child, to go through the days believing one thing, while knowing another.

"You are talking about me." Ada raised one hand and tapped her own chest.

"Yes, dear."

"Why was I given to you?"

"Your mother decided to bring you to another town, to people who had the means . . . she wanted you to have a chance in life, and to be loved. She found me—through friends—and asked for my help." Violet stopped, as though wearied by the search for words. Then she braved a small smile. "Perhaps she thought a lady who had three boys, and whose own daughter had died, needed a little girl."

"*Did* you need a little girl?"

"Oh! From the moment I laid eyes on you, I was—" Violet's throat tightened. She began again. "The loss of Caroline was most painful to all of us. You were a beautiful baby, and I wished to help the mother, whose situation was a hard one. That is why you must not blame her, Ada."

Finally, Ada looked surprised. Until that moment, she had not thought of blaming anyone. Blame would involve taking an interest in the identities of her real mother and father, whereas the immediate impact of this news had been to heighten her affection for the continuity of known people and things. Mama, as she called Violet, Lon and the boys. The front porch of their simple, but spacious and comfortable house. The Thornapple River. The seasons. Cousins and friends. As she sat at the table that afternoon, Ada had been inwardly wrestling Violet's words to the ground, strangling them before they took hold. But when Violet spoke sympathetically of the lost mother, curiosity got the better of Ada.

"What was my mother's name?"

"Her name was Alice Green."

Now Violet faltered. She knew, in the instant before she spoke the next words, that a dry, dead fact was about to be given life.

"But everyone called her Allie."

"Everyone?"

"Her . . . family and friends."

"Did you know them?"

"No . . . not well. I only know that Allie set off alone for Chicago, when you were less than a year old. I prayed every day that she made a new life there and found a measure of happiness. But the truth is, I just don't know. I wrote to Allie at her last known address, but her letters stopped after she arrived in Chicago. I am so sorry, dear, but I cannot even tell you whether she is still alive. Certainly, things did not go well for her after she left Grand Rapids. Judging by her last letter—"

Violet stopped to steady her voice. Speaking aloud in Alonzo Shaw's farmhouse, in her mother's kitchen, hearing such words in *this* room, years later—this was unexpectedly shocking to her. She was shocked to find herself so far beyond the moral universe of her parents. She was shocked by the brutal severity of Allie's loss. Of course, she had *known*, but somehow, keeping the letters in the leather satchel on top of the wardrobe had held it at bay. Now, she was face to face with events and decisions and her own part in the destruction of a life. Moreover, truth was, and would remain, a partial player in these exchanges. Violet was well aware that she was releasing some of the facts, but not all, that she was still organizing the information, still withholding.

"So, Ada. These are the letters your mother sent after she left you here with me. I have kept them for you. Certain passages may be distressing to read, but they will tell you something of your mother's devotion, the difficulties she faced, and her unbearable sorrow at losing you."

Violet slid the letters across the table so that they rested in front of Ada. It was a handing over, however halting and unsatisfactory.

"Open them when you are ready, Ada, whenever that may be. They are yours to keep. And now, I think we have said enough. If you have more questions, you may come to me. But I must ask you not to speak of this to your brothers, or to anyone else."

"Do the boys know?"

"Yes. They remember your arrival in our family. And they all doted on you. You were quite a spoiled little girl, you know!"

"Even Lon? Did Lon dote on me?"

"*All* the boys did," Violet repeated, rising from her chair.

"Why did Lon not want you to tell me?"

It was Violet's turn to look surprised.

"Lon . . . is complicated. Perhaps we had best leave that question for now."

But the girl remained seated, patient but willful. When Violet took over the care of Ada, all those years ago, a strange and unjust set of alliances and exclusions had been set in place. Violet had taken responsibility, even got something she wanted, but now the cruelty of her choice was played out in Ada's reaction. The girl was laying claim to information about the wrong person. Violet tried again to say just enough to bring the conversation to a close.

"It's true that Lon is unhappy about my decision to tell you. I suppose he . . . does not want to upset things. He adores you, and perhaps some part of him fears this information will change you or take you away from us." Violet paused to calm herself and gather conviction. "You know, Ada, Lon would go to the ends of the earth for you. But he will not wish to talk about this history. My advice to you, for the time being, is to keep him out of these discussions. Leave Lon and the boys to me."

Ada listened, her expression hard with concentration; then she slowly pushed her chair away from the table and stood. "Please keep the letters, Mama. Destroy them if you wish. I don't want them," she said.

That was when Violet knew for certain that Lon's hold over Ada ensured the daughter would never go looking for her mother. To please her beloved Lon, Ada would reject the letters and any further revelation. There was an undeniable promise of relief attached to that simple realization. For Violet, the pressure would ease gradually, as in a series of sighs, a physical uncoiling over a period of time. Lon's initial anger would subside, and the painful disagreement between them would be left behind, if not entirely forgotten. Now that Ada had been told, Violet could expect an occasional awkwardness and some small adjustments in the family, mostly unspoken ones, rather like shifting one's weight to find the contours of a new chair.

However, Violet felt such relief would come small, disproportionately small to the low-lying dread of the preceding sixteen years. Yes, she might put the letters away; she might rest on her bed without the constant grating of another woman's last, exacting request. But sleep—that was another matter. Ada's apparent lack of regard, immediately comforting though it was, prevented any final sense of exoneration.

Picking up the letters from the table, having kept her promise to Ada's mother, and seemingly to little effect, Violet knew that no one but she would ever weep for Allie Green.

Ada turned away from Violet's stricken face. The girl's limbs ached from sitting still for too long, and she was anxious about Lon. He had set off for Grand Rapids without saying goodbye. She would have to wait an entire week to scrutinize his mood, to know if things had altered between them. She had yet to determine whether he looked at her differently than before, whether he still wore the expression of alarm that had appeared when she dressed in her graduation gown. She longed to be far from the letters, out of the house, under the sun.

From early childhood, she had been dimly aware of the clues and signs scattered across the years, such as the way Aunt Lizzie and Mama caught each other's eyes over her head as she unwrapped a birthday present. Or the September morning, some ten years earlier, when a census enumerator came to the house and Violet, looking flustered, sent Ada outdoors until he was gone. The day a girl at school called her a "doorstep baby" and the others giggled behind their hands. The look of pity on the teacher's face as she pulled the bully out of the classroom and Ada's private decision not to relate the incident to Mama. But some weeks later, at a school pageant, she watched the mothers grouped together in the small audience, and finally allowed that Mama was considerably older than the other women, and marked by some unnamed difference.

There were a handful of such incidents of whispering and name calling over the years, and each time Ada had swatted them away like flies at a picnic, ducked the arrows that could be nothing more than the cruelty of girls with stirred imaginations. She had said such things herself, to other girls. Finally, there was the permanent silence surrounding James Parker, until he seemed never to have existed at all. The events of his life and death did not fit, so he was turned to powder. Ada could not recall being taken to visit his grave. If Mama went there, she did so alone.

Now, all of these apparently disparate signs began to draw together, suggesting a discernable pattern and purpose and giving Ada confirmation that one story can live, very simply, *inside* another. It was like wearing a protective, extra layer of skin. A person might spend a very long time peeling away the outer layer. But when she finally exposes what was previously concealed, she is not surprised.

Ada and her friends had arranged a walking party along the river. Pausing briefly in front of the hall mirror as she gathered her things, she noted that her brown, summer face, dark eyes, and thick mass of hair were unchanged. The gray woman standing in the kitchen was Mama, just as she always had been. For Lon, Ada would never wear that graduation gown again, never grow up, and never speak her mother's name. When he came home next weekend, he would see instantly that he had nothing to fear. She would wait for Lon on the front step, just like every other Friday. And that evening, sometime before they all sat down to supper, Mama would quietly inform him that the letters had been refused, put away unread.

Ada squeezed her eyes shut, then opened them to the same scene, herself, in front of the mirror on a warm day in June, looking forward to next Friday and Lon's return, and all the Fridays and seasons ahead. She planned to lie on the grass in summer, pick a dandelion, hold it beneath Lon's chin, and say *tell the truth, do you like butter?* She planned to cool her feet in the river, plunge into piles of autumn leaves, and make angels in the snow. Against these coming times, Allie Green was nothing.

DR. THISROY

DR. ELMER THISROY, WHOSE WRITINGS ARRIVED AT THE END OF August, proved to be an inventive and colorful character, a working psychiatrist with a scholarly interest in Johannes Hofer's pioneering work on nostalgia. In just two published articles, Thisroy achieved what, as far as Kay could see, no one else had managed. He resurrected the lost history of nostalgia, claimed that it continued to make people ill, and finally proposed a new diagnostic category to address its latest manifestations.

In his first article, "Nostalgia Ain't What It Used to Be: Medical Discourse and a Lost Malady," Thisroy demonstrated the literal truth of Yogi Berra's famous quip by mapping the historical path of nostalgia after Hofer's 1688 dissertation. For two centuries, nostalgia remained a medical concern, although the discourses surrounding it began to change. In physicians' writings, the understanding of nostalgia crept beyond the immediate physical complications of homesickness, to include pathological, spiritual pining for the vanished past. The typical sufferer of nostalgia, a student, soldier, or other exile, experienced symptoms that belied a profound confusion between home as a physical, geographical place and home as a remembered, imagined place. People afflicted with nostalgia might see ghosts, hear the voices of loved ones, shift from past to present without being aware of it, or even lose the ability to distinguish between the two.

According to Thisroy, the link between nostalgia and memory was identified early and most evocatively by Immanuel Kant in his *Anthropology from a Pragmatic Point of View* (1798). Kant noted that when homesick people revisit the places of their youth, "they are greatly disappointed in their expectations and so cured. Though they think this is because everything has changed there, it is really because they cannot relive their youth there." This statement was crucial to Thisroy, because it supported his view that, with the widening of its symptoms and meaning, nostalgia "morphed, quite early in its history, into a malady of space and time, a fever that had its origins in the normally healthy attachments a person holds for remembered people and places, for cherished objects, distant events, and even for sense memories." An image or a piece of music, a voice, a taste, texture, or smell—all of these might have potent effects on the "nostalgiac" (Thisroy's term). So far, so good, claimed Thisroy. These were "valid permutations" that remained consistent with Hofer's original insights, lending them greater reach and complexity.

The diagnostic challenge was to spot an imminent attack of nostalgia in the victim's descent from healthy remembering into obsessive yearning. In the century before Freud and Breuer and the invention of the "talking cure," treatments included purging, leeches, sweet wine, opium, restorative sojourns in the mountains, and the avoidance of affective images or musical strains. Some physicians advocated *forgetting* as a form of therapy, but there was little agreement as to how, and in what measure, this ought to be achieved. Thisroy remarked that "even pre-Freudian physicians appeared to grasp the danger in attempting to compromise or eliminate in the sufferer, what we now know to be the core of his identity, the *memory of his memories.*"

Increasingly, nostalgia came to be associated with military experience, with French physicians recording its frequent appearance in soldiers during the Napoleonic Wars. In the field, it was contagious and sometimes occurred as epidemics among the troops. In the recorded cases that he could locate, Thisroy found that homesickness remained a persistent symptom for these soldier-sufferers, along with fever, ringing in the ears, loss of appetite, hysterical sobbing, and a fear of falling asleep accompanied by "an anxious, watchful attitude."

During the American Civil War, doctors diagnosed more than two thousand cases of nostalgia on the Union side alone, a number of these ending in death. For army surgeons, it was an accepted diagnostic category, a form of melancholia. In some camps, measures were taken to limit nostalgia-inducing activities such as letter writing, while camp bands might be instructed not to play "Home! Sweet Home!" or other suggestive musical pieces. Individual treatments varied from the granting of brief periods of convalescence to the infliction of physical punishment or a swift return to battle, for what some officers considered to be malingering. In retrospect, according to Thisroy, it might be argued that nostalgia, in the military context, was a variant and precursor of what would later be termed *shell shock* or *soldier's heart* in World War One, *battle fatigue* in World War Two, and *post-traumatic stress disorder* after Vietnam. (In a footnote, Thisroy called for further research into the historical connections among nostalgia, war, and trauma.)

After the Civil War, medical interest in nostalgia declined, as did the number of recorded cases. Observers at the time believed that better hygiene and education helped people to fight the ailment, while advances in transport and communications promised to prevent the kinds of extreme separations that seemed to trigger outbreaks of acute nostalgia. More important, physicians had become excited by the study of hysteria, a promising and newly fashionable disorder. In the years leading up to World War One, nostalgia lost its status as a medical term and eventually disappeared from the professional literature. "Search the latest edition of the *Diagnostic and Statistical Manual of Mental Disorders*," commanded Thisroy. "You will find no recognition given to nostalgia in that bible of the psychiatric profession." Of course melancholia and hysteria also disappeared in their turn, while nostalgia's possible links to those terms as well as to shell shock and post-traumatic stress disorder were lost.

In 2002, as the *fin-de-siècle* mood was overtaken by the post-9/11 mood, Thisroy published his second study of nostalgia, "Hofer's Condition: A New Pathology of Longing." He opened his article with the latest general definition of nostalgia, taken from *The American Heritage Dictionary of the English Language,* 4th edition, 2000:

nos-tal-gi-a
   1. A bittersweet longing for things, persons, or situations of the past.
   2. The condition of being homesick; homesickness

Declaring himself gratified that the American Heritage editors had preserved at least something of the original definition, Thisroy went on to lament the larger "cultural demise" of the term. He argued that this had resulted in a "serious distortion and loss of meaning" in relation to nostalgia, leaving genuine nostalgiacs unrecognized and untreated by a medical establishment increasingly disconnected from its own history.

Plainly nostalgic for nostalgia, Thisroy claimed that the concept had been "hijacked by consumer capitalism and twentieth-century political ideologies of both right and left." The commercialization of the term resulted in its radical separation from the disease itself: the term and the complaint no longer referred to one another. Diagnostic coherence was lost, and the malady was driven underground. Here is an extract from Thisroy's fretful account:

> Beginning in the late nineteenth century, and continuing throughout the twentieth, while humanity busied itself with steam engines and ticker tapes, advanced weaponry, war, stocks and shares, advertising, buying on credit, moon landings, and oil prices, there was a series of assaults on nostalgia, chasing it along back highways into the ages before Freud. In his seminal, *Mourning and Melancholia* (1917), Freud passed up an opportunity to rescue the lost affliction from obscurity. Here, nostalgia might have been reinvented for the age of the "talking cure," restored to its rightful place in our individual and collective experiences of memory and loss, in the pathology of melancholy and the psychology of mourning. The larger gain would have been a psychoanalytic strategy for treating the nostalgiac and returning him or her to a healthier, more productive relation to the past. But this was the road not taken.
>
> In the decades following the birth of psychoanalysis, and especially during the fifties, when Freudian theory was, in turn, crassly popularized, the historical meanings and usages associated with nostalgia were finally mangled beyond recognition until its chief purpose became the parceling out of discount memory via television, heritage theme parks, and the K-Mart warehouse. Nostalgia became kitsch and suburban, trivial and reactionary: hardly the stuff of a meaningful, if at times perilous, engagement with the workings of memory.

Finally, Thisroy claimed that although nostalgia, the *word,* had "jumped aboard a runaway train to Disneyland," the *malady* it originally described had been "left standing on the platform, holding an awful lot of baggage" (Thisroy had an undeniable corny streak). The doctor's recent caseload confirmed that signs and symptoms bearing a striking resemblance to Hofer's original findings continued to manifest themselves in large numbers of patients. Moreover, Thisroy argued that virtually *all* people experienced one or more acute symptoms at particular points in their lives.

> The world is full of what we used to describe as nostalgia cases. They live in towns and cities, loosely strung like blinking Christmas lights, long since forgotten by our medical and psychiatric professions. They have gone the way of melancholics and hysterics, their symptoms subsumed under new diagnostic categories. Those who present themselves at clinics and hospitals are either treated for the latest in depressive and obsessive-compulsive disorders, or dismissed as the worried well.

Recognition and assistance for nostalgiacs would only come, continued Thisroy, when the symptoms were "reclaimed, drawn together again and placed under a new name." As a diagnostic term, nostalgia was irretrievable. Thisroy proposed a clean break and a novel, unspoiled term: Hofer's condition. The old physician's surname, unlike his invented word, had passed into obscurity and this was the very source of its potential in the here and now. Research into Hofer's condition would work backward, reclaiming the rich history of the malady, beginning with Hofer himself, and *forward,* developing a renewed understanding for the twenty-first century.

There was an urgent need for funding, professional recognition, and scholarly inquiry, Thisroy argued. He did not wish to foreclose future developments by fixing methods or predicting outcomes. However, a working definition would prove a useful starting point for physicians, therapists, and researchers. Thisroy proposed that Hofer's condition be defined in the first instance as *"a pathological or dysfunctional longing for irrecoverably past times, people and places."*

Thisroy added that diagnostic distinctions between acute and chronic forms of Hofer's should be developed in order to identify and treat sufferers. In his own practice, he had already seen that there were acute cases, triggered by life events involving loss, grief, and trauma, but that there were also chronic cases, people constitutionally predisposed to an obsessive attachment to the past. In sum, future work should recall the old nostalgia *and* move beyond it, revising it for the new century and offering treatment and practical help to people experiencing Hofer's condition, whether mild or severe. For Thisroy, this was a "new chapter" in the history of nostalgia:

> The only way to manage this ailment in its latest guise is to examine it with fresh eyes, critically engage it, get right inside it for a while. The ailment is currently mutating in as yet unexplained ways, not least because of the onslaught on memory by the *nostalgia industry.* But we can safely begin with this notion of *longing,* the timeless, predominant symptom of a timeless affliction, now termed Hofer's condition. Ultimately, it is longing that may prove to be both malady and cure, for longing can be reconceived as memory with its healing powers restored: the *working through* of what we have lost.

By the time Kay finished reading the second article, she had formed a mental picture of Elmer Thisroy. She imagined him as Frank Morgan, the gray, bumbling, kindly actor who played both Professor Marvel and the Wizard in *The Wizard of Oz.* She was also pretty sure that Dr. Thisroy was a wack job—as wacky as any of his patients—but Kay was prepared to overlook that problem because he was so obviously a wack job for her team. He had interested her, *named* things, legitimated some of her tics and habits, and perhaps even suggested a way forward.

She thought about writing to Thisroy, telling him all about her reckless flight from Los Angeles back home to Garden City, her doomed love affair, Jacques and his leap from the bridge, Violet and her lie, Bell and her notebooks, her own collection of notebooks—in the hope that he would look inside an old-fashioned doctor's bag, say what have we here, *what is it this time, Tootie,* then gently dismiss her with a twinkle and a reminder that it is very common for people to read about ailments and think they have them. There's a word for such people, he would say, and like the Wizard stumbling on the word "ph—

ph—philanthropist" and settling finally for "good-deed doer," the roguish doctor would wave her away and chuckle, say there was absolutely nothing wrong and everything would turn out fine. But Kay feared Thisroy was an imposter, in the same way that Professor Marvel and the Wizard were, hiding their goodness behind curtains and crystal balls, making wild, unsubstantiated claims and manipulating the runaway souls who came calling.

OBITUARIES

Kay showed Joe a photograph of James Parker's grave, one of a black and white series taken at Parmalee Cemetery after Marion's funeral.

"Let's see. Well . . . the headstone looks so worn I can't read the inscription. It's not helping that the shadow of you—holding the camera—is falling on the grave."

"I know. It's practically illegible. But I mean *this.*" She pointed to the lower left of the photo, to an area of dark grass beside the headstone. There, barely discernable, was a small object fixed into the ground, a rusted metal stand, topped by a five-pointed star-shaped medallion. Joe peered closely.

"Oh. The star. Didn't see it at first. You'll find that star in graveyards all across the North. It means Violet's husband was a member of the G.A.R.—the *Grand Army of the Republic,* an organization for Union soldiers founded after the Civil War. I believe it was pretty influential at one time. You should look into it if you want to know more about James."

But Kay thought no more of it, until a few days later when Joe returned to the subject, having stopped at the library on the way home from work and conducted some searches of his own. He said that as a member of the G.A.R., James Parker would have received a hatpin and a badge, the latter being a metal eagle, from which was suspended a tiny flag and the same five-pointed star seen at his gravesite. The star was cast from melted-down Confederate cannons. Joe believed that the word *veteran* had been used first by the G.A.R., and that the tradition of decorating soldiers' graves on Memorial Day also originated with the organization. But its members weren't only interested in patriotic displays. They lobbied for pensions for veterans and widows, and at the height of their activism, helped to put a fair number of politicians in or out of office. However, by limiting membership to Civil War veterans, the G.A.R. effectively wrote its own obituary, as the last members died in the 1950s.

Joe wanted to know how James had died, and Kay was at a loss to tell him. She had already tried various searches, but to no avail. Violet's silence about her husband's death appeared to replicate itself in the available archives. To satisfy Joe, Kay made one last attempt, spending a long afternoon at the library, bent over a huge reference book entitled *Michigan Veterans' Obituaries*. She was hoping against hope to stumble across an obituary for James. It didn't happen. There were several Barry County veterans listed, but no mention of James Parker.

Kay tried numerous times to close the heavy tome and return it to the shelves. But she could not stop reading. Just one or two more, she would think, only to look up at the clock afterward and discover another hour had passed. These were not ordinary obituaries. Her curiosity piqued, Kay spent the next few days back at the library, studying more obituaries in old newspapers on microfilm and then comparing them to current newspapers. From this brief exercise, it seemed clear that the art of obituary writing had changed dramatically over the course of the century.

The current obituaries regularly withheld information about how the person had died, passing quickly to a colorless score sheet of life, a checklist of milestones and outward achievements. Regional and religious affiliations, educational degrees and diplomas, working life or career successes, club memberships, activities since retirement, the names of spouse and children and numbers of grandchildren, typically cast as "survivors." *Mr. So-and-so is survived by four children and thirteen grandchildren.* Great . . . they outlasted the poor bugger.

These were obituaries to numb and soothe the survivors about the entire project of life and death. In other words, those left behind were working hard to convince themselves that it was all worth the effort, that this was no time to mention suffering, sickness, fear, poverty, family secrets, skullduggery, or feuds. Reading the recent obituaries was like being moved along from the scene of a car wreck by a burly policeman who blocks your view, crossing his arms with reassuring authority. *It's over now. You can all return to your homes. There's nothing more to be seen here.* It was death with life removed. It was death with *death* removed.

In marked contrast, the old obituaries were rich in detail about the death itself. Ruptured organs, deliriums, freak accidents, suicides—all were rendered in florid and graphic passages. Men stumbled and bled through their final act, and the death rattle was heard everywhere. Grieving friends and family reported signs and omens, calmly spoken last words, or final acts of generosity. It was taken as given that disease, decay, and random violence hung around everybody's back door. Luck and fate waited there too. In the end, Kay was no wiser about what had happened to James Parker. But she possessed material for dozens of intriguing death stories, and a sense of how his contemporaries might have given drama and color to whatever end fell to Violet's husband.

Kay decided that in the absence of a death notice for James, she would show Joe a selection of veterans' obituaries from Barry County. When he expressed reservations about this solution, she said that these notices brought them closer to James than anything else they had found. Besides, maybe one or more of the veterans had known James. Perhaps one of them had once shared a drink or gone fishing with him, and they had traded war memories. Perhaps like one or two of Joe's friends at the Rouge Plant who were Vietnam vets, the men in these obituaries, even if they had not been close to James, understood something about him that his own wife and family could not. Kay forced herself to look straight into Joe's eyes as she made that last point; he bit his lip and read the three obituaries she had already chosen for him:

1. *Hastings, Michigan, April 4, 1899.* Death came yesterday to Roddy Kane, a long-standing resident of our town. He arose early in order to take the train to Grand Rapids, where his brother lives. A few minutes after 7 a.m., workmen on State Street found Kane sitting alone in a narrow lane behind the houses, eyes staring vacantly ahead, the strength all but gone from his limbs. A policeman on nearby patrol was

hailed and duly notified the nearest doctor, who arrived only in time for the final death rattle. To the dismay of neighbors and passersby, Kane was pronounced dead on the street. When told of the tragic loss of his brother, Alfred Kane of Grand Rapids said he had noticed of late that Mr. Kane's breathing was labored and that he seemed weary of this world. He added that during his brother's last visit to Grand Rapids, the two men had visited a palmist. Upon reading Roddy Kane's hand, the palmist had told him to prepare for death in the not too distant future.

2. *Plainwell, Michigan, September 22, 1896.* Captain Augustus Carver was shot and killed by accidental discharge of his own gun while hunting on Monday. The dreadful accident occurred in Johnson's Wood on River Road, near the county line. The discharge from the gun entered the top of the head, blowing a hole over two inches across Carver's skull, causing immediate death. He was accompanied by his hunting dog, Sam, and his friend John Stimpson, but the two men had become separated and lost sight of one another in the dense wood. Stimpson saw nothing of what caused the tragic event. Upon hearing the shot, he called out to his friend. When no reply came, save the whimpering of the captain's dog, Stimpson grew alarmed and fought through the undergrowth to find the grievously wounded man lying face down on the ground. He turned Captain Carver over and tried to speak to him, but the only response was a long, low gasp from deep in the fatally wounded man's chest, as blood poured down his face and neck. By the time the coroner was called, the captain was no more. The terrible ca - tastrophe has left his poor dog in a state of despondency, and friends report that John Stimpson suffers greatly too, and walks aimlessly around the town, as though in a trance. It is thought that Captain Carver must have tripped in the undergrowth, causing the charge to explode as he fell. Suicide has been ruled out as the captain had long been a keen hunter and was often heard to boast that he would not rest until he had covered every trail in Johnson's Wood. Captain Carver was born in Detroit and, during the War of the Rebellion, served with Company A, Fifth Michigan Infantry, and held medals for bravery in actions at Williamsburg and Sailors Creek.

3. *Yankee Springs, Michigan, December 29, 1891.* Premonition of death seemed to come to John Gumm late last night. His wife, Ellie, went to bed about nine o'clock, but he remained up for a time, reading the family Bible. At midnight, Mrs. Gumm heard him climb the stairs and enter the bedroom. She opened her eyes to see her husband at the foot of the bed, a solemn expression on his face. In a low but steady voice, he said to his wife: "I believe the end is near. Good Bye. Meet me in Heaven." After speaking these words, he collapsed on the bedroom floor. Blood was flowing from his mouth and nose. His wife rushed to his side, but Gumm was already dead. Neighbors reported hearing the tragic weeping of the widow throughout last night. Mr. Gumm saw action at the first battle of Bull Run and was an active member of his local G.A.R. chapter.

Kay soon had cause to regret showing Joe these death notices. The following Saturday, he rose early, drove to the library, and spent the entire day poring over the volume of veterans' obituaries. He made copies of further examples and brought them home. Nor did her tactic pry him loose from James Parker. If anything, he was more determined than ever to develop a picture and a history of Violet's lost husband. He clearly felt that—as one veteran, acting on behalf of another—he carried some responsibility to complete research that Kay appeared to have abandoned.

She was anxious to move forward, away from James and Violet and, especially, away from Allie Green. Kay longed to return to Fred Gaillard and bring him together with Ada. Joe, however, was digging his heels into the wet, grass-covered mounds of Parmalee Cemetery. He was stuck there, with James and his cold, illegible headstone and the rusted G.A.R star. Joe was still insisting that they learn at least the basic facts of James's whereabouts during the Civil War.

They knew from a history of Barry County that a number of local men had served in the Twenty-first Michigan Regiment, including Violet's brother, Lansing Shaw, and her future husband, James Parker. Joe made further investigations and eventually found both names on a list of about a hundred Barry County men who served in Company C. Of these, about ten men, Lansing Shaw among them, were either killed in action or died later of wounds. Two or three were listed as dead with no explanation given. Twenty more died of disease. Three men went missing in action, while seventeen were "discharged for disability." Taken together, these losses amounted to more than half of the men listed.

While Kay silently fantasized that a regimental bout of nostalgia might be responsible for the deaths from disease and discharges for disability in Company C, Joe doggedly pursued its battle history, reporting back to her in grim detail. He discovered that the Twenty-first Michigan was involved in some of the heaviest fighting of the war, with numerous casualties and losses at Stones River, Murfreesboro, Tennessee, in 1862 and again at the Battle of Chickamauga, Georgia, in September, 1863. The Twenty-first also took part in Sherman's March to the Sea in 1864, and the subsequent siege of Savannah.

"At Stones River, Confederate troops attacked at dawn on the last day of 1862," Joe said. "Some Yankees died half dressed, trying to get away. By the end of the day, the Union right flank was destroyed and the ground covered in corpses and dead horses. Later, witnesses compared the scene to the slaughter pens in the Chicago meat yards. If anything saved the Yankees, it was the place of battle. Dense cedar woods and rocky ground slowed the Confederate advance. The Union counterattack, when it came, was mainly by cannon fire. On January 1, 1863, nearly two thousand Confederate men were killed or wounded within an hour of the first cannon shot. Two days later, the North took Murfreesboro and declared victory."

"Some achievement," Joe muttered. "More than three thousand dead and twenty thousand casualties altogether. Some of the wounded lay on the battlefield for nearly a week before help arrived."

Kay reached for his hand, but he pulled away without looking at her.

"Chickamauga was a bloodbath too. The Union side was pushed back and defeated, its ranks broken during three long days of crap military judgment and confusion on both sides. The result was more than sixteen thousand casualties for the North and eighteen thousand for the South. At the end of the first day of fighting, those still alive went to sleep to the sound of moans and crying coming from the battlefield. When the Yankees retreated, they left behind a carpet of bloodied human remains, some still moving."

Following these initial finds, Joe turned morose, but would not be shifted from the Civil War. They spent a miserable weekend during which Kay made a number of feeble attempts to progress to another topic, while Joe paced up and down, reading battle history aloud, knocking back beers, and insisting that she make notes. Kay realized that Joe was trying to shock her, rub her face in things she could not possibly hope to visualize or grasp. She saw that he was speaking to her of Vietnam, and hard as she fought it, she also sensed that Joe wanted to drive her away. He wanted her to *choose* to leave him.

In between accounts of particular battle scenes, he returned again and again to regimental details that must have jarred with his own experience: the mention everywhere of horses, the colors of blue and gray without a hint of khaki, the presence of military bands playing at nightfall as men on both sides rested before the next day's fighting. At Stones River, an infantryman reported hearing music in the dark, coming from both sides, until one of the bands stopped to listen to the other side play "Home! Sweet Home!"

Joe found other, similar accounts of "battles of the bands" that ended in plaintive renditions of that song. He looked up the lyrics and asked Kay to sing them, but she refused. Stubbornly, he recited a verse:

> *I gaze on the moon*
> *As I tread the drear wild,*
> *And feel that my mother*
> *Now thinks of her child;*
> *As she looks on that moon*
> *From our own cottage door,*
> *Thro' the woodbine whose fragrance*
> *Shall cheer me no more.*
> *Home, home, sweet sweet home*
> *There's no place like home,*
> *There's no place like home.*

"I guess James Parker heard that song a hundred fucking times," Joe said, bitterly satisfied.

Kay sat in silence, watching Joe's angry mouth and thinking about those Union surgeons and commanders attempting to ban the song in a feeble effort to rid the men of nostalgia. At that time, nostalgia still predominantly meant homesickness, even if the symptoms and treatments varied. In the nineteenth century, probably culminating in the Civil War, "Home! Sweet Home!" might have been a final anthem for sufferers of Hofer's original disease. Army doctors considered the song a menace to troop morale.

Yet by 1939, its last line was deemed the ideal "closer" for *The Wizard of Oz*. "There's no place like home," emotes Dorothy every time without fail, dark lipped and puppy fattish for all time, her bosom bound and hidden beneath a corset; a painfully perfect-for-the-part Judy Garland squeezed into little-girl gingham. An old soul. An almost woman playing a child as though both were a hundred years old. Clutching Toto, she taps her ruby heels together, topples back through a hole in the universe to Kansas, and finally opens her eyes on her old room, waking in that little bed on the MGM set.

The fifties kids, cross-legged on the living room carpet, watching the annual television broadcast of the film, got really messed up trying to work out which side of the rainbow was best. Meanwhile in that final scene, Dr. Thisroy, in his Professor Marvel rags, makes a house call.

"She got quite a bump on the head," Uncle Henry informs the professor. "We kinda thought there for a minute she was going to leave us."

"Yeah, Dorothy nearly escaped the compound," Joe had cracked when they caught the end of the movie on cable a few weeks earlier.

"Oh," Professor Marvel replies, ineffectually. He leans through the window of Dorothy's drab little room. "Oh," he says again.

Kay kept these various musings to herself, staring at Joe's face flushed with beer, moving her eyes with his pacing, tuning in and out of his tirades about the Civil War. Eventually, he began to tire, and his voice lowered and trembled. But he turned next to a series of regimental photographs in a pictorial record of the Union Army, including two pictures he had managed to locate of Company C, James Parker's unit. These showed the soldiers *before* Stones River and Chickamauga, not especially healthy looking with their drawn faces, but still in one piece. The photos must have been taken on a cold day; the trees in the scene were bare, and the men stood pale and hunched on frost-hard-ened ground. The uniforms and boots were touchingly familiar gear, but the faces were of mute strangers. Nevertheless, Kay and Joe examined each one with a magnifying glass, Joe aching for a face that might belong to James Parker. But of course, they had no chance of settling on a soldier. James could have been any one of them.

Six weeks earlier, at the beginning of Kay's searches, Joe had been a supportive and easy-to-please listener. Now, as the summer drew to an overcast, muggy close, and the days shortened, he filled her with doubt. It was hardly surprising that he chose James Parker as an object of interest, but the Civil War connection agitated Joe more than she had anticipated. He began looking over her shoulder, burying her in extraneous facts and figures, insisting on new lines of inquiry. He chased down information that was tangential at best, casting his own heroes and villains. Kay didn't say it to Joe, but she thought his pursuit of the Twenty-first Michigan was an unsettling diversion and that its true purpose was to recover or exorcize—who knew which—something in his own past. In any case, their efforts had failed to turn up any specific information about James, while Joe seemed even more restless and unhappy than before.

They argued, usually about small, mundane things, and made up several times over. Joe was increasingly unpredictable with his affection; one minute, he gathered Kay in his arms, the next, he refused to touch her. But much of the time, he was simply preoccupied, not fully present. He drank several beers each day after work, not to outright drunkenness, but enough to numb him. The bad nights continued too. Sometimes they sat up late together, watching the Tigers play out a losing season. Joe had given up complaining about pitchers, batters, and fielding errors, preferring to sit through the remaining games in dogged silence, the way diehard fans do, as if they must share in the humiliation of their team. More often, Kay went to bed alone and lay awake, listening to the muffled sounds coming from the television—baseball scores, dispatches from Iraq, or old movies, the ghostly voices of stars from the 1930s and 1940s, repeating lines she knew by heart.

Like Bell Gaillard after her father died, Kay passed the lonely times by making up conversations and lists in her head. One night, she spent hours recalling references to early, classic Hollywood movies in later movies. Whether consciously placed or not, deliberate or not, there were dozens of obsessive quotes and borrowings: particular camera shots, cuts and angles, inserted lines or images, bits of costume or set, a stairway here, a wide-brimmed hat there, the name of a character or place. Not surprisingly, *The Wizard of Oz* topped the list. Kay found more movies about that movie than about any other movie. She lay on her back in the dark, ticking them off, rowing across America on a glittering green river. Not getting America at all; getting it wrong. Pining for things about it that never really existed to begin with. Behind every screen was another screen. There wasn't a single tree, building, goodness, or belief she could reach out and touch.

Another night, she turned to closing lines, making a mental catalog of her favorites, such as "This is Eddie Bartlett. He used to be a big shot," delivered by Gladys George over Jimmy Cagney, the World War One hero turned bootlegger, dead on the cathedral steps at the end of *The Roaring Twenties.* Or the estranged, light-skinned Sarah Jane Johnson in *Imitation of Life,* stopping her mother's funeral procession in the streets of Harlem, distraught and out of control. "Miss Lora, I killed my mother . . . Now she'll never know how much I wanted to come home." And finally, the apposite "Maybe I'll live so long I'll forget her. Maybe I'll die trying," from *Lady of Shanghai.* Kay must have compiled nearly a hundred last lines. She had a powerful urge to phone her brother and ask for his favorite last lines, but Sid was still keeping a distance, and she did not want to admit to him that cracks were multiplying in the relationship with Joe.

Most mornings, after Joe left for work, she cleaned the ashtrays and empty Budweiser bottles from the floor around his chair. The shift at the Rouge plant was the daily event that kept Joe going. It kept him away from her too, and Kay guessed that he felt more at ease at the massive Ford factory than at home. He was an experienced and responsible line worker, and no matter how sleep deprived or beer soaked the previous night, he seemed able to get up early, drive to Dearborn, and operate the massive, steel-limbed machinery that assembled Mustangs. He once told Kay there was a measurable sense of achievement in the hard-wired repetition of tasks, the ritual of auto bodies moving steadily past, and the clean fact of a river of Fords flowing out onto the nation's roads.

But the Rouge complex was changing. The original assembly plant was being scrapped, while a new one for production of the F-150 pickup truck was starting operation. Mustang assembly was about to be transferred to the Ford-owned Mazda factory in nearby Flat Rock, and the Rouge workers would most likely be switched to the F-150 on the new line. Joe and his friends at the plant, powerless over these latest developments in the long history of River Rouge, muttered among themselves about the loss of the iconic Mustang to the Japanese.

They muttered about the union leadership too. United Auto Workers Local 600, traditionally a militant branch that included the Rouge workers, had passed a motion opposing the invasion of Iraq, but received little support from union executives. Joe belonged to a small but tight circle of workers, some of them labor activists with more than twenty years' seniority. They were capable and opinionated. They stuck together, talked union politics over a beer after the shift, and covered for one another if anything went wrong on the line. A few of them had served in Vietnam. Joe said that at the plant, vets almost always recognized other vets, without much being asked or answered.

After he left for the Rouge plant each morning, Kay went into the makeshift study, sat at the desk, and tried to push her own work along. She was hoping to wrap up the Middleville part of the story and return to Fred Gaillard, but found increasingly that she could only manage a few hours at a time. When her concentration broke, she took long walks around the old neighborhood. She walked the six blocks to the school playgrounds, and to the baseball diamond everybody called the Lighted Field because of its tall electric lights allowing for night games. She stopped outside the windows of the first-grade classroom, closed for the summer, cupping her hands against the glass, straining to see the tables and chairs stunted for small people, the cupboards packed with finger paints and safety scissors. At the Lighted Field, usually deserted under a blanket of afternoon heat, Kay sat alone on the bleachers, baking her bare, outstretched legs, and gazing at memories of Sid and Joe in their Little League uniforms.

LATE

ON THE FRIDAY FOLLOWING HER PARTY, ADA PERCHED ON THE
front step, waiting for Lon. The Thornapple Valley finally dropped into
dusk, the last of the long summer sun having reddened the western
end of the fields before draining from sight. Lon was more than an
hour late, several deepening shades of light late. Soon the fireflies
would illuminate his ticking lateness, and the cicadas would sing the
alarm. Already, Violet had stepped out onto the porch twice, the first
time glancing anxiously up the road as she pretended to tidy a cushion
on the wooden bench, then returning some minutes later to move the
watering can from one corner of the porch to the other. When she
came out a third time, she remarked that the Grand Rapids train must
be delayed; supper was getting cold. She asked Ada to come inside, but
Ada refused to move, and Violet did not insist.

Lon's lateness was the kind that crawls inside the bodies of the
people who wait. It begins with a flutter, but soon turns a grinding
dread. For Ada and Violet—each carrying a private, separate sense of
culpability going back to the previous weekend, the party, the morning
after the party, and in Violet's case going back years before, to raw
motherhood—the transition from flutter to dread was terrifyingly fast.
Within the first hour of Lon's lateness, they knew he was gone.

It is a fact that people who wait often believe in those early, pump-
ing minutes that their lives are about to be broken. They begin to ex-
plore the feel, the sensation of a missing person—devastation and desire too, for who has never been tempted by the idea of cutting loose
from those who come close? They glimpse a possible future: barren
freedom, brutal separation, years of straining to hear every footstep
outside the house, every voice in the downstairs hall; of waiting for the

mail delivery, examining postmarks, checking newspaper reports of accidents and crimes, following the backs of strangers along station platforms. Ambivalence, rage, terror, and regret. Wondering whether there will be a point of no return, years in the future—a point at which one no longer *wants* the return. And then, when the brain is pounding, the late one walks through the door, innocent and apologetic, with an explanation that utterly fails to measure up to the preceding torment of the waiting person.

But once in a while, the late one does not walk through the door. He was in the train that derailed or the building that collapsed; he was the fisherman on the winter lake who broke through the ice, the boy who went swimming in the old reservoir, the child who chased a ball into the woods. At least in these cases, the outcome is known, and waiting turns to grief. But what of the girl last seen walking home from town, never found? The son who went away angry the week before? When lateness goes unresolved and waiting turns to a permanent state, some, like Violet, will turn to prayer and remembrance; others, like Ada, will refuse God, church, and the passage of time itself, spitting hot, whispered obscenities at the steeple and sky.

For Violet, Lon's lateness threatened to divide the world permanently into two times, before and after, where before is the once-unappreciated golden time. When people say, *oh but that was before,* they are referring to a world locked behind tinted glass, to be viewed only with the bitter knowledge of after, with this wretched *hindsight* that causes them to walk up and down and wish they had not said or done certain things. And in later years, when the mother who waits has grown too sick or weary to wait any longer, this same hindsight will be there when she dies in bed, with or without God, sleeplessly replaying all the before times, when she saw or held the loved one.

CRYSTAL PALACE

INCREASINGLY STANDARDIZED, INTERCHANGEABLE PARTS; GOOD suspension; vanadium steel; a sturdy, but light car for the rutted roads beyond Detroit. All four cylinders contained in a single block that could be opened on top and bottom for easy service. The transmission consisted of a brake, forward pedal, and reverse pedal. A skilled driver could leap straight out of forward and into reverse.

Priced at $825, the Model T was a winner, with ten thousand sold in the first year. It made the Ford Motor Company so successful that it soon outgrew Piquette Avenue. Henry Ford commissioned local architect Albert Kahn, the son of a German rabbi, to design a new factory for a fifty-seven-acre site on the outskirts of Detroit, in Highland Park. Kahn opted for reinforced concrete in his design. This allowed for large, open factory floors and external walls made primarily of glass. There were some fifty thousand square feet of windows in the Highland Park plant, which opened at the end of 1909 and quickly became known as Detroit's own "Crystal Palace."

At Piquette Avenue, Fred had been one of a team of workers who built engines. The men would cluster around a large, stationary cradle holding a single engine. Each completed engine would be hauled to the next shop and fitted with axles and wheels. Once the wheels were on, the whole thing could be rolled to the upholstery shop, where seats were installed. Until components were fully standardized, the automobile engine was a crafted product; nearly every part that arrived needed filing, grinding, or adapting in some way. Fred had loved that aspect of the job, figuring out why a part did not fit or work, judging and measuring the adjustment to be made, sizing and resizing it until the match of part and product was complete. He had a knack for the work that went back to boyhood, to the age of six or seven, when he used to follow his father around the house, mending things and learning to handle the tools.

At the Crystal Palace, Fred was moved to another job, the assembly of the same flywheel magneto he knew to be the creation of Spider Huff. He missed the larger role of building an engine and the collaboration with members of a team. But the new post brought its own rewards: better pay and the recovery, however thin and belated, of a sense of connection to the mechanic who had taken his part in the bet against Ralph and given him his first job at Ford. The magneto might be Spider Huff's design, but it was also Fred Gaillard's skilled handiwork.

Each morning at the new factory, Fred assumed his place at a large workbench, handling a full range of magnets and bolts, and by the end of the day, he would complete thirty or forty magnetos. Simply put, he made the device—that made the spark—that made those Ford automobiles jump to life when they exited the factory to putter along the streets of Detroit and the rest of the nation. There was satisfaction in that.

In 1913, the flywheel magneto makers were set a new task. Instead of gathering around the workbench, each working on his own product, they were lined up, one next to the other, facing a row of flywheels placed waist high, on a shelf. The flywheels were shunted from one worker to the next, with each man allocated a container of components—magnets, bolts, nuts—below the shelf. Along with the others, Fred was assigned two of the twenty-nine operations that went into the production of a single flywheel. He placed a particular magnet, and then he tightened it, before pushing the flywheel to his neighbor, who would perform a similar operation with a different magnet. Fred had never thought of his work that way, as twenty-nine separate pieces, but *someone* had. So he held tight to his place on the line and set out to prove he could perform as efficiently as the next man.

The time it took to make one flywheel magneto dropped immediately, from fifteen minutes to thirteen. There were further refinements, including the introduction of a motorized conveyor belt to replace the metal shelving. Now there was a continuously moving line of flywheels. Fred learned to adjust to the motion, the increasing division of tasks, and the dreaded "speed-up." Soon, the production time for a new flywheel magneto was reduced to five minutes.

In the months that followed, Fred saw the same principle being applied to nearly every aspect of production and assembly: axles, crank-shafts, transmissions, dashboards, even the body of the automobile. It seemed that any job could be broken down into a series of small operations and placed on a conveyor. The Crystal Palace became a vibrating network of advanced power tools and moving assembly lines. And although Fred would not forget how to make a flywheel magneto from start to finish, he was never asked to perform that job again.

STRANGER

THE CARTOON, PRINTED IN THE *NEW YORK GLOBE AND COMMERCIAL Advertiser,* showed a group of fat, fur-coated, cigar-smoking Ford workers waiting at a cashier's booth. Another man, similarly attired and sitting at the back of a car, speaks to his chauffeur: "Hawkins, will you step over to the pay window and get my wages? I quite overlooked the matter last week."

Fred never saw that particular cartoon. But he knew the papers were full of Henry Ford's Five Dollar Day plan, announced with fanfare on January 5, 1914. The columnists argued about it, politicians and bankers also; people in shops and on the street put in their two cents' worth. Everybody had an opinion about whether or not it was good for industry and good for the country to pay a working man such a high wage. Ralph gave Fred an earful about it. "Don't believe 'em for a minute, Fred," he said. "There's a hitch. I ain't figured it yet, but there's a definite hitch."

Fred said little and waited to see what happened next. The company directors were looking to recruit some four thousand new workers and move from two shifts to three eight-hour shifts in order to keep the assembly line operating without pause. During the Christmas layoff, two new lines, moved by chains and elevated to waist height, had been installed at Highland Park. These were visible changes, but none of the Ford workers were yet aware that the directors anticipated a reduction in assembly time to a few hours for a single Model T engine, and less than one hundred minutes for a chassis. The directors also hoped the new pay plan would address the problem of employee turnover, which was running at nearly 400 percent by the end of 1913.

Fred, twenty-five years old and one of a minority of long-standing employees, had no idea what the announcement meant for him, whether it heralded a change in his working arrangements, more speed-ups, perhaps even a gradual replacement of the existing fifteen-thousand-strong workforce by a new set of men with fresh blood and rumbling stomachs. Or, if he did keep his job, would his current wage of $2.50 for a nine-hour day be raised, as the new pay plan promised? Fred had learned to avoid "second-guessing" the bosses, but the Five Dollar Day made him nervous. He suspected that Ralph was scratching at the truth: there must be invisible strings attached to the new pay plan. Perhaps only a select group of workers would prove eligible for what Ford had declared "the greatest revolution in the matter of rewards for workers ever known to the industrial world."

Henry Ford was once again the talk of the town, but it was with some apprehension that Fred watched the crowds of unemployed men gathering outside the Highland Park factory in the days following the announcement. There was nowhere for them to shelter from the gusting winds, snow flurries, and freezing temperatures that had blown in with the new year. On the third day, the directors ruled that only those who had lived in Detroit for at least six months might be hired. It was a qualification that came too late; disastrously late for some. Jobless men had already streamed into Detroit from all over the Midwest. They were underdressed and underfed; many had no contacts in the city, nowhere to stay, and certainly little prospect of help from Mr. Ford.

Soon there were ten to fifteen thousand men outside the gate every morning before dawn, jamming the roads around the Highland Park plant. The older ones applied boot polish to their graying hair and stuffed newspapers inside their shirts to pad thin shoulders. Others drank and swore. When Ford agents went undercover in the crowd, quietly slipping hiring papers to handpicked recruits, rumor spread from one line of men to those behind. They pushed and shoved; fistfights broke out as everyone jostled for position.

On the morning of January 10, Fred approached the corner of Woodward Avenue and Manchester Street, removed his metal work badge, and placed it in his side pocket. He had seen other Ford employees attacked by the desperate job seekers outside the factory, and he had no wish to flaunt his privilege now. He made himself as small as possible, kept his eyes down, and quietly picked his way through the throng; he winced at the hacking coughs and foul smells. When one of the company guards boomed through a megaphone, "We are not hiring today! Go away!" the crowd groaned and moved in a single, agitated mass. Fred bobbed and gasped for air in a swell of bodies as menacing as the Detroit River in a storm. He was knocked from left and right, but at least no one recognized him as a hated Ford worker.

It took Fred twenty minutes to cross Manchester Street and head toward the heavily guarded employee entrance. He paused to reach inside his pocket for his work badge, when something cold and sharp clipped his right temple. He reeled and turned to find a wall of furious job seekers moving toward the entry gate, some wielding bricks or stones. A tiny trickle of blood moved down his face and neck. Caught between the gate and the advancing mass of men, he was grabbed by a Highland Park policeman, who dangled him by his collar. Fred held his badge up for the man to see.

"I'm a Ford worker! Just tryin' to go inside!"

"Then pin that badge on and get out of our way before we throw you to these wolves."

The uniformed man laughed and released Fred's collar, now stained with blood. Fred fumbled with his badge as he ran for the entrance, where a Ford personnel officer allowed him in, just as the men at the front of the crowd began chanting "Jobs! Jobs!", then linked arms and surged toward the line of police. Securely inside the gate, Fred noticed that "No Hiring" signs had been posted in several languages. He turned to gape one last time at the scene from which he had narrowly escaped. That was when the man caught his eye.

It was not the first time Fred had seen him. He had been there the morning after Henry Ford's announcement, when the earliest hopefuls began to gather outside the plant. There was no immediate reason why this person should stand out from the groups of men milling about that first day, except he was the only one who did not turn away from the blasts of wind that blew snow up from the ground, stinging their faces. He stood apart, his feet planted and arms crossed, while the others covered their noses and cheeks, bumped shoulders, and complained, even as they huddled together for warmth.

It was impossible to guess the stranger's age. Fred changed his mind completely each time he stole a glance: first the man was older than he appeared, then no, thought Fred, he was younger. His skin was chapped and dried, like that of a tough laborer who had spent the last cold months outside in the elements. He was haggard and unsmiling, with dark shadows beneath his eyes and deep lines pulling his face downward. But he was broad in the chest and muscular, as though a youthful body refused to make way for age and unhappiness. Fred saw that he adopted a public attitude of belligerence rather than the hungry obedience required of new recruits. When one of the company agents finally paused to look him over, the man stared back into the agent's eyes. That was when Fred knew for certain the stranger would never be hired to work at Ford.

But here he was again, several days later, alongside more than ten thousand madmen, all of them straining to read the "No Hiring" signs. Again, Fred thought there was no obvious difference between this stranger and all the other strangers. His clothes were like those of the men nearest him. Except for his nose pinkened by cold, there was no bright color to draw the gaze of bystanders. They all had pink noses on pallid faces, whether caused by cold, drink, or both. But again, Fred noticed the man, and this time, the man looked straight back at Fred. It was as though they had chosen one another. He watched Fred run the gauntlet, hang like a puppet from the policeman's extended arm, wave his badge in the air, and finally, retreat to the safety of the other side of the gate. The stranger stood off to the side of the advancing line of desperate men, his arms folded like the first time. If he was frightened by the mob, he did not show it.

Finally, the police unrolled a fire hose and aimed it at the crowd, dispersing thousands under an ice-cold jet of water. The water froze almost instantly as it struck the men's clothes and faces, shot between their legs, and skimmed the ground. Men ran, slipped, and fell over one another, screaming in the winter streets. As they retreated, some overturned the lunch stands placed by opportunist vendors at various locations around the factory. Fred shrank from the scene and took several steps back, trembling. One of the company officers ordered him to get to work or he'd be washed away with the others. As he retreated inside the factory, Fred looked for the stranger one last time, certain he would be gone. But there he was, pulling himself up from the ground, still watching Fred, a bitter smile finally cracking his face. His hair, moustache, and clothes were white. The water from the fire hose had turned him to ice.

LOW

IN THE BARS AROUND THE FORD PLANT, WORKERS PAID A QUARTER for two shots. They stumbled out of the factory in small groups, cursed the cold, and headed for the nearest saloon to buy a burn of whiskey. It soothed the coughs, diminished the taut, binding sensation in the chest, and as warmth worked its way through the veins, dragging fatigue turned to a more agreeable, heady tiredness. The men stood on sawdust floors, hovered near the stove, and timed their orders to stay inside as long as possible.

Although he was a quiet young man, Fred had gradually learned to enjoy a little company and a drop of beer or whiskey. He also liked a smoke now and then. It felt good to commune, without fear of reprimand, with men who worked at his side for eight hours. In the saloon, he could slow down, shake the mechanical movements from his aching limbs, and find solid footing in a building that did not vibrate from floor to ceiling or drown his thoughts in the roar of machinery. An hour or so spent in the bar after work made it possible for Fred to climb aboard the Woodward Avenue streetcar, head home, swallow some food, drop onto the bed, and find sleep.

Fred was not married. Together with another Ford worker, he rented a room in a two-story house on Calvert Street, just west of Woodward Avenue and south of Highland Park. His landlord was also a Ford employee, a German engineer, married with a baby boy. It was the latest in a series of lodgings since Fred had moved from his mother and Ballantine's household in 1911. He stayed with his sister, Bell, and her new husband for a brief period, then with Ralph's family, but finally, Fred preferred the relative independence of lodging with strangers. Until the German, all Fred's landlords had been American born, English speaking, and opposed to mixing with immigrants. But Fred liked the German and his wife. The husband had been in Detroit a number of years and knew the general run of things, but his wife was a more recent arrival from her husband's town in Bavaria. She was frightened of the city, the signs and street cries and banter, all in a language that was still beyond her grasp. But she was a fair and reliable landlady; for four dollars a week, Fred could count on clean sheets and a blanket, steam heat, an electric light bulb suspended from the ceiling of his room, and a regularly cleaned privy at the back of the house.

It was a harmonious household, and Fred considered himself pretty fortunate. He lived comfortably in comparison to the new immigrants, or "the ethnics," as they were known, the Russians, Poles, Italians, Rumanians, Bohemians, and dozens of other nationalities, most of whom lodged in densely populated neighborhoods and overcrowded boardinghouses. Fred had heard that some landlords filled every available space with bunk beds that were occupied twenty-four hours a day, in eight-hour sleep shifts, rotating with the shifts at Ford. The alleyways and privies in the poorer areas were rat infested and smelled of rotting waste. For those hours when men were locked out of the factory because it was not their shift, and locked out of lodgings, again because it was not their shift, there were hundreds of bars and brothels, opium dens, and "blind pigs"—the local term for unlicensed drinking houses.

During the week, Fred took meals with the German family; Saturdays, he went to a restaurant, and Sundays, he visited his mother or Bell. During the baseball season, together with Ralph and several other boyhood friends, he attended games whenever the Tigers played at home. In winter, they met at Curley's Poolroom, down on Jefferson Avenue. Sometimes Fred went to the movies and dreamed of playing piano or even one of the new Wurlitzer pipe organs at a grand picture palace. In the dark of the Cadillac Theatre on Michigan Avenue or the Empress on Woodward, unaware that his dream pulsed down each arm and into his hands, Fred lightly played his knees as through they were a keyboard, ten fingers flying along with the chase scenes on the big screen. If Ralph was there, he would elbow Fred and complain loudly and hoarsely, "Watch the movie, will ya?"

In fact, Fred no longer had time or energy for the piano. Once in a while, he got the chance to play at a party or in a saloon. But mostly, he forgot about it; only the movies reminded him. He found he could never lose himself in laughter at a comedy. When everybody around him roared, clutched their sides, and pointed at the screen, Fred either indulged his fantasy keyboard or sank into his seat, regretful and lost in the musical accompaniment, until the house lights brightened the auditorium. The piano was impossible, so he played the rhythm bones instead. The bones could be carried anywhere, just like the words to popular songs. Fred and his pals sang "Peg o' My Heart," "Snookey Ookums," "Love Is Like a Firefly," and "My Melancholy Baby," and whenever he felt like it, Fred pulled out those bones.

He thought of himself as a Detroiter, a *native,* as some liked to say, a native with a job, a map of the city printed on his brain, with long-standing friends, a modest savings account, money in his pocket, a mother and adoring sister to fret over him on Sundays, even a few girls who smiled when he strolled down Woodward Avenue. The electric signs at Grand Circus were reflected in his eyes on Saturday nights. On Griswold Street, the ridiculous heights of the Dime Building made him giddy. The Hammond Building, which had so impressed his father in the old century, would be dwarfed by the new skyscrapers. At the top of the Detroit Opera House, a massive sign showed a beautiful woman driving an automobile, her scarf flying, with a caption that read *Watch the Fords Go By.*

With the exception of Ralph, who never lost his hostility to Ford, most people regarded Fred with envy when he mentioned he worked for the Ford Motor Company. Ford workers were widely believed to be the richest of all the factory hands in Detroit. But in the months following the announcement of the Five Dollar Day, Fred began to trip on those invisible strings attached to the pay plan. First, he discovered that each and every worker, no matter how long he had been with the company, must prove his eligibility for the five-dollar wage. The basic wage would be $2.34, less than Fred had made before the grand announcement. A further $2.66, in the form of a "profit-sharing" bonus, would be made available only to those workers who conducted themselves in a manner approved by the company.

It was not long before Fred's landlord was visited by an investigator from the newly formed Ford Sociological Department. The investigator, carrying a clipboard and accompanied by a translator, arrived in a chauffeur-driven Model T. He questioned the German and his wife, Fred, and his fellow lodger. They were asked about marital status and intentions, health, religion, hobbies. The men were requested to produce their savings books, and these were carefully scrutinized. The investigator also wanted to know how frequently each member of the household bathed, and whether they smoked or drank. He recorded each answer, sometimes adding worryingly long notes. He inspected the rooms, the state of the bed linen, the cooking facilities, food stores, the yard and privy. The German blanched with anxiety, while his wife grew increasingly flustered, constantly pleading with the translator and her husband to explain. Then the investigator visited the neighbors on each side of the little house on Calvert Street and asked further questions about the German, his lodgers, and his household.

The German, a hard worker of some standing in the factory, was put on probation for keeping lodgers and for allowing his wife and baby to use the same privy and bathing facilities as single men, the latter being the two lodgers. Husband and wife were given a handbook entitled "Helpful Hints and Advice to Employees," and warned they had six months to reform, after which the husband risked being discharged from Ford. Fred and his fellow lodger were also put on probation, for a long and varied list of faults. Both lived in lodgings when they had family in the city. Both were unmarried, smoked, drank, and were infrequent churchgoers. Like the German, the two lodgers were told to expect regular inspections, with a final decision in six months as to whether they might qualify for the Five Dollar Day.

There never was a kinder termination of a tenancy than the one delivered by the German. He apologized in a broken voice and hung his head. His wife cried, not only for the lost rental income, but for the two young men who had been good lodgers, reduced her loneliness, and acted as a buffer between her inexperience and the shock of the city. Fred, in particular, had always taken time to say hello, ask about the baby, explain American words and ways, and help to decipher the myriad signs, letters, street noises, and interactions that regularly threw the German's wife into confusion. But on May 31, 1914, Fred shook hands with his landlord for the last time, picked up his bag, and headed for Tuxedo Street and a large boardinghouse much closer to the factory.

A few weeks later, on a Sunday, Fred joined a picnic party at Belle Isle. Some of his friends arrived with girls on their arms, including Ralph. Ralph's girl brought along her sister Mary, who blushed deeply when introduced to Fred. But she made sure she sat next to Fred at the table and turned her delicate face toward him as the contents of the picnic hamper were passed along. Like most people, she thought Fred was a Five Dollar Day man, probably the richest man at the picnic that day. She asked him about his job and whether he had met Mr. Ford personally. Mary was so pretty and pristine in her summer frock, Fred found it hard to make conversation or look her in the eye. He stole a glance now and then, and shyly replied to her questions, but kept quiet about his true position at Ford—a probationer, with far too many vices to meet with the approval of Henry Ford and his army of investigators.

Fred kept quiet about his wage, the German's wife and her tears, the thin, soiled mattress in the boardinghouse on Tuxedo Street, and the speed-ups on the assembly line. He kept quiet about the new recruits paraded naked before company doctors, the dizzying babble of the ethnics who now seemed to outnumber him at the factory and on the streets around Highland Park, their "old country" clothes, the way they panicked at the barked orders of the foremen, exhausted themselves, and allowed themselves to be degraded for the five dollars and American citizenship. Fred had heard there were forty or fifty nationalities at Highland Park. He could not think of that many nations, but knew for certain there were Germans, Poles, Italians, Russians, Swedes, and Greeks. To say nothing of the trainloads of Negroes arriving from the South, men forced to work in the foundry, a place surely hotter than an Alabama cotton field.

Fred said nothing to Mary about his father and Belle Isle Bridge, the same bridge that had carried them all to the picnic. He never mentioned the curious hole in his mind about the bridge; no one there, while Bennett Park was haunted. Other locations were haunted, particular street corners and buildings. But not the bridge. Finally, he kept quiet about the stranger, immoveable before the fire hose at Highland Park. In Fred's memory of that day outside the factory, the stranger had grown grotesquely tall and broad, a man made of ice.

Fred found it remarkably easy to think about all these things, without saying them aloud, all the while making polite conversation at Belle Isle. The girl's attentiveness, the powdery quality of her face and clothes, drove Fred inside himself. It was easier to return to these passing thoughts, bleak but reassuringly familiar, than to reach for the sunny present. In the months following the Five Dollar Day announcement, the dismal thoughts had moved more freely, seeped downward, taken root, and spread unseen, waiting only for Fred to dig them up. It was funny how a halting exchange with an eager girl you never would marry could bring on the darkest state of mind, just because you would rather *think* than talk to her.

Later, after the girls had been seen home, Ralph and Fred walked along together, hands in pockets, heads down, keeping a steady pace. The downtown streets were busy with people strolling, out for the evening and enjoying the warm weather. Each passing group left tiny flashes of movement and color, snatches of conversation, footsteps. Finally, without slowing his stride, Ralph gently but deliberately bumped his friend's shoulder.

"When did ya get so low, Fred?" he asked.

FORD ROAD

JOE DROVE SLOWLY THROUGH THE RESIDENTIAL BLOCKS, PAST THE hospital, schools, and playgrounds. He followed zigzag routes, crawling along the back streets where old schoolmates once ran, finally arriving at Ford Road, Garden City's largest east-west thoroughfare.

His expression tightened when they reached Kroger's supermarket. Joe loved the inside of his car and driving, but there were a number of places where he preferred never to arrive, and Kroger's was one of them. As they walked across the parking lot toward the entry doors, Kay looped her arm through his and tried to jiggle his mood. He stiffened slightly and grumbled about the traffic noise and planes overhead. Then he grumbled about the blast of arctic air upon entering the store. Joe disliked all grocery stores and shopping malls, but it was the size and scale of the aggressively air-conditioned Kroger's that bothered him the most.

"It's hotter than blazes outside and freezing in here," he muttered. "And I hate these goddamned aisles. I mean—there must be *fifteen* unnecessary aisles! You can't tell what the hell is going on in the other aisles or who you're gonna run into next. They oughta remove all the crap people don't need. Then they could lose at least half of the aisles, departments, and checkout lanes. Everybody'd be a lot happier."

Kay closed her ears to Joe's gripes, because she enjoyed their weekly outing to Kroger's. She enjoyed finding a place to park, getting out, and padding across the large, sunny lot. She liked to comb the supermarket shelves and try the latest in self-improvement foods. Kay wanted Joe to stay healthy and live as long as the next guy. And thanks to her parents and her former employers out in California, she was rich enough to buy the top brands, reached for them without reserve, and always arrived at the checkout with a cart full to bursting, ready to make small talk with the pimply high school girl at the cash register. Joe, embarrassed by her excesses, refused help from the packers and avoided the checkout girl's eyes. He couldn't wait to get back to the car.

Kay enjoyed shopping, but like Joe, she was happiest when they went for a ride in his used metallic green car. There was no shortage of aimless riding around to do in suburbia. Car windows down, radio on, past the front lawns and picture windows, driveways, mailboxes, street signs, grocery stores, drugstores, and parking lots, stopping for ice cream. The car was Joe's sanctuary and probably the only place Kay ever saw him look completely at ease. He drove some kind of old Ford, she knew that much. But she never did learn to distinguish between models, other than the most striking designs of the sixties, the Thunderbirds and Mustangs. And of course, the used Ford Falcon Pam bought in 1964, after she found a sales job at the Hudson's store in downtown Detroit. But the most memorable feature of all their past automobiles was not the model or make, but the color.

When Model Ts flowed off the first moving assembly line at the Highland Park plant, Henry Ford famously remarked that customers could have any color they wanted, as long as it was black. In the fifties and sixties, such sobriety was finally jettisoned in favor of the garish tones of postwar chewing gum packed with additives and dyes. Sticky pinks and yellows and turquoises. Kay could recall lounging against Pam's powder blue Falcon in the driveway, summer of '66 or '67, barely pubescent in shorts and sleeveless top, a candy cigarette dangling from her lips, the strap of her first bra, a "starter" bra, according to the label, purposefully slipped from the shoulder onto her upper arm, so that Joe would think she was "developing," as her mother liked to put it.

Behind the wheel of his Ford, Joe never complained and never got lost. It was as though he had mapped the entire metropolitan area himself, as though roads existed because he wanted them to; he had only to turn the car in a particular direction, and the next stretch of highway would unfurl just ahead of his front bumper. Outside the Garden City borders, Kay possessed no mental map or navigational powers. Within its six square miles, she knew the layout and texture of the place almost as well as Joe. But she was a poor driver; her competence was in her limbs. Kay could, in her imagination at least, still run five or six blocks at the speed of a skinny girl with strong legs. Without breaking stride, she could hook the toe of her tennis shoe into the chain-link fence at exactly the right height required to swing the other leg over the top and hurl her body from one backyard to another. With her eyes closed, she could skip all the way to school. The same for dozens of other places—the park, Tastee Freez, Silver Lanes bowling alley, the municipal swimming pool and ice-skating rink.

At the beginning of the summer, thrilled to be back in Garden City, Kay had purchased a local history guidebook from the Chamber of Commerce. At the time, she told Joe she planned to "read up on it" and look at their hometown through the fresh eyes of a stranger.

"What are you talking about? The whole point of a place like Garden City is that strangers never come here. Most of the people in this town are terrified of strangers, even though they never actually meet any. Then they end up seeing some guy outside the gas station or in a parking lot somewhere, and they think *he* might be a stranger, because *'you never can tell these days,'* but the *guy*, who is *also* terrified, probably lives on the next block. So you see, the only strangers in Garden City are the ones who live here. Hell, I guess I've talked my way around to your position. Gimme that damned book!"

Joe laughed at himself, and she played along by handing him the guide. He held it up in the air like an artifact, turned to her, and said, "I bet there's not a single mention of *the sign* in these pages."

The sign, they both knew, was a wooden placard that had once marked the town line between Garden City and Inkster. Inkster, one of the few black suburban enclaves in the metropolitan area, bordered Garden City to the south. The sign read *No Negro Shall Ever Enter Garden City*. Joe and Kay had never seen it for themselves; it was removed before their time. But there were still some old-timers around who remembered, even if they kept quiet about it. Joe flipped through the pages of the book, quickly at first to confirm the sign's omission from historical record, until his interest was caught by something else.

"Keep it," Kay said. "I'll buy another copy."

He was too busy reading to hear her.

"Ha! Check this out. In 1956, the city held a slogan contest, and guess what the winning slogan was."

"I wouldn't know."

"*City without Strangers*. I'd say that's code for city without black people."

"Times have changed—" she began feebly.

"Like hell they have. How often do you see somebody around here who doesn't look like you and me? When we were growing up, there were no black people in this town. Now, there are two, maybe three black guys, if that."

Kay changed the subject by pointing to a little red star on the guidebook's fold-out map. The star announced the corner of Ford Road and Middlebelt to be the Garden City Town Center. Joe said that was straight out of Disney, and he was right. At no time during her childhood did Kay experience Garden City as having a center. When Pam ratted her hair, pulled on her jeans and a mohair sweater, and headed downtown, that usually meant somewhere along Ford Road, with its strip shopping developments, Shafer's Cinema, Big Boy diner, Joe D's Bar, Fox Hole Record Shop, Moose Lodge, and Orin's Jewelers. Downtown was a wide highway named after Henry Ford's father.

Garden City was *without* a center. In its peak growth period, it was what Jake and Marion Seger and all the other optimistic, busily pro-creating, accumulating, and commuting postwar parents liked to call a "bedroom community," a "womb with a view," "vetsville." Now, it was *post*-postwar, post–baby boom, post-historical sprawl. Of course there were still people in town, including Joe and Kay, living neither more nor less meaningfully than the previous generation. But Kay could not shake the feeling that if history had happened in this place, it was over.

The guidebook featured two local landmarks: an original Kmart outlet and a McDonald's restaurant, both of which celebrated cars and suburban consumption. Kmart had started as a five-and-dime store in downtown Detroit, opened in 1899 by Sebastian Spering Kresge. But as early as the 1930s, when the automobile was already pulling people away from the cities, Kresge located one of its stores in the Country Club Plaza near Kansas City, the nation's first suburban shopping center. And the first Kmart discount department store, Kmart as it is known today, opened in 1962, "right here in our own Garden City, on Ford Road," boasted the author of the guide.

McDonald's, located west of Kmart, further along Ford Road, was included in the guide as a cautionary tale. With its emblematic golden arches, it was a landmark belonging *not* to Garden City, but to neighboring Westland, another optimistically named suburb. The guide writer lamented the fact that in 1952, the town council had passed up an opportunity for territorial expansion which would have annexed portions of railroad and the River Rouge Parkway, along with six thousand new inhabitants. The assessed valuation of the town would have increased by some twenty million dollars, making Garden City the fourth city in the county. And the McDonald's outlet would have been situated in Garden City rather than Westland. When a plaque commemorating the McDonald's trademark was dedicated in 1990, there were probably still a few early residents who, like the guide writer, regarded the 1952 council decision as a failure of nerve, and the golden arches of Westland a deep-fried reminder.

One Sunday, when Joe seemed in lighter spirits, Kay asked him to take her there for a drive-in meal.

"What? And fuzz your arteries with nasty shit? What's the point of all that expensive health food you buy?"

"Just one burger and a chocolate shake," she pleaded. "Sitting in your car. And after we eat, I want to make out with you in the McDonald's parking lot."

With fast food spread between them and Smokey Robinson on the car radio, she told Joe that when he got his first driving license at the age of sixteen, all those years ago, she used to dream of him taking her on a date to McDonald's. "Wow, you were a real gold digger," he said, tossing a French fry at her. When they carried their used cups and containers to the parking lot trash bin, he showed Kay the plaque:

> *This golden arch sign is recognized by the city of Westland Historical Commission as a sign of an era of time that led the way for the fast food and franchise businesses. This sign was installed at the McDonald's restaurant at 33921 Ford Road in Westland on the 11th day of October, 1968. Dedicated 16th day of May, 1990.*

Below the engraved inscription were the names of the members of the Historical Commission. Kay photographed the plaque while Joe paced around her like a maniacal tour guide.

"You see what I gave up when I went to boot camp? I mean, we had it all here. I'm tellin' you—we had *signs of eras* and *eras of time*. Front-row seats to the decline of Western civilization. And everybody who turned up got a Big Mac."

Then he took his wad of napkins, messy and soaked red with ketchup, like an exploded softball, and raising his left leg in an exaggerated pitcher's windup, hurled it at the waste bin. Kay came up behind him, grabbed his pitching arm, led him back to the car, opened the back door, and pulled him in next to her. She kissed and stroked and guided him, slowly, slowly, until he gently pushed her arm away and took over, sliding his hand under her summer skirt.

As they drove home from McDonald's that Sunday, again crossing the intersection of Ford and Middlebelt, Kay closed her eyes and forgot she was all grown-up. She forgot about the guidebook and the local stories and monuments to postwar capitalism. Joe's car smelled of their fondling, and the motor hummed. The gritty surface of Ford Road was pleasant, like sandpaper beneath the wheels. It struck her then that the most telling thing about Garden City *was* Ford Road. Ford and all the other *through* roads. The ones that stretched far beyond the town line into other suburbs, ending invisibly somewhere near the horizon, flat, unchecked, and uncelebrated, off the historical clock. In her memory, the stream of traffic was perpetually moving east or west, north or south, out of Garden City. Nobody looked to be staying. So why had she spent so many years longing to return?

At that point, Kay had not yet stumbled on Johannes Hofer or Elmer Thisroy, but she already held the obvious answer: nostalgia for childhood, first places, mother and father, first love. Unappeasable homesickness. Garden City might be a pretty fucked-up place, lawned comfort with an undeniably nasty side. But it was *her* fucked-up place, her rosebud and Kansas. It was also an abstraction. A fabrication, in the way that all childhood memories are fabrications. There was little need to seek further explanation. And Kay knew very well that until her last days, the dream of Garden City, a suburb known for little more than its Kmart store, would cause her pulse to race, her throat to tighten, and her eyes to well.

It's true that Kay's longing ran beside a grinding distrust of the place, suspicion seeded at an early age—as early as the sixties—that the town possessed an ugly underbelly. She was learning, too, that the story of Garden City was inseparable from the story of the automobile. It began before Fred's bet on Henry Ford's racer back in 1901, before the encounter with Spider Huff. It swept its long arm backward and forward through time. Tin Lizzie, Piquette Avenue, and Highland Park were in its path, as were the moving assembly line, the Melting Pot, the Great Migration of black workers to the northern factory towns, the Depression, the wars, the GI Bill, and the baby boom, right through to her father's executive career at Ford corporate headquarters and Joe's job at the Rouge Plant.

After she told Joe about George Bissell, Detroit's first auto fatality, and how it reminded her of *The Magnificent Ambersons,* Kay could not stop thinking about that movie. She returned again and again to a particular scene, the one in which George Minniver tells Joseph Cotton, the handsome inventor and early car manufacturer, that "automobiles are a useless nuisance. Never amount to anything but a nuisance and they had no business to be invented." Because he is courting George's widowed mother, the hostility of the son is an obstacle, and Joseph Cotton is wounded by the remark. But, being a far gentler hero than Henry Ford, he cedes to the son, and in his wistful reply, the future decay of the Ambersons' world is foreshadowed:

> I'm not sure George is wrong about automobiles. With all their speed forward, they may be a step backward in civilization. May be that they won't add to the beauty of the world or the life of men's souls. I'm not sure. But automobiles have come! And almost all outward things are going to be different because of what they bring. They're going to alter war and they're going to alter peace. And I think men's minds are going to be changed in subtle ways because of automobiles. And it may be that George is right. It may be that in ten or twenty years from now, if we can see the inward change in men by that time, I shouldn't be able to defend the gasoline engine, but would have to agree with George that automobiles had no business to be invented.

Just as in the movie, cars had taken people away from the old city centers. The young roads that cut across the woodland surrounding Detroit enabled the suburbs to spring up and grow. Money flowed along those roads, away from the city, to take root in building plots and housing developments for white people. The men of Garden City put up a race-exclusion sign to keep out the men from Detroit and Inkster. Ancient forests were mowed down and the footprints of native chiefs finally erased. Wild animals fled, raced across lanes of traffic, dying beneath the wheels, balls of matted, bloodied fur. Corn by the roadsides withered and turned brown.

Eventually, people would try to put nature back. The yards and verges along the new residential lanes would be replanted with bald young trees. Grass seed would be lovingly sprinkled and watered. Commuter cars would be carefully reversed out of driveways, turning back toward the city office blocks. It was as if the entire scene were trying to run itself like a bomb blast in reverse. The mushroom cloud caved in on itself. Leaves flew back to the branches. Babies careered back into mothers' arms.

As a Ford brat, Kay had once happily played with the toy Thunderbirds and Lincoln Continentals brought home by her father. She rolled plastic models along the griddle-hot pavement in imaginary shopping trips and Barbie and Ken scenarios. Sid and Kay liked to perch on the bumper of Jake's Mercury, its shiny metallic heat warming their thighs while they waited for Joe to come along. Nighttime, at the drive-in, they ate popcorn in the backseat, dressed in their pajamas, while Jake and Marion watched the movie. Riding up north one summer, Kay kneeled up in the backseat to kiss and cling to her father's neck while he drove. Marion told her to sit down, and muttered, in weary and faintly injured tones, "You don't like your dad much, do you, Kay?" When a Christmas-morning surprise went awry one year, and Jake told the children to wait in the kitchen because Santa's sleigh was "stalled" in the front yard and he was waiting for a mechanic, they believed him. Forget the reindeer. In Michigan, Santa ran on gasoline.

Kay now realized that Ford, GM, and Chrysler had bound themselves perfectly to notions of Manifest Destiny and to the idea that if you don't like a place, you move to a new place. You get in your car and drive away. Westerns and road movies. If you do like a place, you just drive around it a lot, call it home, distort it, and develop an unhealthy obsession about it. Frank Capra movies. *American Graffiti.* You spend the rest of your life deeply confused, torn between Kansas and the

Emerald City, never quite sure where you are or what to believe. "The Yanks have colonized our subconscious." So says a character in Wim Wenders's *Kings of the Road*. It was the German filmmaker's insight about growing up European after World War Two. What he surely knew equally well was that the Yanks pickled their own brains first.

Around 1970, Kay began to think mean things about the company. The first holiday season after the family moved further away from Detroit, out to the new suburb, leaving Joe behind, her father made it onto the executive Christmas-card list. At the time, a personalized piece of mail from the second Henry Ford and his wife served to confirm Kay's vague suspicion that moving from Garden City constituted some sort of class betrayal. To her surprise, her father, too, was unmoved by the card. At Christmas dinner, when Sid reached for the salt shaker at the start of the meal, Jake repeated a story they had heard dozens of times—that Henry Ford once fired a man for salting his food before tasting it. But several glasses of Burgundy and two platefuls of turkey and stuffing later, their father grew morose. "I never really cared for cars," he slurred, out of the blue, apropos of nothing.

In *The Magnificent Ambersons,* when the arrogant George Minniver finally gets his comeuppance, the people who once prayed for it are either dead or scattered by the cars and roads that have turned the town into ugly sprawl. It is a final insult that George is felled by an automobile, the invention he once described as a useless nuisance. The movie, made in 1942, became part of Hollywood legend after the studio vandalized it, cutting and destroying some of the original footage shot by Orson Welles, changing the ending. But Kay loved it anyway, this film marked by deep ambivalence, unsure whether the old, aristocratic, small-town complacency of the Amberson era was better or worse than the automotive age that followed.

JEFFERSON AVENUE

ON A SATURDAY NIGHT IN AUGUST, 1914, FRED SAW HIS FATHER IN A crowded tavern on Jefferson Avenue. Jacques Gaillard was at the bar, holding a beer and making idle conversation with the man next to him. Both men stood with their backs to the room. Fred lifted onto his toes to get a better look, brushing away the curls of smoke that drifted in front of his face. Then he pushed slowly through the groups of drinkers and came to a stop within feet of the bar, afraid to move closer or breathe. He had fallen through darkness, all the way back to the flat on Concord Street, where he used to wake in the night to find his father asleep, but upright, on the end of the bed. It was terribly important not to speak or stir the air in the room. You must remain absolutely still, if you hoped to keep your father.

Fred watched as Jacques rested both elbows on the bar, leaned his chin on his hands, looked down at his half-empty glass, and then turned to say something to the man next to him, finally revealing his face in profile. It was a face Fred recognized, but not the one he craved. His mood went into freefall, an old and familiar sensation, regularly experienced from childhood, even before his father's death. In fact, no one had ever understood it except Jacques, who could steady his son simply by placing a hand on the back of Fred's boyish, thin neck. Who now could soothe him with a touch to the neck? Who could help him not mind that the man at the bar was not his father? There was the rub. Fred had come up against it before. So, although he felt like an orphan child, he closed his grown-up eyes and pulled himself into the present by silently repeating a mantra he had used on other occasions when he thought he saw his father: the actual date, year, and place he happened to be, in this instance—a drinking hole on Jefferson Avenue, opened several years *after* Jacques Gaillard's death. Fred let the mantra do its work until a single wave of the old grief washed over him, causing his eyes and throat to sting for a moment. Then it was gone. He looked around self-consciously, but no heads were turned in his direction. And as for the man at the bar—that was never Fred's father. That was Paul Gaillard, Fred's brother.

Fred saw immediately how his mind had been tricked. A little grayer and thinner, Paul was finally, grudgingly, beginning to resemble their father. He stood the same way Jacques used to stand, with the weight shifted to the left side, everything marginally tilted, head bent forward. Perhaps it had only come lately, with growing older, and that was why Fred had never noticed it before. Or maybe all those nights he had hidden in the dark street and followed his brother, hoping for signs, he had tried too hard, looked for more than could reasonably be expected. But finally, in his posture if in little else, Paul Gaillard was surprisingly like his father. As though the dead man's ways of moving had slipped into this younger frame and begun to alter it ever so slightly.

"Hey!" Paul said, finally catching sight of Fred. "What do ya know? How 'bout I buy a drink for my little brother?"

Paul's next words were for the benefit of the man standing next to him at the bar. "No, wait a minute—maybe my brother should buy one for *me*. He's one of Henry Ford's boys."

Now the other man turned to look Fred up and down. "*Well*, look who it ain't," he said.

It was the stranger, first seen outside the Highland Park plant after the Five Dollar Day announcement. The same man who had folded his arms across his chest, stared down the hiring agents, taken the full force of the fire hose, and turned to ice before Fred's eyes. For these incidents alone, Fred surely would have remembered him. But the stranger had also turned a hard gaze on Fred that day, effectively challenging him to disappear inside the factory and forget all they had witnessed. A silent dare, like a wire stretched between them.

Face to face with the stranger again, Fred found himself thinking not about that cold moment back in January, but about a more recent, summer evening. Walking home after a picnic, Ralph had asked, "When did ya get so low?" The question was perhaps the closest Fred ever came to the old sensation of his father's hand on his neck, the feeling that someone had *noticed* him. But Fred's reply, "Last Tuesday, four o'clock," was designed to make his friend chuckle and retreat. Now, he returned to Ralph's tender-hearted question and his own evasive answer. Maybe it *was* as sudden as that. From the instant the stranger turned to ice before his eyes, Fred had been *low.*

Of course, he was aware that unhappiness runs deep and tends to take hold incrementally, over long periods of time, the layered outcome of actions and incidents, large disappointments and small ones. Sometimes unhappiness delivers a violent blow—the untimely death of a loved one, for example—to gain a heavy and lasting advantage. But Fred sensed that even without his father's suicide, he could look back over the years and revisit the muted defeats and compromises that, sooner or later, would have caused him to "get so low," as Ralph put it. Indeed, this was the nature of Jacques Gaillard's unhappiness too— the very thing that had sent him tumbling into the river. Like his father, Fred found that unhappiness was always present. It ran beneath the surface, but now and then reached up to grab his ankles. Most of the time, he was pretty adept at shaking it off, hiding it, and hiding *from* it. Or so he had believed—until a stranger outside the factory gate locked onto him, a lovely girl at a picnic failed to move him, and his best friend posed a question. Three moments, occurring between January and June, like a stretch of road signs. Doors closing behind him. Afterward, unhappiness seemed harder to dodge.

Fred did disappear inside the factory that January morning. He was back on the assembly line before the fire hoses were stored away. He worked and stuck to his old routines. He needed the job; that was a plain fact from which there was no escape. In the following months, some workers declared Ford a tyrannical employer and quit Highland Park to look elsewhere, cursing the time-study men, the sociological investigators, and the company *Americanization* program that was obligatory for the immigrants. But Fred stayed. He stayed and stayed, even though countless times over the months and years, before the stranger and after the stranger, he had witnessed things at Ford that made good men leave. In the eighteen years following his father's death, from Piquette Avenue to Highland Park, he had become a smaller and smaller fish in a bigger and bigger pond. And swallowed an awful lot of water, while wiggling up and down, decreasing in size and getting nowhere. No wonder Ralph, although not a natural-born worrier, had lately grown anxious about his oldest friend.

"You two know each other?" Paul asked, glancing back and forth between Fred and the stranger.

"Let's just say we've bumped into one another before," the stranger answered.

"Where's that, then?" Paul asked.

"Outside the Ford factory, back in January."

Fred tried to shake free of his thoughts, stepped forward, and extended his hand. "Yes, that's right. But we did not meet. My name's Fred. Fred Gaillard."

"Lon."

The stranger ignored Fred's offer of a handshake.

"Lon. What's that short for?" asked Paul, who evidently had not exchanged names with his drinking partner.

"Short for nothing that I can remember. Just Lon," the stranger replied, shifting his weight from one foot to the other.

"So *Lon*, you work for Ford too?" Paul asked.

"No. I turned up with all the other damn fools hopin' for a Five Dollar Day job. But I saw right away it was a hoax. If they'd offered me a place, I would've told 'em what to do with it. Say, you earnin' five dollars yet, Freddie?"

"No. They've got me on probation. They check how you're livin' outside the factory. And if they don't like it, you don't get the full pay."

"Then that makes you a bigger fool than I ever was," Lon said.

"Lay off him. Fred's all right."

Fred glanced at his brother in surprise. It was always odd to find himself in company with Paul, someone so hard to fix, yet so singularly important. Odder still to hear Paul defending him. Then he looked back at the stranger, also important, this phantom he had been inwardly battling for months, suddenly made flesh. He was a little thinner than Fred remembered. Older too, perhaps forty years or so, to Fred's twenty-five. It was a distance Fred had not previously considered, but it was heartening. He guessed Lon would use his age as an advantage if given half a chance. But Paul and Lon were becoming old men; Fred had more time ahead than both.

"Most of the men outside the plant that day were not from Detroit. Where did you come from?" Fred asked.

"Most of 'em were ethnics. And look at 'em now. You can't walk across Detroit these days without being peddled a newspaper in some foreign language or landing in the middle of a fight. It's got worse lately, with everybody in Europe declarin' war against each other. The French and Belgians hate the Germans. The Germans hate them right back. The Italians hate the Austrians and vice versa. And the Irish, well, they hate anybody who sides with the English."

"But where are *you* from, Lon?" Fred tried again.

"I'm Michigan born. Western part of the state. Quit it a few years back."

"Why'd you leave?" Paul asked.

"Let's just say I'm not a farmer."

"But don't you have family out there?" Fred pressed a little harder.

"Do *you* stay with *your* family?" Lon batted the question back.

"I board over on Tuxedo Street. In Highland Park—near the factory. But I visit—"

"Seems to me you haven't seen your brother here in some time."

"Well, no, but—"

"Our family busted up years ago," Paul said. "When our father killed himself. Jumped into the river like a damn loon, back in '96. Fred was his favorite. Our mother remarried—get this—with the lodger who lived downstairs. You never much liked ole Ballantine, did ya, Fred?"

Lon put his glass down, tilted his head, and peered at the two brothers. Fred stared at the floor in silence, his face and neck flaming. Paul had crossed an invisible line, stating aloud and with cruel detachment the time, place, and manner of Jacques Gaillard's death. Fred found it almost impossible to *think* these facts, let alone expose them to a stranger. And the remark about Fred being his father's favorite. Anyone might think Paul hard done by, a rejected son, but the truth was that Paul had never wanted his parents, Fred, or Bell. He had always behaved like an unwilling member of the diminished Gaillard clan, biding his time, taking meals, waiting for circumstances to change. Now, telling the stranger their history, Paul painted a crude picture; he stripped away these complications of family—the shaded enmities and alliances that can never be fully explained.

Although Fred was visibly injured and angry, his brother, fueled by drink, was in a gregarious mood. Paul continued talking to Lon, but kept one eye on Fred, as though measuring the impact of his words, verbally elbowing his younger brother to make room for a dissonant version of their shared past.

"We never knew *why* he did it, though I can't say I was too surprised. But Fred was pretty young at the time. I guess it's tough to lose a father you look up to. And Ballantine was never gonna cut the mustard. As for me, things got real simple after my father took his big leap and my mother remarried. I figured I didn't owe anybody and I could get out on my own. Fred'll tell ya—I'm no family man."

Paul glanced at his brother one last time and took out a cigarette.

"It's true, Paul," Fred said, his mouth dry and tight. "You're no family man. So let's not talk about family *now*."

Paul shrugged. "Okay, Fred. Have it your way." Then he burped loudly.

Lon, the stranger, laughed. "Hard to make you two as brothers."

"So what about *you*?" Fred turned again to Lon.

"Nothing to tell."

"Well, what about your people?"

"As I said," Lon sighed impatiently. "Nothing to tell."

"Well . . . how did they feel when you left for Detroit?"

"Never told 'em."

Lon averted his gaze, and for the first time, Fred saw that he could be made uncomfortable. Normally, the smallest sign of unease in a person would cause Fred to draw back, but his brother and the stranger had muscled him into a corner, and he felt the need to battle his way out of it.

"So your people . . ." Fred persisted. "They don't know where you are?"

"That's right."

"Don't they care to know?"

"I couldn't say."

"So they might be desperate with worry, searching for you. Why don't you at least let them know you are alive?"

"It's not that simple. It's . . ." Lon started to reply, but his voice trailed off.

Then he tried again. "It's none of your beeswax, Freddie. But all I can say is back home, they might not . . ." But he choked on his words. A small sob, barely audible, caught in his mouth, and he brought his fist down hard on the bar.

Never before had Fred seen a person lose their composure as rapidly as the stranger did now. The tough fellow who had faced up to the Ford agents and the fire hose, turned to ice that day back in January, yet held his ground. But here in a warm tavern on Jefferson, with no more threat than a question or two from Fred Gaillard, he dropped his head in his hands, clearly distressed, unable to recover his voice. Fred and Paul glanced at one another. Paul grimaced and shook his head in disdain. The stranger had been put in his place by the two brothers. But that was not how Fred saw it. He felt implicated; he suddenly felt bad, bad enough to begin to *like* the stranger, this man who had fixed him with an unforgiving stare outside the factory and troubled his thoughts ever since.

It was true the tables were turned. Fred had tapped into some piece of private history, and he sensed that Lon was strongly tempted to round on his heel and quit the bar, yet equally tempted to stay and unburden himself. But whatever Lon might do, Fred decided then and there that he would not walk away from the stranger this time. He shifted position and gestured Paul to leave. His brother looked surprised, but did not argue.

"Think I'll find a card game. See ya around, Freddie."

After the street door closed behind his brother, Fred turned to the stranger and reached out to tap his shoulder. Lon brought his arm down and roughly pushed Fred away. Fred saw that his face was wet.

"How 'bout I buy us a drink?" Fred asked.

Lon gave no reply. He wiped his face with his sleeve and pushed his large body against the bar to steady himself. Then he reached into his inner vest pocket and produced a photograph, printed on stiff card. Without showing the card to Fred, he studied it for a long minute, oblivious to a final teardrop he had failed to rub away, now hanging bulbously from his stubbled chin. Fred saw that he was exhausted.

"I have a daughter," Lon said finally, his voice shaking.

He sounded tentative and fearful, as though the statement might break into a thousand pieces. Then he held out the photo, close enough for Fred to see that it was worn around the edges, and that it showed a tan-faced girl with strong bones and a square jaw, very like the stranger's jaw.

"What's her name?" asked Fred.

"Ada."

"Ada . . . I like that."

Fred looked at the photograph a second time.

She wore a formal, white dress and clasped a diploma in her gloved hands. The photograph was obviously intended to celebrate an achievement, but the girl's expression did not quite match the intention. Yes, there was a shy, proud half smile on her face, but her eyes were caught by something other than the diploma and the occasion, or perhaps by a person, someone positioned slightly to one side of the photographer, tripod, and camera. Fred saw all this too quickly to form a coherent impression. He grasped Ada's mouth and eyes, and the disunity of purpose between them; he grasped this not in lines or phrases, but in a flash of recognition. But when he leaned forward to focus his attention, Lon appeared to change his mind. He snatched the photograph away from Fred's direct view and held it in both hands, so that only he could see it.

"She's pretty," Fred said carefully. Then, in a small attempt to make Lon smile and save him from the embarrassment of his tears, Fred nudged him slightly and added, "Even if she does look a little like you."

"She was beginning to remind me of her mother," Lon replied, unsmiling. "The day this photograph was made, I saw it, and it spooked the hell outta me."

"How long ago was that?"

"Four years ago. 1910. I left for good the next morning. Haven't seen Ada since."

"She must be missing you something awful. Don't you think you should go home?"

Lon looked up from the photograph and stared hard at Fred for a moment.

"Ada grew up believing I was her *brother*. I never told her the truth. And I'm more than sure that to this day, nobody else will have told her about me. About her mother maybe, but not about *me*."

"What made you leave?"

"I never did right by her. Never did right by her mother. These things . . . have a way of catching up on you. My hand was forced a little, but I was already reaching the point where I couldn't stay and look Ada in the eye."

"But don't you think Ada deserves to know?"

"Ada was always crazy about me—she looked up to me. What do you think she'd say if she knew the truth?"

"But that's unbelievably cruel and selfish!" Fred said. "You let her idolize you in ignorance. Then, you disappear and leave her to wonder where you are. All that—to *protect* yourself? How can you do that to your own child? If you went home now, *told her now*—you might still do some good."

"But I'm not a good man. Surely you've figured that by now."

Lon gave Fred a sharp glance, a warning glance, then shook his head, signaling an end to the questions. He returned to the photograph, looked at it one more time, head bowed, thick forefinger resting on its surface to touch the face of the girl. Fred felt him slip away.

"I have a daughter," Lon repeated to himself finally, with greater conviction than the first time, but also with terrible remorse, as though he had been waiting a hundred years to utter those words, but only pain could follow them. As he put the photograph away, back into his vest pocket, he appeared lost and shattered, no longer aware of Fred's presence. His body weaved slightly. Then he let go of the bar, turned into the packed, smoky room, and walked blindly toward the tavern door.

Fred watched him leave, the stranger who carried a photograph next to his chest like a secret scar. He had forgotten about Fred and clearly did not wish to be followed. So Fred forced himself to remain behind, cling to the bar, and wait several long minutes, until he felt sure there would be no sign of the stranger along Jefferson Avenue. But stepping out of the bar after, Fred looked right and left; he walked up and down, checking the alleyways and side streets.

With racing heart, he grasped his dreadful mistake. A person in trouble should *always* be followed. How many times had he wondered if someone had seen his father that night in April of 1896, seen him and guessed? It was a bitter suggestion that sometimes caused Fred to resent each and every person who carried on living afterward, the inhabitants of Detroit, his mother, brother, Bell, and himself. Horace Ballantine, who Fred *knew* had been seen talking to his father outside the house on Concord Street that night.

IT WAS AN EXCRUCIATING WEEK THAT FOLLOWED THE ENCOUNTER on Jefferson Avenue. Fred agonized about his failure to pursue the stranger, thought of things he might have said or done differently. Gradually, this was replaced by a low-grade guilt and anxiety, then by notions about Lon himself. The old menacing image of the iced figure outside the factory gate was gone, to be replaced by a smaller, desolate one, still unnerving to Fred, but no longer a cold judgment against him. If anything, from his first appearance to his last, Lon had tucked into Fred's mind and kicked him awake. Fred must do everything in his power to find the stranger. He had no idea what might happen when he found him, or even if he would know what to say or do. It did not matter that Lon was likely to reject Fred with incivility, maybe even with violence. It mattered that Fred try. And after that, whether Lon wanted his friendship or not, *because* he had tried, Fred would be released, free to change his own life. He could quit Ford forever.

He possessed no specific clue or lead, no last name or address. The only information was a first name, Lon, and a passing mention of western Michigan and farming. But the state of Michigan, the towns and rural counties beyond the city, did not really exist for Fred. In any case, he felt certain the stranger would remain in Detroit. Every night during that interminable week, he returned to the tavern on Jefferson. He tried other bars. He checked Champlain Street, where the brothels were. He even walked up and down the river shore, worried that Paul's account of Jacques Gaillard's suicide might have lodged inside the stranger's head and given him ideas. Fred revisited the bridges and docks and the places where you could watch the water breaking on the edge of Detroit. He knew the city like the back of his hand, and no one could say he didn't try to find the stranger. But it was a dense, tough town, and it could swallow anybody, even a fighter like Lon.

As the days and nights dragged into the second week after the stranger vanished, Fred became more and more agitated. He grew haggard from loss of sleep. He neglected to change his clothes and shave. His landlady threatened to evict him for staying out late, then waking her when he crawled home in the early hours. He took a decision to stop paying rent and force the eviction. He would put the money aside for Lon, maybe buy him a train ticket back to the daughter in western Michigan. At the plant, Fred slumped over his work, exhausted and constantly fearful for Lon's well-being. His feet ached from hours of walking, and his hands shook. Whenever he grabbed a tool or a part and held it up to the light, it shimmered and made him dizzy. He found he could not recover his usual rapid, habitual movement or keep pace with the line. But it did not matter how much the foreman threatened, because Fred planned to leave as soon as Lon was found and helped. At Ford, he was secretly approaching freedom.

At the end of the second week, Fred was pulled off the line as his shift finished and told to report to the cashier's office. *So, this is it. They get me before I get them,* he thought, with a wry smile. *You can't beat a Ford in any kind of race.*

"There's a person here to see you," the cashier said from behind his window.

A young woman in a nurse's uniform rose from the wooden bench against the wall and approached Fred.

"Are you Fred Gaillard?"

"Yes. What's this about?"

"May we talk outside?" she asked.

They stood on Manchester Street, close to one another, face to face in fading light. To passersby, they might have been a couple, intimate. They knitted together immediately, because she had come looking for him; come to speak of someone. But there was no urgency in her face or voice, just the leaden look of someone about to deliver bad news. Fred understood she had come to tell him of a death, not an injury or illness. His mother was dead. She had looked gaunt and tired of late. Or was it Paul? How would it feel to be the sole surviving son of Jacques Gaillard? To *have* to stay alive? The white bib of the nurse's uniform glowed in the dusk, making her bosom large and bright. Fred felt weak and dirty in her presence, but she did not seem to notice.

"I work at Harper's Hospital," she began slowly. "And last night, I tended a man who I believe may be known to you. He carried no papers and refused to provide a name. I was hoping you could identify him, or help to locate his people. The only clue we have is a photograph, found inside his vest."

She paused, but Fred said nothing. He had turned stone cold, and his mind slowed to treacle as he adjusted to unanticipated news. Forced to pull his thoughts away from his mother, Paul, and the family, he found he could not manage it immediately, not without an inward tug of war.

"He was discovered in an alley down near the riverfront," she continued. "Alone. He may have been set upon by criminals or involved in a brawl; we have no idea what happened. Only that he was the victim of a serious stab wound to the chest. And he . . . he *died*. About two hours after admittance to hospital.

"The patient was conscious when brought in, but he could not tell us who had attacked him or why. I don't think he knew. I don't believe he cared. But he was very agitated about the photograph. He wanted me to hold it for him to see. I'm afraid I damaged it a little when I tried to clean his blood from it."

Then she opened her bag and took out the picture of Lon's daughter. There was a brown stain in the top right corner, a faint rubbing, where she had tried to remove the blood.

"When I asked if we should contact the person in the picture, he became very distressed. *No*, he said. *Please, no*. Then he pleaded with me. *Give it to Fred. At the Ford plant*. I pressed him for a surname and address, but he did not seem to know. *Fred at the Ford plant*, he repeated. *Fred . . . Gaylord or Gayard. Some such name. Find him at Ford. He'll know what to do*. I have no idea what you are to this man, but he wanted me to come here. He left me no choice, you see. I've never been here before. The cashier went through the employee list and helped me to find you."

She stopped talking and waited, noting that Fred's face had lost its color. He was the person her dying patient had asked for. Fred felt dizzy, as though the blood had drained from his head to his feet, and all his frenetic activity of the previous two weeks had somehow led to this terrible outcome. He bent forward, doubling nearly to his knees, to keep from passing out. Finally, he pulled himself upright and found the nurse's eyes again.

"Did your patient say anything else before he died?" he asked.

"Yes, but not to me—not to anyone. After he made me promise to find you, he only talked to himself, private-like. And low. So low and weak I could not follow. Then, nothing more."

MIDDLEVILLE NIGHT

SEPTEMBER 1914. THE WARM, DRY WEATHER PERSISTED, A PROMISE of Indian summer. Violet Parker lay very still in her cotton nightdress, silvery hair sprayed on the pillow, curved hands hugging a packet of letters to her chest. Sometime after Lon's disappearance four years earlier, she had taken to sleeping with Allie Green's letters.

One night, nobody knew when, Violet would die in her bed. Slip away quietly, leaving no dent other than the faint imprint of her body on the mattress. She would disappear, having lived long and cautiously, after a single remembered moment of girlish recklessness, when she looked into the eyes of James Parker, a frightened farmhand just out of uniform, dared him to look away, married him, and soon delivered Lon, a willful and beautiful son. Thereafter, she found that a husband was nothing, compared to a child.

She began motherhood with an excess, a near-violent devotion to her firstborn, only to be forced to step back. She gave birth again, again, and again, each time without question, to Eugene, Caroline, and Merritt. She tried to spread herself evenly, across this number greater than Lon, this family group. The three sons were sturdy, but Lon was always larger, more central in her mind than the others. The daughter became ill, could not survive. Violet looked for James once more, and lost him. Marriage and motherhood had made her cautious. She did things by degrees, always faltering and deliberating, measuring the effects of her feelings and choices on the ones she loved, especially Lon. He put her through the mill. She *partly* defied her son, *partly* deferred to him, *partly* helped Allie, *partly* stole from her, *partly* told Ada. It left an awful lot of gray.

In due course, Allie would be given the final word. This was Violet's

197

sole, remaining purpose: to force the letters on Ada. Otherwise, what was the point of all the hurt and shame and holding back and deception? What was the point of losing a son, if Ada never accepted the letters? But for Allie to be heard, Violet would have to die. It did not matter whether it took months or years, her last wish would be plain as death itself. One morning, Ada would find the letters, locked in cold fingers, impossible to refuse.

It always took Violet hours to fall asleep. The dawn chorus might begin long before she drifted off. Her weak eyes fixed on the cream-painted ceiling of the darkened bedroom, but she saw nothing but her years, rolling out nightly in a memory scroll. When an aging person no longer sleeps, but finds in thoughts of death a comfort and a plan, and wonders at how long she has lingered, how few friends are left, how she has crossed from one century to another and lived up to 1914—all this becomes no different from dreaming. She dreams awake, staring at the ceiling.

So on this particular night at the end of a hot summer, as was her habit, Violet breathed, moved her lips without sound, and sifted through a number of vivid and ready scenes before finally settling on the picture of another night—white, gusting, and frozen—all the way back in 1885:

Two feet of snow already, drifts forming along the fences in the fields. The elm tree, its dark, bare, winter arms pelted by driving snow. The blizzard crashes around the house, trying to get in. Cold drafts fly up the stairs and under the closed doors to loosen the quilts on the beds. Violet and her mother clear the table after supper. Violet's husband sits with her father, the two men warming themselves by the cookstove after evening chores. Her husband cleans his pipe and listens to the storm. Her father, a muscular man with scaly, red skin on his face and hands, rubs his aching joints.

Young Alonzo, named after his grandfather Shaw, but everyone calls him Lon, sits cross-legged on a colorful rag rug between the two men and their chairs. Aged ten and Violet's eldest, Lon is the only child unafraid of the burly grandfather. The little ones cling to Violet's skirt and shrink with shyness when Alonzo Shaw addresses them. But Lon looks every adult in the eye, his face wide open.

There is a snap, followed by a knocking sound at the kitchen window, as a sudden gust hurls itself against the glass and shakes the frame. Everyone stops what they are doing and looks toward the window.

"Who's out there?" laughs the big man, Alonzo Shaw. Then Alonzo leans toward his defiantly brave grandson. "You think this is bad, Lon? Imagine a blizzard in a log cabin."

"Did you live in a real log cabin?" asks Lon, knowing the answer already, but liking to hear his grandfather's stories.

"Yessir. And right here, where this house is stood. Built that cabin myself, with help from my brothers and the Reds."

"Indians?"

"Yessir," Alonzo repeats. "And I can recall, like it was yesterday, another blizzard—must have been about 1838—when snow blew through the logs on one side of the cabin, the side exposed to the wind. It even came through the roof! That night, snowflakes fell on our faces, right there on our mattress in the loft. So I got up to plug the roof and check the fire, went down the ladder, and guess what I found?"

"What did you find?" the lad says, unblinking, his chin cupped in his hands.

"Four Ottawa braves! Fast asleep by the fire. Snoring contentedly. They had crawled in to escape the storm, and there they stayed until morning."

Then Alonzo sweeps his arm across the room to indicate the space to his grandson. "Mighta been right where you're sitting now, Lon," he says. "It was the old cabin, of course, not this house. But it was the same ground."

Lon looks at the floor, stretches his farm-boy arms beyond the border of the rug on which he is seated, touches the wood, and flattens his hands on the boards. Violet, her mother, and her husband watch in silence. Only the storm keeps to its business.

"Think on this, Lon," Alonzo continues. "When we arrived at this place, back in 1836, Michigan was not yet a state, and there were probably no more than a thousand whites in the whole county. The Ottawas lived in small bands and encampments north of the Kalamazoo River. They kept to their hunting and planting. Right near us. We had backbreaking work to clear the land. It was thick with oak, elm, and walnut trees. But the Indian traders kept us supplied with venison, fish, berries, maple sugar, and other foodstuffs. We traded dried goods and whiskey.

We traded, and we got along. I made friends with one or two, and they made friends with me. Every autumn, the northern Ottawas sailed down Lake Michigan, all the way from Mackinaw to here. They fished in the streams, and their ancient hunting grounds lay all around these parts. So in winter, there were more Indians than at any other time of year. The woods stayed busy with their hunting throughout the cold months, even though more than one of 'em told me the white settlers were scaring away the game."

Alonzo leans back in his chair.

"It's been many years since the Indian hunters stopped coming down here. Long before you were born, Lon. And the traders stopped calling long before that. But to this day, when the blizzard howls, I swear I can hear Ottawa voices in it, calling to be let inside. That's my abiding memory of the old tribes."

Gray light moved slowly into Violet's room, while outside the early birds told that no one had died in the house that night. Nothing will happen today, they sang. Violet listened for a time, lightly moving one of her fingers back and forth on the packet of letters. Then she sighed and closed her eyes. Alonzo Shaw by the fire in the kitchen and his clear-eyed grandson. Her father liked to tell boys' stories, and Lon was always hungry for them.

Violet slept a few hours. Later, as she dressed for the day, slow and careful, because her bones ached, she glanced from her window toward the road. There he was again, the same young man she had spied the previous evening, wearing his Sunday clothes, fighting the dust blowing off the dry fields, until he finally turned away and disappeared in the direction of town. He was back, this young man, a person unknown to her, watching the house, trying to decide whether to approach, climb the steps to the porch, and knock on the door. He walked up and down the road a few times, stopping regularly to look back at Violet, though she drew back from the window so that he could not actually see her. She would not help him.

But it was already out of her hands. So Violet finished dressing, sat down on the edge of her bed, and waited.

THE LIGHTED FIELD

SEPTEMBER 2003. SUMMER CLOSED WITH A RUN OF THUNDERSTORMS
that finally broke the heat. There were tornado watches and warnings.
The sky yellowed, and then darkened as gusts of fierce, hot wind rattled the screen door. No funnel cloud swept along Maple Court to tear
Joe's house from its foundations and send it spinning above the subdi-
visions and freeways, but when the rain came, it pounded so hard that
it kicked back off the pavement. Afterward, the days turned cooler, and
Joe talked of packing the window fans away for another year. It soon
became clear that he regarded the change of season as a turning point
for the two of them.

"So what are you going to do next?" he asked, as they dressed one
morning.

"What do you mean?"

Alarm sprinted from each of Kay's words to the next. Joe's rhythm
was slow and deliberate, by contrast. His question had been prepared
beforehand and would not be hurried.

"I mean . . . when you finish looking into your family's past. What
are you going to do after that?"

"I don't know. I haven't given it much thought. There's still so
much material to dig into."

"*Really?*"

"Yes. *Really.*"

Half dressed and feeling vulnerable, trying to steady herself, Kay
stood in the middle of the bedroom. The walls seemed to have drawn
back, cutting her loose. Joe pulled his shirt on, staring hard at her as
he did so.

"You're looking thin," he said.

Kay glanced down at her bare legs and placed a hand flat across her belly.

"You don't eat enough," he continued, a note of irritation in his voice. "That's your responsibility, Kay. It's not up to me. You do know that, don't you?"

"Of course I do, Joe. I never asked you to take care of me."

He sat down on the edge of the bed, fully dressed except for his shoes.

"I'm worried about you. You don't look well."

She saw that Joe's words did not come out of the blue. There was thought behind them, days of thought, maybe longer.

"I wonder if you are burying yourself in things," he said. "Losing direction with your project. I mean, what you do every day, the way you spend your time. Your stash of papers and notebooks and old stories. You never seem to finish anything. Not one story has actually ended. And it seems to me you're unhappier than when you first arrived. None of it seems to be helping you."

"Joe, I have never been happier!"

Kay crossed to the bed and sat down beside him.

"And anyway, wasn't I supposed to be helping *you*?" she said, touching his arm.

He smiled weakly and shook his head.

"That was a way for us to buy back some time together. But by now, you should have figured out that I have . . . limits."

And as had happened before, Kay heard a lonely bitterness slide into his voice.

"To be honest," he added, "you bumped up against my limits some time ago, not long after moving in here, truth be told."

That stung and made her quarrelsome.

"I don't get you, Joe. You are good to me, so good to me, nearly all the time. But every so often, you punch below the belt. Then you're sweet again, then back with the punch. It can happen from one minute to the next with you, from one *word* to the next. I never see it coming, and it hurts. It's not fair."

"Oh," he replied flatly. "I didn't realize we were discussing what's *fair*. In that case, maybe I *would* like to go back to 1970."

He stood up, reached for his shoes, and headed for the bedroom door.

"I'm running late."

She followed him, anxious now.

"I'm sorry, Joe. I know you're only trying to help. Maybe I do seem unhappy at times; I read things that throw me a little off course. The old pictures and mementoes sometimes make me blue. But really, it's like that old Sinatra song—I'm *glad* to be unhappy."

"Oh, *Christ,* here come the songs and movies."

He was exasperated. She had tried to shrug off his apprehension and bad feeling as though they were nothing. It wasn't working.

"Okay. Listen, Joe. I never meant to make you worry. I would hate to do that to you. Believe me—I'll think about what you say. And I swear—I don't expect you to help me."

"Good. Because I can't do that. Try to understand, Kay. It's not that I wouldn't *want* to help. But it's all I can do these days to look after myself. And I'm not sure you really see that."

"I'll try, Joe. I give you my word. I'll try not to cause you any worry."

He nodded, but looked miserable, perhaps disappointed by her faint promises. He stood at a distance, wary, as though it were dangerous to come close.

"I really do have to go," he said. Then guiltily, "I'll see ya tonight."

He picked up his keys from the kitchen counter and hurriedly left the house, the front door crashing shut behind him, making Kay jump. She remained there, trembling and unhinged, praying he would return to take her in his arms before leaving for work. But seconds later, she heard the car door click and the motor scrape and start. She ran to the picture window in time to see his crappy old Ford disappear at the end of the street.

IN THE FOLLOWING DAYS, KAY RETURNED TO JOE'S REMARK ABOUT her weight, isolating it, perhaps because it was less frightening than his larger intimation that their time together was nearing an end. She stood before the hall mirror, turning right and left, lifting her t-shirt to inspect her waist and hips, straining to look over her shoulder at her backside. At first, she found nothing in her shape or size to cause alarm. But gradually, she noticed that her skin was paler and her clothes looser fitting than usual. She began to realize, too, that her appetite was smaller than before. So, almost as a distraction, Kay revisited the idea she had entertained on and off throughout the summer, that there might be something wrong.

She decided *not* to see a doctor. That would be the worst course of action, the one certain to make disease come true. She had promised Joe not to give him any cause for concern. Whatever ailed her would have to go away on its own. But she fretted intermittently, looked at self-diagnosis charts on medical websites, set her pulse racing with the occasional morbid notion, only to slap herself out of it. *Shut up*, she would think. *You're fine.* Kay knew she was messing with her own recent good fortune, what she sometimes termed her "money, love, and Maple Court." She recognized the perverse tendency of the moneyed, loved, and Maple Courted to entertain fantasies of losing it all. Fantasies of not being alive. Losing Joe. Absence. Missing out on things. Like when the Tigers next won the series and everybody in the bars hugged each other like old friends. *Shut up*, Kay scolded again. *You'll be there. With Joe by your side. So shut up.*

But she could not block the hectoring voices, shrill taunts that this particular silver lining had a cloud. At her most anxious and irrational, Kay thought she might be contagious. She tried not to breathe on Joe or share a beer, even turned away from his kisses once or twice. But then sometimes, she felt like breathing all over him, so she would not stumble and fall alone, so he might never be with anyone else. Back and forth, every next thought as unsafe as stepping out onto a newly frozen lake.

At other times, Kay wondered if Joe was real at all. Perhaps he had died in Vietnam. Their late love affair was a reverie. Joe was her Harvey, a six-foot rabbit, invisible to everyone but Kay. Her sister Pam, the neighbors, and the girl at the supermarket checkout—they only pretended to see the handsome companion who wasn't really there. They humored her when she conversed with the air above her left shoulder. She had come home to Garden City only to take up the post of village idiot. Then again, maybe *none* of it was true. She had *not* moved away from Los Angeles. No, she had duly returned there following her mother's death, but in a fugue. For weeks, she had been wandering up and down Hollywood Boulevard, carrying a soiled blanket in a black plastic bag and loitering outside Grauman's Chinese Theatre, waiting for the next film premiere. Talking to herself; spitting studio history like venom—like Norma Desmond in *Sunset Boulevard*. Or it might be a simple trauma to the head, a car accident or a fall. Perhaps she had fallen in Parmalee Cemetery at Marion's funeral, cracked her skull on an ancestral grave stone, *never* made the return flight to LA, and was now in a coma. Out like a light in some back ward in western Michigan. Visited less and less by Pam and Sid, who had given up hope. Years had passed. Perhaps she was dead. Together with Joe after all. At least he wasn't a rabbit.

Alone in the house one morning, Kay pinched her arms until she raised painful welts. She was not feeling self-destructive or depressed; no, she needed the pain to prove she was still there. Later, having hidden the sore, red patches under a long-sleeved cotton shirt, she began to wonder if her ailment might be one of the spirit. A bygone ailment, involving humors, bile, and nerves, such as Johannes Hofer would have recognized. It could be that some new, virulent mutation of nostalgia was slowly wasting her away. Dr. Thisroy was right after all. It might explain why lately she was so weighed with regret, so bogged down, and not by the large questions that might be raised by the fear of illness, but by the small things, or rather, the *accumulation* of small things.

Taken together, Kay's small things had produced a mound of patently mediocre results. Not the results she had planned for or wanted, back in the days as a high-strung but promising child of the baby boom. She needed another round; who on earth was capable of getting it right in one? She wanted a chance to relive the so-called small things. Make some changes. Learn piano. Sing like her mother, like Frank. Become a radio singer, swing style, of noir music—those forties lyrics and melodies seemingly light as a May breeze but for some dark idea embedded there, some nightmare view of the world, bang in the middle. Sing jazzy noir songs. Like there was no tomorrow. Resist the movies. Try, for once in life, to think freely and awake— imagine and invent America freely—from *outside* the conventions of Hollywood. Was that even possible? Read more, but stay away from universities. Spend more time with her grandfather. Ask him about his father and the Ford factory and Detroit, and in a brown leather note-book, write down his words, every one of them, exactly as pronounced. Sneak back into their homemade tent in the yard when Sid and Joe are sleeping boys. Crawl in noiselessly, lean over and, without waking him, whisper, *Joe Chase, I'll love you till the day I die.* Just like little Mary Hatch in *It's a Wonderful Life,* perched high at the soda fountain in Bedford Falls, declaring her secret love to the boy, in his deaf ear. Stay away from the fucking movies. Later, at fifteen years of age to Joe's seventeen, whisper it again, this time with kisses and alarming, adolescent wetness. Natalie Wood and Warren Beatty in *Splendor in the Grass.* This time, Joe gets past first base, behind the clubhouse at the Lighted Field, a diamond like no other, a heart's hold, where night crackles, mosquitoes swarm and fry on the electric bulbs high above the outfield, clouds of dust swirl around the hitters and base runners, sandaled and sneakered feet of all sizes dangle between rows of bleacher seats, and bats pop and spectators hum. At the Lighted Field, there are no movies, only people inventing life. So, Joe and Kay run away together. To Canada. Make love all over Canada. No more movies. And when his draft notice arrives in the Chase family mailbox on Maple Court, there is not a single soldier boy to enlist, because of a series of *small things* over the years, ending with a one-way drive in a trusty Ford. All the way down to Detroit, through the Windsor Tunnel and out the other side. Next stop is Vietnam? No. Memory? *Fahget about it!*

Kay thought about that expression people like to use, "Don't sweat the small things." Yet to her, the gaping disappointments and wounds, the fuck-ups and failures, could only be explained by traipsing backward, link by historical link, along the chains of small things. Charm bracelets of mistakes, dangling and clinking, growing heavy with time. Now, when it was too late, she sweated the small things, sweated hard, pumped herself full of regret, and missed things about home that really ought *not* to be missed because it wasn't such a great place after all. And she attempted to bury her regret in cranky diseases, spooked herself with medical dictionaries, and reread Hofer's description of nostalgia.

All the while, Allie Green's letters remained, delicate and dry as chalk. Of the countless documents and artifacts Kay had retrieved and examined, Allie's letters were the most troublesome. They shadowed Kay and stripped her of power. Joe had cared about Allie, and nothing could be done. Kay felt herself refusing Allie. Why did everyone refuse Allie Green, one after another? Beginning with Lon, then Ada, and ending with Kay. Yet the letters had survived; there was something in that. Perhaps Violet had died insisting they be preserved. So Ada grudgingly kept a promise to Violet, who had kept a promise to Allie. By the time they reached Marion, Fred and Ada's daughter, the letters were little more than memorabilia. There was no life in them, nothing at stake anymore. To Marion, they were just an affecting story to pass on. She sometimes wondered whatever became of poor Allie Green, and took another sip of wine.

Beyond the problem of Allie Green, Kay continued to harbor a curious grudge against her mother, and increasingly against *all* the dead ones. They could not rescue her, and she could not rescue them. How could she save them from the decades to come, when strangers would motor past the graveyard without stopping? She could not even protect the ancestors from her own actions! Already, it was possible to say, think, or write anything she chose and find no one to disagree. She might choose *not* to think about them, maybe even to forget them. But sooner or later, she'd be right there too, and the same neglect and distortions would be committed against her. Sure, people in families tried harder; it might take longer to prise the fingers apart. But each one of us falls from the cliff alone and misunderstood.

During the bright, chilly afternoons of early September, wearing jeans and a large flannel shirt belonging to Joe, Kay spent hours on his plastic lounge chair in the backyard, watching the sky and thinking about the sin of oblivion. She made lists of dead people, chanting their names over and over in her head. But mostly, she thought about Joe. In secret, she broke the rule and dwelled heavily on the years up to and including 1970. Her passing estrangement from the ancestors, the sense of having failed them, these were mirrored in what she had done to Joe when they were young. She had gone away and forgotten him.

LOVE

"I CAN'T," JOE SAID, FINALLY.

They had been trying to make love.

"It's all right. You're tired—don't worry about it. Let's just get some sleep."

"No, I mean it, Kay. This has gone on too long. I can't touch you anymore without feeling I'm going to break you. I reach for your skin, but I find something brittle. Like glass."

He stood to his feet, put his clothes on, and left her alone. Kay found a nightshirt and followed him into the living room. He was on the sofa, upright and staring at the late news on TV, the sound muted. She approached slowly and sat down next to him, but not too close. They stayed there for some minutes in silence before he turned to her, low and remorseful.

"I made a terrible mistake when I let you come here. I swore I would never make that mistake with you. Not with *you*."

She had known this was coming. Yet panic shot through her insides all the same. She felt sick with dread of what he might say next and tried to block him by going there first.

"What is it, Joe? Is it that you don't love me? Maybe now is the time to ask you why, during this beautiful summer we have spent together, you have never once told me you love me."

He replied with deliberate patience. "You have been living on my love your whole life, Kay. And you know it. Just try to find one childhood memory that is *not* touched by my love for you. But it's like a buried treasure. I can't find it anymore; I can't *add* to it."

"Because you can't forgive me."

"There's nothing to forgive. We were kids."

208

"That's not an answer."

"I'm sorry."

"I don't know what you want me to do, Joe. You seem to blame me not only for the past, but for what is happening now. You say I make you worry; I'm too thin, breakable as glass. You say I shouldn't stay here because I am unhappy. But that is not fair. *You're* the one in trouble. You know what I mean—the flashes of temper, bitter remarks. The nightmares and loss of sleep. Crying out in the dark, completely out of touch with your surroundings. And it starts all over again the next day. You work too hard, come home exhausted, and then you can't sleep. I know you have bad memories—why won't you tell me about them? You almost never talk about Vietnam. I'm more and more afraid to ask. Why should that be? You have made it impossible to ask about the war."

Joe's face hardened, but his reply was measured.

"What I saw in Vietnam, what I did—that's mine. I never wanted to give that to you. And if you need any more proof of my love, well . . . there it is."

Kay felt her eyes fill with tears. Like a swimmer too long in rough ocean waves, she was tired. Joe had been waiting all summer for her to flag and give up. He was immoveable, there on his corner of the sofa, watchful and sorry. Finally, he appeared to reach some private decision.

"I'll tell you this much, Kay. Then maybe you can let go. When I arrived back here, everybody was so happy I made it home alive. My mother cried and hung on to my neck till it ached. She was so fucking happy. *I* was happy! I was actually happy at first. I even allowed myself to believe that it would only be a matter of time before I saw you again and kissed you. I guess I thought we'd meet up somewhere, kiss and work it out. We'd finally know if we were meant to be together. But whatever happened, *things would work out*. Maybe I could still go to college. I'd make it through. I mean, how fucking naive can a person be? I guess I was so relieved to be home, it made me stupid. But that didn't take long to pass. In fact, I can remember the exact moment it passed. I was at a convenience store on Ford, buying cigarettes."

He stopped for a minute or so, lost in retrospection, placing himself back in the store on Ford Road.

"Anyway, there I am. I've been home a couple of weeks, and I'm doing okay. I'm helping out around the house—I'm driving my car—I'm in a store buying a carton. I'm *okay*. But now I'm in this store, and I bump into our old little league coach at the checkout counter. He's holding a basket with a loaf of bread and a six-pack in it. Maybe a couple of other things. He's looking a little older; he's got a beer belly, and he's balding. But he recognizes me and gives a big, friendly grin. And then he says, 'Say Joe, you been on vacation? That's some tan you picked up!'

"So, I'm standing there, wondering what I'm supposed to say about my 'Vietnam tan,' and I notice a big clock on the wall behind the cash register. It's shaped like an old-fashioned Coca-Cola bottle, and it has huge red hands. And I suddenly remember how, early in my tour, time seemed to stop. I never knew the day of the week, often had no idea what month it was. Sometimes I thought my whole life had been spent in Vietnam, and it would never be anywhere else. But as I neared the end of my tour, I made a conscious effort to locate time again. When I got down to my last month, I even started marking it on a calendar, along with a friend of mine, Donnie Perrone. Donnie wasn't my closest friend over there, but we got along. And we were due to be discharged the same week. Every night after midnight, we crossed off another day. Donnie was superstitious as hell, convinced he was gonna die when he got to single digits. He always said to me, 'When I hit nine days, Joe, start watching my back. That's when they're coming for me.' He made it down to six days, with everybody teasing him about it. Then he stepped on a land mine.

"So, I'm thinking about Donnie and staring at the Coca-Cola clock and my old little league coach, all at the same time. Here's this man I always looked up to and liked. And he has no idea where I've been. He doesn't want to know, and he doesn't stop to think. All he can see is I've got a tan. It's not his fault. In fact, a lot of people commented on how healthy I looked when I first came back. My face and arms were so brown after a year over there. But now, we're standing in the liquor store waiting to pay, and I look at my old coach and find him despicable. But *I'm worse*. *I'm* the guy who made it home in one piece. And now I'm driving around town like nothing happened. I'm not about to explain to him how my skin turned brown. But I finally get it: I have more in common with Donnie Perrone, a dead man, than with this fellow who has known me all my life.

"I'll never know why that incident turned things for me. It was nothing. A chance encounter, an innocent remark. Other people had made similar remarks, stupid remarks. But this one brought me up short. I stopped feeling happy to be home. It was over. After that, I started to go downhill. I blamed everybody else for what had happened to me. Blamed you especially. Changes arrived so close together—your moving away, my getting drafted. The two things were locked together in my head, and I held that against you. I'm glad now that you never saw me during that period. Your brother knows. He was about the only person I could stand to be around. But even with him, my best friend, even with Sid, things were never quite the same. He went back to college, but that was no longer a possibility for me. I was in a pretty bad way for a few years. By the time my brother Lenny died, I was too fucked up to grieve or miss him or help my parents. I just saw it as my punishment for making it home alive, with a fucking tan."

Joe stopped talking, reached for Kay, and pulled her close.

"You want to know about the war? It finished me. Vietnam broke my life in two."

He touched her cheek. "It's funny, Kay. You came home looking for the past. You've been running backward, so *hard*. And there was no need. The past was right here beside you. *I'm* the past. All the love I have for you—that was made in the past too, a long time ago, *before* Vietnam. Because after . . . is impossible. I'm finished. And there's really nobody to blame. But that's the reason you can't stay here any longer."

Then Joe, more generous than anybody Kay ever knew, more generous than she deserved, tenderly helped her one last time.

"Ask yourself this, Kay: do you ever wonder why you care so much for Fred Gaillard? Why you started with him and you'll end with him? I think it's because he stayed alive. And that's what *you* have to do."

FORWARD

KAY STOOD WATCHING HIM FOR THE LONGEST TIME. HE WALKED UP and down Shaw Road outside the town of Middleville, kicking at the dirt, occasionally stopping to adjust his hat or feel his coat pocket, carefully checking for something inside it. Of course, he was familiar to her; she knew him, but even a complete stranger would guess that the young man wished to approach the farmhouse, but was fearful for some reason. He was on the road there, *mustering his courage,* as they say. Kay knew that because she, too, was mustering courage, but in her case, to walk *away* from the farmhouse. There was nothing inside that place for her.

She had taken up position only yards from him, under bright fall sunshine. It warmed them both at the same time. She was so close to him that she could see the dust start from the dry, unpaved road with each nervous step. She watched it settle on his leather boots in a fine coating. She could tell that he wore his only suit, his Sunday best; his hands and face were scrubbed, and he was slightly built. She was so close she might reach out and touch him, but she kept tight to her spot and did not move. Once he looked directly at the place Kay stood. She looked back, right into his eyes, her heart banging in her chest. But he saw no one and turned away again, scuffing along in the opposite direction. The next time he walked toward Kay, his gaze fell on another part of the road, several feet to her left.

Finally, he appeared to make up his mind, took a step toward the house, then another and another. Gathering pace and resolve as he neared the wide porch of the two-story frame house, with its big barn and fields beyond. He was off the road and along the front path, growing distant. Only once did he pause and glance back—again, straight at Kay—a quizzical look on his face as though someone had called his name—as though *she* had called his name and he had heard her. But Kay had said nothing, and there was no one else on Shaw Road that day. Just the two of them out there in the country. She saw him shrug, as though this were a familiar sensation. And it seemed to encourage him, because now he returned to his task more assuredly and mounted the steps to Shaw Farm.

He sent faint noises drifting out to the road—the tap of his soles on the porch, and creaks in one or two of the boards. Then Kay heard his knuckles rattle the loose window glass in the door, as he knocked to see if anyone was home. Shortly, a young woman of strong build appeared, cautious behind the door, holding it half open. *Ada.* She had thick brown hair and wore a cleaning apron over her plain cotton frock. They talked for a moment, low, too low for Kay to make out the words, just his voice, her voice, back and forth. Finally, Kay saw the expression on Ada's face change and drop. There was a long pause. Then Fred was asked into the house, and the door closed behind them.

It was lonely after Fred Gaillard disappeared inside the old farmhouse. But she found she could not move from her spot. The sun shone wonderfully warm for the time of year. She noticed now that the house had been recently painted white; the barn was bright red. There was a shiny Ford pickup parked at the barn side of the house. The leaves were beginning to turn, and she could imagine the reds and golds to come, then frozen fields, and finally the first snowfall. Kay was just thinking how beautiful this place would be under heavy snow, how much she should like to see that, when she heard a voice, very close behind her.

"Are you ready to go now?" it asked gently.

Kay started and swung around quickly, but there was no one. It was only her own voice, helping her along.

ACKNOWLEDGMENTS

Ford Road is set in Garden City, Middleville, and Detroit, Michigan. I felt no need to change these place names, preferring to credit them with inspiring strong feelings in this writer and her characters. As for the detailed histories of these places, I was careful in my research, but not slavishly bound to my findings. Of the three towns, Middleville remains the least known to me, but I apologize in advance to the inhabitants of all three should they find any errors of fact or understanding. For a broad narrative history of Detroit and its people, I consulted Robert Conot's *American Odyssey* (1974). Robert Lacey's *Ford: The Men and the Machine* (1986) provided a detailed account of Henry Ford and the Ford Motor Company, while Clarence Hooker's *Life in the Shadows of the Crystal Palace, 1910–1927: Ford Workers in the Model T Era* (1997) gave added insight into the experiences of Ford workers during that early period, the Five Dollar Day, and the notorious Ford Sociological Department. Spider Huff's role in Ford's early innovations is documented in Lacey's book, as is the Grosse Pointe race of 1901. Richard Bak's *A Place for Summer* (1998) provided a history of Tiger Stadium, the teams that played there and the fans. *Detroit across Three Centuries* (2001), Richard Bak's illustrated history of the city, proved especially useful as a guide to Detroit's street and cultural life in the late nineteenth and early twentieth centuries. Thomas Sugrue's book *The Origins of the Urban Crisis: Race and Inequality in Postwar Detroit* (1996) provided a wealth of additional information. Although most of the Detroit stories are set during the automotive revolution, I hope that what I found holds some interest to Detroiters now, as the city undergoes yet another period of profound change. If a place and its people can be said to have heart, soul, courage, and the capacity to reinvent urban life, Detroit has these in abundance.

For the history of Garden City as a postwar suburb, two publications by the Garden City Historical Commission proved helpful: *Early Days in Garden City* (1962) and John Macfie's *Garden City Chronicle* (1976). I also made use of my own previous research, the result of which can be found in *Dreaming Suburbia,* a work of nonfiction published in 2004. I am also indebted to Raymond Kenyon and Fred Kenyon and to Pavanne Lapham, along with numerous early friends, for generously sharing their memories of Garden City.

For the history of Middleville and Barry County, I consulted the *History of Allegan and Barry Counties, Michigan: With Illustrations and Biographical Sketches of Their Prominent Men and Pioneers* (1880). To learn something of the settlement of western Michigan, I read the Kenneth E. Lewis study *West to Far Michigan* (2002) and Susan E. Gray's *The Yankee West: Community Life on the Michigan Frontier* (1996). I am especially indebted to Mr. Lewis, who kindly answered my inquiries as to the routes Alonzo Shaw might have followed to Michigan and the early practices of land purchase and settlement. It should be added that any inaccuracies in this material are my own. All of the above-mentioned works gave additional information about the early relations with local tribes. Alonzo Shaw's story of finding four Ottawas asleep before his fire during a blizzard is based on an incident related to me by a descendant of Duncan Campbell, a Thornapple Valley settler.

The three obituaries that Kay shares with Joe are composites of some of the death stories recounted in *Michigan Veterans' Obituaries: 1898–1939* (1989). I drew liberally from a few obituaries to produce Kay's selection, altering names, dates, places, and numerous details.

Johannes Hofer's "Medical Dissertation on Nostalgia or Homesickness" (1688) was translated for the *Bulletin of the Institute of the History of Medicine* in 1934. In subsequent studies, there is some disagreement as to whether it appeared in 1678 or 1688, but this has no bearing on my use of it.

The history of nostalgia after Johannes Hofer, as narrated and interpreted by my fictional Dr. Thisroy, was drawn from a large, cross-disciplinary, and growing literature. A handful of studies should be mentioned here. Ed Brown, a specialist in the history of psychiatry, wrote a short Internet piece titled "Notes on Nostalgia," which I found enormously helpful, not only in providing an introduction to this material but in noting some of the important questions raised by this history. I also found insightful historical and conceptual work on nostalgia in the following: Svetlana Boym, *The Future of Nostalgia* (2001); *Descriptions*, a collection of essays edited by Don Ihde and Hugh J. Silverman (1985); Willis H. McCann, "Nostalgia: A Review of the Literature," *Psychological Bulletin* 38 (1941); Susan J. Matt, "You Can't Go Home Again: Homesickness and Nostalgia in U.S. History," *Journal of American History* (2007); Constantine Sedikides, Tim Wildschut, and Denise Baden, "Nostalgia: Conceptual Issues and Existential Functions," from *Handbook of Experimental Existential Psychology*, edited by Jeff Greenberg (2004); Linda Hutcheon, "Irony, Nostalgia, and the Postmodern," *University of Toronto English Library* (1998); and Jean Starobinski, "The Idea of Nostalgia," *Diogenes* 54 (1966). Kant's remark about homesickness is also noted in Linda Hutcheon's discussion of nostalgia.

To gain insight into the experience of coming home from Vietnam, I consulted James F. Behr's *Vietnam Voices* (2004), Aphrodite Matsakis's *Vietnam Wives* (1996), and Christian G. Appy's *Vietnam: The Definitive Oral History Told from All Sides* (2003). However, I owe the greatest debt of gratitude to the late Bill Crowell, who shared some of his memories and reflections about Vietnam and coming home. Only a few small details of Bill's account appear in this book, but the care and generosity he showed in our conversations did find their way into the character of Joe Chase.

Ford Road had its start in the discovery of two past events. My great-grandfather committed suicide by drowning in the Detroit River. My great-grandmother had a child out of wedlock and disappeared, leaving behind a packet of letters that is now in my possession. Beyond these key events and locations, this is a work of fiction. I make no claim to knowing or presenting the "truths" of any persons in the past, but I do hope the stories in this book have delivered something of the times in which my ancestors lived, their Michigan *places*, and the real complexities of family.

I am grateful to Colleen Mohyde of the Doe Coover Agency, Rosemary Keeler, and Alison Bennett for critical comments and advice. At the University of Michigan Press, thanks are due to Ellen McCarthy, Marcia LaBrenz, and Scott Ham, and to the copyeditor, Carol Sickman-Garner. Above all, I wish to thank Ricardo Blaug and Isaac Kenyon Blaug for reading, love, and encouragement.